"The Great Plan?"

Grant crossed his arms over his thick chest. "That's apparently what Sam calls it. The plan to eventually control all of humanity—homo sapiens and homo superior. Both new and old humans are in the same boat—marked to be ruled or destroyed."

Baron Sharpe's eyes clouded over with the intensity of his emotion. "Academically, I can see a certain logic to it. If the control mechanisms are installed at key points throughout history, then the nukecaust will not be necessary."

Quietly Brigid said, "I know we've dropped a lot on you. Some of our claims are very wild and impossible to prove. The final decision as to whether we're right or wrong is up to you."

Baron Sharpe blinked, then his eyes frosted hard. "What do you expect me to do?"

"Spread the word to all the other barons," Brigid answered. "Form a consortium of barons and pool your resources to occupy Area Fifty-one. Do whatever you have to do to fight the future, to keep the Imperator's adaptive Earth from coming to pass."

"And what of you?"

"We have our own fronts to fight on," Grant responded brusquely.

Other titles in this series:

James Axler
Outlanders

SEA OF
PLAGUE

Heart of the World
BOOK 2

A GOLD EAGLE BOOK FROM
WORLDWIDE®

TORONTO • NEW YORK • LONDON
AMSTERDAM • PARIS • SYDNEY • HAMBURG
STOCKHOLM • ATHENS • TOKYO • MILAN
MADRID • WARSAW • BUDAPEST • AUCKLAND

First edition August 2003

ISBN 0-373-63839-6

SEA OF PLAGUE

Printed in U.S.A.

SEA OF
PLAGUE

The Road to Outlands—
From Secret Government Files to the Future

Almost two hundred years after the global holocaust, Kane, a former Magistrate of Cobaltville, often thought the world had been lucky to survive at all after a nuclear device detonated in the Russian embassy in Washington, D.C. The aftermath— forever known as skydark—reshaped continents and turned civilization into ashes.

Nearly depopulated, America became the Deathlands— poisoned by radiation, home to chaos and mutated life forms. Feudal rule reappeared in the form of baronies, while remote outposts clung to a brutish existence.

What eventually helped shape this wasteland were the redoubts, the secret preholocaust military installations with stores of weapons, and the home of gateways, the locational matter-transfer facilities. Some of the redoubts hid clues that had once fed wild theories of government cover-ups and alien visitations.

Rearmed from redoubt stockpiles, the barons consolidated their power and reclaimed technology for the villes. Their power, supported by some invisible authority, extended beyond their fortified walls to what was now called the Outlands. It was here that the rootstock of humanity survived, living with hellzones and chemical storms, hounded by Magistrates.

In the villes, rigid laws were enforced—to atone for the sins of the past and prepare the way for a better future. That was the barons' public credo and their right-to-rule.

Kane, along with friend and fellow Magistrate Grant, had upheld that claim until a fateful Outlands expedition. A displaced piece of technology...a question to a keeper of the archives...a vague clue about alien masters—and their world shifted radically. Suddenly, Brigid Baptiste, the archivist, faced summary execution, and Grant a quick termination. For Kane there was forgiveness if he pledged his unquestioning allegiance to Baron Cobalt and his unknown masters and abandoned his friends.

But that allegiance would make him support a mysterious and alien power and deny loyalty and friends. Then what else was there?

Kane had been brought up solely to serve the ville. Brigid's only link with her family was her mother's red-gold hair, green eyes and supple form. Grant's clues to his lineage were his ebony skin and powerful physique. But Domi, she of the white hair, was an Outlander pressed into sexual servitude in Cobaltville. She at least knew her roots and was a reminder to the exiles that the outcasts belonged in the human family.

Parents, friends, community—the very rootedness of humanity was denied. With no continuity, there was no forward momentum to the future. And that was the crux— when Kane began to wonder if there *was* a future.

For Kane, it wouldn't do. So the only way was out— way, way out.

After their escape, they found shelter at the forgotten Cerberus redoubt headed by Lakesh, a scientist, Cobaltville's head archivist, and secret opponent of the barons.

With their past turned into a lie, their future threatened, only one thing was left to give meaning to the outcasts. The hunger for freedom, the will to resist the hostile influences. And perhaps, by opposing, end them.

Prologue

Sam, the imperator, turned slightly toward the helmeted guard standing just outside the balcony. Instantly the uniformed man stepped forward, hefting his SIG-AMT rifle. His boots, coveralls and helmet were midnight blue with a facing of bright scarlet. A batonlike club hung from his belt.

In sharp contrast to the soldier's garb, Sam's tall figure was draped in an impeccably tailored white linen suit. It seemed to shimmer in the borealis-like nimbus exuded by the Heart of the World fifty feet below the balcony. Underlit by its lambent glow, Sam resembled a specter.

Sam was so exceptionally lean, he looked like a poster child for anorexia. His hollowed-out cheeks stressed his high, jutting cheekbones. He had no facial hair to speak of, not even eyebrows. Beneath the brow arches, sunken very deep in his head, as if hiding from the light, haughty golden eyes shone like polished ingots. Below the crag of brows and probing eyes, his face seemed to taper down like a teardrop. A sharp, narrow nose and a long, thin mouth that never curved far from a straight line completed the face.

A white turban covered the top and sides of his head, and light glinted from the blue diamond broach pinned at the turban's forefront. The subtle slant of his golden eyes beneath the prominent supraorbital ridges gave his pale skin a vaguely Asian cast.

His hands were inhumanly long and slender, but the backs and palms were crisscrossed with a network of deep lines like those of a very old man. Yet judging by his smooth, unlined face, Sam could be no more than twenty years old.

Kane pretended not to notice the summons to the guard. He kept his bearded face blank of expression, even when he felt his shoulder-length hair stirring from the static discharge due to the energy field surrounding the Heart of the World. His flesh prickled as if thousands of ants were crawling over every inch of his skin.

He, Sindri, Sam and Tanvirah stood upon a railed balcony that encircled a vast circular chamber more than two hundred feet across. Positioned all around the balcony were arrays of consoles, power conduits, displays, switchboards and computer terminals. Some fifty feet below, in the center of the chamber, yawned what appeared to be a pit or a pool. On closer inspection, the pit looked more like a sphere of dense black, its obsidian surface dotted with pinpoints of intense light. A swirl of white vaporous dust formed a long, sweeping curve that cut through the center of the black mass.

The black mass wasn't solid, nor was it liquid. It gave the impression of being utterly empty, and yet it was sprinkled with a multitude of tiny sparks shining and glowing within it. There was the impression of motion, as if each spark were moving and as if the central spiral misty mass slowly revolved, each glittering facet of it alive and fighting against the eye-hurting blackness—which, according to Sam, was not so much blackness as the complete absence of color. It was a deep emptiness, a total lack of existence.

The pool lay at the bottom and precise center of the twelve-hundred-foot-tall Pyramid of Xian, the largest megalithic structure ever found on Earth. No one really knew who had constructed it or precisely when, but apparently it had been built to protect the Heart of the World.

Many years before, Sam had described the pool as a nexus point, a convergence depot of geomagnetic energy, from which a hub of ley lines spread outward across the planet. Now, after Sam had altered it with technology, he referred to the center of Earth energies as the microcosmos, penetrating the space-time continuum. The pool contained a slice view of the universe, compressed and condensed, visible through a dimensional window he had created.

Only moments before, Kane had been rooted to the spot by terror at the very concept of the power at Sam's command. He claimed he could enter the coordinates of a particular point in space or even a time period and inject whatever elements he chose. It was the final component in what he referred to as the Great Plan, a dream to create and then control all of reality.

If dwarfish Sindri was intimidated by Sam's casual proclamation of guiding human destiny, he gave no sign of it. Nodding toward Kane, Sindri impatiently said to Sam, "You didn't answer his question about the plague."

Sam sighed. "It's not quite the horrible genocidal act you might think it is. I merely borrowed a few lessons from history. When a disease ravages a society, economics shatter, poverty moves in and trust in governments and fellow human beings dissolves."

"Not to mention," Kane said darkly, "new messiahs and messengers from God emerge from the chaos, especially if some kind of religious prophecies were apparently fulfilled during the plague times."

Sam gave him a fleeting, appreciative smile. "Exactly. In the Middle Ages, a century of progress was brought to a crashing halt by simultaneous outbreaks of the bubonic plague. When I inject my own virus into the various key points of time and place, I will effect changes just as major…but the nukecaust will be avoided because the circumstances that led up to it will have been averted.

"There will be waste, of course, and that is to be deplored, but the plague victims will be mostly from the underclass of the stricken societies who contribute the least."

"The useless eaters," Kane drawled. "That old saw."

Sam chuckled. "But I want you, Kane, to be part of the Great Plan—especially as it moves into its final phase. If you're my ally, the temporal-ripple backlash will be minimized. I will give you whatever you want. Just name it."

Kane forced a contemptuous smirk to his face. "Can you give me back Brigid?"

When Sam's smile faltered, Kane stated, "What I want is not within your power to give. And even if you tried to convince me that it was, all you'd do is hold the possibility of returning her to me over my head like a sword."

Sam began clicking the memory cards together again. "Then what can I do for you?"

Kane shrugged. "There are some questions you can answer, suspicions I've harbored for many years that you can confirm or deny. I'd like to find out why you financed the Nirodha movement…what the significance of the entire Scorpia Prime alter ego and Tantric sex deal was all about."

Sam opened his mouth as if to reply, but Kane held up a hand. "But as much as I'd like to know those things, the fate of human civilization, maybe even of all humanity, rests with me. That's not something I ever bargained for. But I've come to accept it, and I'll do what I can."

Kane moved with the blinding speed and the controlled explosion of near superhuman reflexes that had been his as a younger man. He hurled himself forward, shoulder-rolling between Tanvirah and Sam. He caught a glimpse of fearful desperation on the face of the soldier when the man realized he was Kane's objective.

He tried to bring his autorifle to bear, but Kane rose smoothly to his feet right in front of him. The edge of his left hand lashed out, catching the man full across the neck. There was a mushy snap, as of a stick of wet wood breaking, and the red-and-blue-garbed trooper dropped dead after uttering only one choked cry.

Kane tried to wrestle the weapon out of the man's hands as he sagged, but they had reflexively tightened around it and he had no time to wrest it from his grip. He caught a blur of movement from behind him. Tanvirah launched an expert kick at his back, and he twisted aside, taking the impact on his hip.

Pain shivered through him, but if her foot had struck solidly where it had been aimed, the impact would have cracked his spine. She wore knee-length stilt-heeled boots, and he already knew she could use them to kill him. The girl was a master of unarmed combat, as skilled as any opponent he had ever met.

Tanvirah's face was full cheeked and bold nosed, her skin the rich brown of coffee and milk, her eyes large and black and flashing with fury.

Her sleek, straight hair was a thick, ebony cascade sheening over her shoulders from a part in the middle of her scalp. She wore a black-and-red uniform ensemble, the colors of the imperial forces. The pants hugged her long, lithe legs, and her waist was tightly cinctured by a red sash. The narrow shoulders of her satiny black tunic were lifted by tapered pads.

The fabric was tailored to conform to the thrust of her full breasts, a goodly portion of them visible due to the tunic's plunging neckline. It revealed not only the smooth sweep of cleavage, but also a silver medallion in the shape of a scorpion.

Kane kept twisting, reaching out for the astonished Sam, putting the imperator between him and Tanvirah. She had started to launch another kick but checked the movement, shrieking in frustration. She stumbled off balance, and Sindri chose that moment to cannonball his small body into her legs. She fell heavily, and Sindri leaped atop her. Kane knew from painful experience that despite his three-and-a-half-foot height, Sindri was far stronger than he looked.

Sam tried to contort himself out of Kane's grasp, twisting and turning wildly. Kane turned with him, locking the man's left arm under his right and heaving up on it. Sam's lips writhed over his teeth in a grimace of pain. His nerve-numbed fingers opened and dropped the data cards.

Kane caught them, snatching them out of the air. Maintaining the pressure on the captured arm, he forced Sam down on the floor grille. "Stay there, messiah," he snapped. To show he meant business, he drove his knee into Sam's pointed chin, slamming him hard against the metal floor plates.

He whirled toward the computer consoles, noting as he did so that Tanvirah and Sindri were locked in thrashing, cursing combat. He swept his eyes across the machines and saw with a surge of relief that they were all networked. Swiftly, he inserted the cards in the proper ports, praying they could be read.

Within a few seconds—which felt like a chain of interlocking eternities to Kane—symbols indicating the cards had been successfully uploaded flashed on the monitor screens. Kane then began inputting the spatiotemporal injection coordinates into the keyboards.

Even he was amazed by how swiftly and surely he moved. "Sindri!" he yelled. "Get over here!"

A hand suddenly closed around Kane's shoulder from behind. Fingers dug in deep, seeming to puncture flesh, muscle and bone. He was too engulfed by the pain even to cry out. Then a force hauled him violently away from the keyboards.

He didn't fall, but he staggered nearly the entire breadth of the circular walkway. He saw Sindri lying on his face, breathing hard with Tanvirah kneeling on his back, holding both of his arms in hammerlocks. And he saw Sam, the imperator, saunter toward him, carrying himself with the completely confident manner of a lion approaching its prey.

"You are such a fool," he said. "I was your salvation, your only hope and you threw it all away." He shook his head in pity. "All away."

Kane leaped at Sam in a dropkick, throwing all of his weight against the tall, slender man. Both feet impacted against Sam's chest, but he merely took two stumbling steps back while Kane fell heavily on his back.

Before he could rise, Sam sidled in and caught hold of the back of his neck and squeezed. Kane choked off a scream of agony. The sensation was like being trapped between the jaws of a hydraulic bear trap. He tried but failed to prize Sam's fingers apart. Then he pistoned his fists into Sam's midsection as the imperator lifted him clear of the balcony's floor and twisted him around so they were face-to-face.

"You want to know why you were really implanted with the SQUID?" Sam asked pleasantly. The pupils of his eyes suddenly sparked with a familiar crimson glow, like pinpoints of fire.

Agony overtook Kane. He screamed in mindless pain and fury. Forgetting Sindri, even Tanvirah, he bellowed an animal wail of rage and pain, cursing the sleet storm of hot coals that seemed to fill the inside of his skull. He was unable to form words or even to think a single cogent thought.

When Sam released him, Kane fell limply onto the floor plates, writhing and twitching feebly. The imperator toed him onto his back, and Kane gazed up at him blankly, his nervous system overwhelmed. Sam reached up and pulled off his turban—revealing a naked cranium peeled clean of flesh, the skull bone open to the air. Sprouting from it was a series of tiny electrodes, studding it in an orderly pattern. Between the electrodes stretched flat ribbons of circuitry.

In a gentle tone barely above a whisper, he said, "That's why you were implanted, Kane...just like everyone will be one day...so we will be unified and I never need be alone again. No one will ever be alone again. All the units—the human brains in the world—will be linked to me. Chains, enabling my mind to take over that of another, to influence, to guide, to control in almost total assimilation."

The pain in his head ebbed sufficiently so Kane could move and think again. "That's a very old dream," he muttered.

"Yes," Sam agreed. "Many others attempted what I have. But they never completely realized their dream of an orderly world, a controllable and unified universe. Until now."

Kane managed to shamble to a half crouch. Sam negligently drove a knee into his face. He heard and felt his nose cartilage collapse under the impact, and he fell over on his side. The pain was nothing compared to what he had experienced from the superconducting quantum interface device, the SQUID.

"Time will expand my horizons and build on the accomplishments of my predecessors," Sam continued.

"Predecessors?" Kane croaked, slowly trying to climb to his feet again.

Sam grinned, a very human grin, made horrific and macabre by his fleshless cranial bone. "Surely you've figured it out by now, Kane. Remember what I told you a long, long time ago in another place altogether."

Kane wiped at the blood threading his face and tottered erect. He knew now who Sam really was. The imperator had confirmed suspicions he had secretly harbored but dared not even consciously examine for many years.

"I remember," Kane husked out. "You said that you're a program, not an individual entity." He made a statement; he didn't ask a question.

Sam started to nod—then cried out more in shock than pain when Sindri struck him from behind with the truncheon taken from the guard's body. He had performed a truly prodigious leap in order to do it. Sparks flew in a shower from the top of Sam's head.

Sam staggered forward—directly into Kane's left fist. Kane glimpsed Tanvirah grabbing Sindri and hauling him down to the floor, then a fountain of scorching rage erupted out of Kane. He moved to the attack, raining blow after blow on the imperator's face, trying to pulverize it to a bloody mass of pulped flesh. The imperator didn't bleed and Kane hadn't really expected him to, although his pounding fists lacerated his prominent cheekbones and knocked out a couple of teeth.

Kane kept up the battering, driving his fists into Sam's body, then his face in a flurry of hooks, right and left crosses and uppercuts. He was encouraged by the lack of neuronic energy pouring into his brain from the SQUID. Sindri had apparently knocked something askew and Kane wasn't about to allow the imperator the opportunity to repair it.

Sam suddenly swung a fist from the hip, driving a blow into Kane's left side. The cracking of bone was audible, and razors of pain slashed through Kane's torso. He doubled over, jackknifing around the fist. Slowly he fell, coughing up a mixture of blood and phlegm. The blow had been too swift, delivered with unerring accuracy and precision. Kane understood dimly that Sam had been learning while he was being pummeled. He had processed all the finer points of hand-to-hand combat. He knew exactly where to strike.

Kane lay doubled up around where the blow had landed, his eyes clouded with tears of pain. He panted through his open mouth, tasting blood. He waited for Sam to reach down and crush his larynx or kick him to death. Neither happened.

The imperator walked right past him and bumped against the rail. Kane gaped at him as Sam extended his arms and waved them through the air. In a voice high and wild with fear, he cried out, "I can't see! Tanvirah! I can't see!"

Kane almost laughed. The blow Sindri had landed on his SQUID network had damaged the optic nerve feed to his eyes. The imperator was blind. Tanvirah shrieked in horror and tried to hurl Sindri away from her, but he held on by double handfuls of her black hair.

Kane forced himself to his feet, ignoring the grate of bone in his side. He lashed out with a straight-leg kick, catching Sam in the center of the back. Vertebrae crunched under the impact, but Sam didn't scream or plummet over the rail. Instead his mouth opened but no sound issued out. He jerked and fell, long limbs thrashing uncontrollably, like a puppet whose strings had been cut.

Kane guessed his entire network of neuronic energy was disrupted, but not necessarily on a permanent basis. He leaned against the rail to ease the pain of his shattered ribs and called, "Let her go, Sindri…time for us to implement the last phase of our own great plan."

Snarling, Sindri punched Tanvirah in the side of the head before letting her go. She flopped onto her back, arms and legs sprawled. Panting, Sindri staggered over to him. "You've uploaded the data cards?"

Kane nodded. "So you knew that's what I was going to do?"

Sindri snorted, then winced as he touched the welt swelling on the side of his face. "It was pretty damn obvious. I did everything I could to piss Sam off and make him careless.''

"You did a fine job.''

"You might say it's a calling, Mr. Kane.''

"How well I know that.'' Kane forced a smile to his face. From the pocket of his bodysuit he withdrew the CD and handed it Sindri. "Here you go. People's Exhibit A.''

"And I guess I'm Exhibit B…providing I get to where you want me to go.'' Sindri moved along the rail in the direction of the computers, peering over the side into the pool. "How do you figure to inject me into the past?''

"The simplest way is to—''

Kane's words were drowned out by the stuttering report of the SIG-AMT. Tanvirah had pulled it from the soldier's hands and fired it in Kane and Sindri's general direction. She shrieked wordlessly as she did so, the recoil making her upper body shake violently. Bright brass arced from the ejector port and clinked at her feet. Sindri uttered a howl of fright.

Kane lunged forward, kicking himself off the balcony floor, the jackhammering roar of the subgun a thundering drumroll in his ears. Bullets smashed into the computer consoles, gouging through the plastic keyboards and tearing scars in the metal. Two sledgehammer blows landed against his back and hurled him forward. He slammed into Sindri.

The little man toppled over the balcony rail but clung to Kane's hand and held it tightly for a long agonizing moment. The gunfire ended, replaced by the mechanical clack and snap of a jammed cylinder.

Sindri stared up uncomprehendingly into his face. Kane opened his mouth to speak, and blood vomited from his lips. Sindri uttered a short cry of disgust. By summoning all the energy left in his broken body, from toe tip to the crown of his head, Kane managed to gasp out a half-gagged, imploring sentence: "When you get there, tell him—tell *me*—who the imperator really is. He's Colonel C. W. Thrush and—"

Tanvirah shrieked, hurling herself onto Kane. She pounded hysterically at his back with the butt of the autorifle. Kane's hand opened and Sindri plunged down into the maw of the universe. When he struck the pool, the microcosm of infinity, a cloud of star sparks shot up like a stream of embers cast from a burning log. Then he was gone.

Kane hitched around and pushed Tanvirah away from him. She sat down hard on the floor, then crawled over to Sam's spasming body. She cradled him in her arms, but he didn't speak. His eyes were vacant, his gape-mouthed face a blank mask.

Tanvirah burst into tears, burying her face in her hands, sobbing as if her heart would break. Kane hoped it would. Gritting his teeth, he tried to make himself comfortable, but he knew that was an impossibility.

He ruefully eyed the raw, pulsing exit wounds on his chest. They were bleeding profusely, and he thought he saw bits of lung tissue mixed in with the scarlet flow, but he figured he would recover. He always did.

Then he chuckled at the absurd way his mind was constructed. It didn't seem capable of accepting death or defeat even in the face of utter and complete finality.

As darkness crept in on the edges of his vision, he wondered how long he would be dead. Only time will tell, he thought.

Chapter 1

Cerberus Redoubt, twenty-seven years earlier

In the main operations complex, lights flashed and needle gauges flickered on the primary mat-trans control console. In the anteroom, a droning hum arose from the gateway chamber.

Both Bry and Lakesh jumped in surprise. Brigid, seated at the main ops console, spun her chair away from the keyboard and stared at the armaglass-enclosed unit. "Is it a true matter stream carrier," she demanded, "or another quantum fluctuation like happened the other day?"

Swiveling his head, Lakesh stared at the Mercator relief map that spanned the entire length of one wall. Pinpoints of light shone steadily in almost every country and were connected by a thin pattern of glowing lines. They represented the Cerberus network, the locations of all indexed functioning gateway units across the planet.

His eyes searched for any light that blinked steadily. A flashing bulb indicated a transmitting gateway, but there was none. However, lights of all colors of the spectrum blinked and winked on the control consoles within the center. The panoply of electronics and lights was watched over by a dozen men and women, most of them wearing one-piece, tight-fitting white bodysuits. They scurried from station to station, consulting the readouts and calling out status reports to one another.

Bry announced stridently, "We've definitely got a matter stream, Lakesh! Coming into full phase!"

"How can that be?" Brigid asked, coming to stand beside Bry.

For a long moment, Lakesh didn't answer. He only shook his head in confusion. The main reason for his bewilderment was pure shock. Long ago he had altered the modulations of the Cerberus gateway unit's transit feed connections so its transmissions were untraceable. Nor could anyone gate into the redoubt's mat-trans, or beam in so much as a molecule, either by accident or design—with one relatively recent and very notable exception.

Recalling that exception kept his mind from working properly, and the bright flares, like bursts of heat lightning on the other side of the armaglass walls of the chamber, distracted him further. The low hum climbed rapidly in pitch to a hurricane howl as the device cycled through the materialization process.

"We've definitely got a materialization," Bry said fearfully, pushing his chair back from the console on squeaking casters. His eyes were wide beneath his tousled mass of coppery curls.

Staring at the flares of energy on the other side of the brown armaglass, Brigid said loudly, "Lakesh, you'd better get an armed detail in here."

The green-eyed woman's terse tone of voice freed Lakesh from his state of mental paralysis long enough for him to thumb down the call button on the trans comm system. ''Armed security detail to operations! Stat!'' he half shouted.

His voice echoed throughout the redoubt. A formal security force didn't exist as such in the installation. All of the personnel, including the recent Moonbase émigrés, were required to become reasonably proficient with firearms, primarily the lightweight ''point and shoot'' SA80 subguns. The armed security detail Lakesh summoned would be anyone who grabbed a gun from the armory and reached the control center under his or her own power.

The electronic wail from the jump chamber faded, dropping down to silence. The bursts of energy behind the translucent slabs disappeared. Within a minute Kane rushed into the complex, wielding a nickel-plated Mustang .30, a memento of his escape from Area 51. He was wearing jeans and a black T-shirt, but no shoes, so he had apparently been relaxing in his quarters.

''We've got an unauthorized jumper,'' Brigid told him, nervously brushing her thick mane of red-gold hair back over her shoulders.

Kane snorted. ''It's happened before, hasn't it?''

''Yes, and it's never been a friendly visit from anyone, either,'' Bry said.

Domi rushed in, double-fisting her .45-caliber Detonics Combat Master. The small albino girl followed Kane's hand signals and took up position on the left side of the jump chamber. She wore a short red jerkin that displayed most of her pearl-colored body. Her short, ragged mop of hair was the hue of bone, contrasting sharply with her ruby-red eyes.

Reba DeFore hustled in, looking both frightened and annoyed. A stocky, bronze-skinned woman, DeFore's usually tidy hair hung in disarrayed ash-blond wisps. Instead of a gun, she carried a medical kit. She hung back in the operations room, watching as Kane and Domi took up cross-fire positions on either side of the mat-trans unit, weapons held at hip level.

Brigid stepped up to the platform and gripped the door handle. "No matter who—or what—is in there, don't shoot until I give you the go-ahead."

Carefully, Brigid disengaged the lock mechanism, lifted the handle and swung open the heavy door on its counterbalanced hinges. Most of the mist produced by the quincunx effect's plasma bleed-off had dissipated, so the figure slouched over against the far wall was easily discerned. Identification wasn't so easy.

Brigid stared at the small man-shape huddled on the hexagonal floor plates, then stepped in, dropping to one knee beside him. Despite the damp coating of blood half covering his face, she recognized the unconscious man. It took her two attempts, but she managed to call out, "It's all right...I think."

Kane peered around the open door, stared in disbelief for a long second and half, then shouted, "*Sindri!*"

Sindri's eyes flew open, wide and wild. Convulsions racked him violently from head to toe. He dragged in a great shuddery breath as if his lungs had been deprived of oxygen for a long time. He clawed out with his right hand, finding Brigid's hands and closing his fingers around them as if they were anchors to life. His glassy eyes asked a silent, beseeching question.

"You're in Cerberus," Brigid told him. "I'm assuming it's where you meant to end up."

Air rasped in and out of Sindri's lungs as he tried to sit up. He managed only a flailing spasm of arms and legs. Kane stepped in and pulled him up to a sitting position by the collar of his shadowsuit, then dragged him out like a sack of corn, letting him use the table as support.

Lakesh and DeFore came in cautiously and joined Kane, Domi and Brigid as they stared at the little man in dumbfounded silence. Despite suspecting they would encounter Sindri again, the notion he would gate right into Cerberus covered in blood had never occurred to any of them.

"How the hell did you get here, pissant?" Kane snarled out the words.

Sindri leaned against the table edge, his eyes passing over the people and guns surrounding him. At length, he said hoarsely, "Mr. Kane, Miss Brigid. You probably won't believe this, but I'm overjoyed to see both of you again."

Lakesh stepped between DeFore and Domi. "And why is that?" he challenged. "Friend Kane and dearest Brigid told me you intended the most ghastly fates for them during your last meeting."

Sindri favored him with a bleak smile. "Yesterday's news. And I mean that in the most literal way possible."

He started to reach into a pocket, but Domi snapped up her gun barrel and he subsided. "Surely none of you think I can conceal a weapon in this outfit?"

"I think if anybody could," Kane snapped, "you'd be the one. Move slow."

Sindri carefully slid out the slip-sleeved compact disk. Lakesh made a move to take it, but Sindri snatched it away. "No," he said firmly. "I have been charged to give this to Mr. Kane and Mr. Kane only."

Brigid arched a questioning eyebrow. "Charged by whom?"

"That Mr. Kane will find out after he reviews its contents."

Kane gazed at the disk distrustfully as if he half suspected it was really a radioactive isotope. Gingerly he took it.

DeFore stepped forward, eyeing Sindri clinically. "I should get you to the infirmary and treat that wound."

Sindri shook his head. "No need. This blood isn't mine."

"Who does it belong to, then?" Domi demanded.

Sindri wiped a bit from his face and looked at it shining on his gloved fingertips. "I believe if you test it, you'll find it belongs to Mr. Kane."

Kane's jaw muscles knotted in angry frustration, and he took a threatening step toward Sindri. "I've had enough of this. Tell us how you got here Sindri— and from where—or I'll do what Grant said he'd do the last time we were in each other's company."

Sindri's brow furrowed as if he were dredging up a memory. "Oh, right. Rip my arms off and hammer them down my throat. Where is the truculent Mr. Grant anyway?''

''He is away at present,'' Lakesh responded gruffly. ''I suggest you comply with friend Kane's request.''

Sindri laughed with genuine amusement. ''Very well. It's worth being pushed around just to see the looks on your faces. I came to be here through the venue of a spatial and temporal dimensional window, cutting across the continuum through a microcosmic pathway. It was put together by someone you know…he calls himself the imperator.''

He paused, apparently enjoying the surprise flickering in all of their eyes. ''However,'' he continued, ''you know him best by the name he travels under— Colonel C. W. Thrush.''

No one spoke or moved or even appeared to breathe for a long, silent moment. Sindri made shooing motions with his hands. ''Off with you, Mr. Kane. Time for you to find out what the future holds and how you can get the hell out of the arrangement.''

All the humor in Sindri's voice, eyes and manner disappeared as he added, ''And believe me, all of you have a very long way to go.''

Kane's pale blue-gray eyes turned cold. His jaw muscles clamped tight as he reached out to put a hand on Sindri's shoulder. The little man started to slap Kane's hand away, but he sensed the violence just below the surface and checked the movement.

''What the hell do you mean?'' Kane growled. ''How do you know about Thrush?''

Sindri nodded toward the disk held between Kane's

fingers. "That should provide you with enough background to contrive your own hypotheses. I'm just the messenger, Mr. Kane, I assure you. You need not fear me."

The two men locked eyes. Sindri's expression remained neutral even as Kane's fingers dug into his shoulder. Standing an inch over six feet, Kane towered over Sindri by almost a full yard. Every line of his supple, compact body was hard and stripped of excess flesh. He was built with the savage economy of a timber wolf, with most of his muscle mass contained in his upper body.

Beneath thick dark hair, Kane's high-planed face was set in a grim mask. A faint hairline scar showed like a white thread against the sun-bronzed skin of his left cheek.

Sindri, despite his small stature, possessed such perfect proportions, Kane's sense of perspective was always confused at first sight of him. Unlike Sindri's fellow genetically engineered transadapts, his legs weren't stumpy, nor were his arms too long or his head too big.

Slowly, reluctantly, Kane relaxed his grip, but he didn't release him. He turned toward Brigid, extending to her his Colt Mustang butt first. "Do you and Domi want to escort our guest to detention?"

Brigid's eyes widened in surprise, but she took the pistol. "I assumed that was a chore you'd look forward to—give you a chance to find an excuse to kick him around a little."

Pushing Sindri toward her, Kane's lips quirked in

a mirthless smile. "I don't need an excuse to do that."

"Me, either," Domi announced, leveling her Combat Master at Sindri's nape, right at the point where his long blond hair was tied back in a foxtail.

The little man turned, eyed the hollow bore of the automatic pistol, then looked Domi up and down. She was a small, curvaceous white wraith, barely a hair over five feet tall. Though petite to the point of being childlike, she was exquisitely formed. One of the genetic quirks of the nukecaust aftermath was a rise in the albino population, particularly down south in bayou country. Albinos weren't exactly rare anywhere else, but they were hardly commonplace.

Chuckling scornfully, Sindri said, "The one characteristic all of you people in Cerberus share is a lack of gratitude."

No one responded to Sindri's oblique reference to how he had once saved Domi's life. They didn't need a reminder of the incident, nor of the fact he hadn't performed the act motivated by anything other than the most conniving of whims.

Lakesh stepped forward, running a nervous hand over his glossy, jet-black hair. "I'll tag along to make sure friend Sindri does nothing to aggravate his escorts."

Sindri looked Lakesh up and down and smiled slyly. "You look far less spry than the last time I saw you, Dr. Singh."

Lakesh's eyebrows knitted at the bridge of his nose. "What do you mean? The last time we saw each other was in the Anthill and I hadn't—"

He broke off, not putting his memories into words. Sindri's smile widened as he interposed, "Hadn't had your imperator-designed makeover yet?"

Lakesh stared at him in wonderment. He nodded but didn't speak. When he and Sindri had last encountered each other, his black hair wasn't thick or glossy, nor was his deep olive complexion clear and relatively unlined. He couldn't hazard even the most extreme of guesses how Sindri knew about Sam restoring him to the condition of his youth—or his early middle age. But Sindri's enigmatic reference to his looking even younger bewildered him.

Impatiently Kane declared, "Get him out of here. Find Farrell or somebody to search him before you lock him up."

"Like I told you," Sindri replied. "I am not here to cause you harm. Quite the opposite."

"Right," Brigid drawled with undisguised sarcasm. "You've said that to us at least three times before." She jerked the short barrel of the Colt Mustang toward the exit. "Move along."

Kane stepped toward a computer station, removing the compact disk from the slip sleeve. "I'll take a look at what's on this."

"Make sure you run a virus scan before you open it," Bry instructed sharply.

Sindri groaned in weary exasperation. "Oh, please. Do you think I risked my life to make an interdimensional incursion here, into the sanctum sanctorum of my most dedicated enemies, simply so I could screw up your computer systems?"

Reba DeFore said flatly, "None of us knows what

to think about you, Sindri.'' She regarded Kane with a challenging stare. ''And not all of us here are necessarily your enemies.''

Sindri snorted disdainfully. ''Name two.''

Nobody answered. Domi poked him in the back with the bore of her gun. ''Move.''

Sindri grimaced at the pressure of steel, but called out, ''Mr. Kane, I intend to cooperate, but might I have a word with you in private?''

Kane glanced toward him. ''No.''

In a hushed, grave voice, Sindri said, ''Mr. Kane, it's imperative you listen to me. All I ask is a few seconds. I have something to tell you, not ask you. What you do with the information is totally up to you, but it has to do with the security and safety of your little sanctuary here.''

Kane gusted out an exasperated sigh and stepped toward an aisle between two computer stations. ''Come over here.''

Sindri did as he was directed. Everyone watched with alert, suspicious eyes as Kane bent and Sindri whispered into his ear. He didn't whisper for very long, only a few seconds. When Kane straightened, he glowered first down at Sindri, then glanced over at Lakesh with a keen, searching gaze.

''Take him to detention,'' he ordered.

Sindri rejoined Brigid, Domi and Lakesh. As the four people crossed the operations center toward the door, walking between a double row of computer consoles, the little man demanded peevishly, ''Can't you at least let me wash up before I'm consigned to durance vile? Although I did not find the sight of Mr.

Kane shedding his blood particularly upsetting, I find wearing it most disgusting.''

"There's a sink in your new quarters," Brigid told him.

They exited the control complex and moved along the twenty-foot-wide main corridor. The walls of the passageway were sheathed with softly gleaming vanadium alloy, and shaped like a square with an arch on top. Great curving ribs of metal and massive girders supported the high rock roof.

From the main corridor, side passages and elevators led to a well-equipped armory, bunk rooms, a cafeteria, a decontamination center, individual apartments and an infirmary. On the bottom level were a gymnasium, a pool and the detention area.

Brigid took the lead, walking in her characteristically swift, almost mannish stride. Despite her gait, the men she encountered in the passageway gave her swift, admiring glances. She was a tall woman, less than half an inch shy of matching Lakesh's five feet ten inches. Her fair complexion was lightly dusted with freckles across her nose and cheeks. Her big feline-slanted eyes weren't just green; they were a deep, clear emerald. A high forehead gave the impression of a probing intellect, whereas her wide mouth with the full underlip hinted at a sensual nature.

A mane of red-gold hair fell in loose waves almost to her waist. She wore a white bodysuit identical to Lakesh's, which showed off her willowy figure to full advantage. It was slender with a flat belly, rounded hips and taut, long legs. Her arms rippled with hard, toned muscle.

Sindri looked around and murmured, "It's quite the improvement over the last time I saw this place."

Domi scowled down at the small man. "You've never been here before."

Sindri smirked impishly. "Very true. Not before. Definitely after."

Lakesh's eyes narrowed and he started to speak, but Brigid put a forefinger to her lips and shook her head. After a second of brow-creased consternation, Lakesh nodded in understanding. He recalled Kane and Brigid once commenting that the best way to persuade Sindri to reveal a plan or a secret was to pretend they had no interest whatsoever in anything he had to say.

They encountered a number of people on the way to the elevator, men and women dressed in white bodysuits. They eyed the procession herding the little man along at gunpoint with curious eyes.

"Are these folks the Moon base refugees?" Sindri asked.

Lakesh and Brigid exchanged swift, startled glances, neither one wanting to answer the question. Sindri cast them an irritated glance over his shoulder. "Well?"

"Yes," Domi said flatly.

"How do you know about them?" Lakesh demanded.

Sindri shrugged. "You'll find out soon enough."

Ever since the destination-lock code to the Luna gateway had been discovered a month before, the immigrants from the Manitius base had been arriving on a fairly regular basis. Whether the people intended to remain in the installation or try to make separate lives for themselves in the Outlands was still an open question. At the moment, Brigid felt that discovering how Sindri knew about them at all was a bit more urgent.

"I'd prefer to find out now," she said, letting ice edge her voice.

"That's a shame," Sindri retorted blandly, "because you won't. This is one occasion where I don't mind Mr. Kane calling the shots. Besides, you won't believe anything I have to say."

"Due to nobody's fault but yours," Domi stated coldly.

As they turned a corner, they met Brewster Philboyd, another émigré from the Moon colony. He was an astrophysicist in his mid-forties, a little over six feet, long limbed and lanky of build. He wore the white, zippered bodysuit, the unofficial duty uniform of Cerberus personnel. Blond-white hair was swept back from a receding hairline. He wore black-rimmed eyeglasses, and his cheeks appeared to be pitted with the sort of scars associated with chronic teenage acne.

He gaped down in surprise at Sindri. "Who is this?"

Sindri eyed him contemptuously. "Who wants to know?"

Repressing a smile, Brigid said, "Dr. Brewster Philboyd, this is Sindri. You may recall hearing about him."

Philboyd's gape became more pronounced. "The little Martian maniac?"

Sindri's blue eyes glittered with sudden anger. "Doctor, if I hadn't been told of the noble sacrifice you made—will make—to save the people here, my hand even now would be removing your scrotum from your groin.''

Philboyd's hands reflexively covered his crotch, and he moved back a pace. His expression twisted in irritated astonishment. ''What sacrifice?''

''You won't get an answer out of him,'' Lakesh said. ''Friend Sindri is enjoying his role as the Sphinx of Thebes too much.''

Philboyd blinked at him in confusion. ''I don't get you.''

''He means,'' Sindri said waspishly, ''that I'm teasing and tormenting you with intentionally cryptic comments.''

''Oh,'' Philboyd said as if he understood.

''You can help us, though,'' Brigid said. ''We're taking him to the holding cells and we need someone to search him.''

''I already told you such a precaution wasn't necessary,'' Sindri growled.

''Kane thinks it is,'' Domi declared. ''But I can do it as well as anybody.''

The hint of a threat in her tone caused Sindri to cast her an apprehensive sidewise glance. With a resigned sigh, he said, ''Oh, very well, then. But for the sake of propriety and my own safety, I request that Dr. Philboyd do the honors.''

Philboyd swallowed hard. ''I don't think I'm comfortable with that.''

Domi grinned and stepped away. ''Everybody has to do their part here.''

She marched away, back in the direction of the

operations center. Lakesh looked to be on the verge of calling after her, but then he laughed shortly. "Let's get it done."

The four people entered the elevator and rode it to the bottom level of Cerberus, some 150 feet below solid, shielded rock. It held the nuclear generators, various maintenance and machine rooms and the air-conditioning core. A semidetached wing contained ten detention cubicles, all of them as nicely appointed as the average flat in the Cobaltville Enclaves.

Lakesh tapped in the sec code on the door leading to the wing. Followed by Sindri, Philboyd and Brigid, he walked through a dimly lit corridor that had once been bisected by a wire-mesh security checkpoint. Only the frame remained now.

He stopped in front of an open cell door and gestured for Philboyd and Sindri to enter. "We'll be right outside," he said, nodding meaningfully to the pistol in Brigid's hand.

Sindri heaved a deep sigh and strode into the small room. Philboyd followed him. Brigid shut the door and the electronic lock clicked and held. She and Lakesh took up positions on either side of the door and regarded each other gravely.

In a low voice, Lakesh asked, "Any ideas on where he came from?"

Brigid shook her head. "None. But it might be more appropriate to wonder *when* he came from."

He angled an eyebrow at her. "What do you mean?"

As she stared into Lakesh's bright blue eyes, Brigid realized she still hadn't grown accustomed to dealing with a relatively youthful Lakesh whose eyes weren't covered by thick lenses and whose voice no longer rose to a reedy rasp.

Brigid said, "The last time we saw Sindri was in the Operations Chronos installation on Thunder Isle. The temporal dilator was running wild, building to critical mass."

He nodded. "Right. There was a venting of its chronon energy, and after the explosion, you found no sign of him."

"It's probable he used the dilator to escape," Brigid declared solemnly. "He either was injected into another timeline or survived in a form of temporal stasis since that day."

Lakesh tugged at his nose, a gesture that meant he found Brigid's speculation intriguing. "A zero time pocket, perhaps."

Brigid raised a questioning eyebrow. "What's that?"

"Basically a state of nontime, a form of nonexistence. Perhaps for the past few months, Sindri was trapped in the temporal dilator's memory buffer matrix, reduced to digital information. He was outside the space-time continuum more or less in a noncorporeal suspension."

"Something like the quincunx effect?" she inquired.

He nodded. "A similar phenomena. In certain circumstances, photons—the particles of which light is made—can jump between two points separated by a barrier and freeze in what appears to be zero time."

Brigid's lips twitched in a wry smile and then compressed into a tight line. "He obviously came from somewhere, as well as somewhen. What do you think he meant about having Kane's blood on him?"

Lakesh lifted a shoulder in a shrug. "Who can say? But since Sindri is the proverbial cunning runt, nothing he says, implies or infers can be taken at face value without a body of supporting evidence."

"So you don't necessarily believe what he said about Sam, a spatiotemporal window and Colonel Thrush?"

"I don't necessarily disbelieve it, either. Sam's true nature has been a mystery for quite some time. If he is Colonel Thrush, that would tend to explain a great deal."

"Like what?" Brigid asked.

Lakesh's brow furrowed for a thoughtful moment. He opened his mouth to reply, but a rap sounded on the other side of the door and Philboyd called, "We're done here."

Obligingly, Lakesh keyed in the unlocking sequence and swung open the door. "That didn't take long."

Philboyd hastily stepped out of the cell. "Good thing, too."

Brigid glimpsed Sindri bent over the tiny sink. The upper portion of his shadowsuit was peeled down from his torso, and he was industriously scrubbing the layer of dried blood from his face.

As Lakesh closed and relocked the door, Philboyd said, "He was telling the truth. He didn't have anything under that suit of his but him. And that was enough."

The astrophysicist's face was a shade paler than normal, and Lakesh eyed him quizzically. "What was enough?"

His eyes blinking repeatedly behind the lenses of his glasses, he murmured, "I thought he might be smuggling something because of—"

He broke off and glanced down meaningfully at his crotch. Taking a deep breath he said in a rush, "Because of what it looked like down there. I had him strip off completely, see—"

"Never mind," Brigid interrupted. "I know what you're referring to."

Philboyd looked at her in surprise and opened his mouth as if to voice a question. Then he thought better of it and kept his inquiries to himself. Brigid was just as glad. Even without her gift of an eidetic memory, she still retained vivid recollections of the time Sindri had tried to rape her—and the sight of his disproportionately huge male member.

If Lakesh knew about Sindri's unusual endowment, he made no comment. He said only, "Let's go back topside and tell friend Kane that Sindri is safely confined."

"I'm not worried about Sindri anymore." The unexpected sound of Kane's voice, echoing hollowly through the corridor, caused all of them to jump and swing their heads around toward the screened-in checkpoint.

Kane marched through it, his face drained of all color. His eyes shone startlingly bright and hard in his face. He had apparently stopped by his quarters before taking the elevator, because he now wore running shoes. He had also made a quick trip to the armory. All of them noticed that his Sin Eater was holstered to his right forearm.

"Philboyd, Baptiste, step away from Lakesh." Kane's flinty tone held an undercurrent of a threat.

"What's your major malfunction, Kane?" Philboyd demanded hotly.

"Do as I say." Kane's response came back as sharp as a whip crack. "I'll explain later."

Lakesh and Brigid stared at Kane with wide eyes, stunned into speechlessness. Neither person moved. "Kane—" Brigid began.

"Do it!" As he barked out the words, Kane's lips peeled back from his teeth. He lifted his right arm, and sensitive actuators attached to the holster popped the Sin Eater into his hand. There was no trigger guard, and when the firing stud came in contact with his crooked trigger finger, the pistol would fire immediately. Fortunately Kane's index finger was held out straight.

"Unlock the cell, Lakesh," he snapped. "Let Sindri out and put yourself in."

After three faltering attempts to speak, Lakesh finally found his voice. His "What?" was a strangulated screech of outrage.

"You heard me," grated Kane. "I'm not going to argue with you, Lakesh. Just do what I say and make it quick."

Angrily, Brigid rushed toward him, eyes glinting like polished emeralds. "Are you fused out, Kane? Why the hell are you doing this?"

When she reached a point in the passageway where

she was within his arm's reach, Kane grabbed her by the shoulder with his left hand and jerked her roughly through the checkpoint frame. She cried out in wordless fury and confusion. He blocked the open gate with his body, preventing her from rejoining Lakesh.

Philboyd, spots of red glowing on his cheeks, started to lunge forward, but he just as quickly subsided when Kane trained the pistol bore on him. Still, he shrilled in agitation, "Have you gone nuts? I thought Sindri was an enemy of yours!"

"This time around, Sindri isn't the menace," Kane declared grimly. "Lakesh is."

Lakesh was too astounded to speak or even to move, but Brigid shouted in fury, "How did you come to that conclusion? Who told you that?"

Kane's tone was steely with conviction as he tapped his chest with a thumb. "*I* did. The me twenty-seven years from now told me. And I see no reason to call myself a liar."

Chapter 2

After five minutes of shouted accusations, matters finally tapered off to a subdued mood of resigned shock and simmering anger.

Kane refused to be swayed from his single-minded insistence that Sindri be freed and Lakesh locked up in his place.

Lakesh seemed to be almost in a condition of somnambulism and didn't appear to be truly aware of what was happening until the cell door closed and locked behind him. Then he began cursing, pounding and kicking. Kane kept Philboyd from intervening by the simple expedient of training his Sin Eater on him, counting on its wicked appearance to intimidate him.

Stripped down to a skeletal frame, the Sin Eater was barely fourteen inches long. The extended magazine held twenty rounds of 9 mm ammo. There was no trigger guard, no fripperies, no ornamentation, no wasted inch of design. The Sin Eater looked exactly like what it was supposed to be—the most viciously efficient handgun ever made.

Sindri stood aside and didn't interfere during the confusion, for which Kane was both grateful and disturbed. He didn't so much as crack a smile at his discomfiture. If Brigid noticed Sindri's unusual complacency, she gave no sign.

"The *you* twenty-seven years from now said to lock up Lakesh?" Her normally melodious, almost musical voice was ragged and harsh.

"He did." Kane directed Philboyd through the checkpoint and closed the gate. "The disk Sindri gave me was recorded by me in the future and sent back as a warning."

"So you're saying the future you sent Sindri back in time?" Brigid's tone was rich with incredulity, but it was underscored by fascination, too.

Sindri folded his arms over his chest and smiled triumphantly. "I told you I was just the messenger."

"How did you—the future you—find Sindri? He looks exactly the same as he did the last time we saw him, only a few months ago."

"He's been trapped in zero time," Kane replied matter-of-factly, as if the answer should have been obvious. "No time passed for him."

Philboyd's mouth worked as if he were either trying to laugh or spit. Finally he husked out, "You're crazy, Kane. You told me a while back you were only a baby step from insanity, but I thought you were joking. You really *are* a fucking lunatic!"

Brigid studied Kane's face closely. His narrowed eyes glittered in a way that made her distinctly uncomfortable, setting her flesh to crawling. She said, "No, he's not."

Philboyd swung his head toward her, expression twisted with disbelief. "Brigid, you can't possibly believe this bullshit!"

Brigid stated crisply, "Kane believes it. That's

enough for me." She paused and added darkly, "For the moment."

Sindri laughed his sinister rattlesnake buzz of a laugh, which raised the nape hairs on all of them. "Quite the testament of trust."

Kane forced a bleak smile to his lips. "Under the circumstances, that's about all I can hope for."

"You'd get a bit more if you leathered your pistol," Brigid told him. "You wouldn't shoot me, and you know it."

Kane's smile widened, but it didn't increase in warmth. "Very true." He shifted the barrel toward Philboyd, who murmured in fear. "But if he gets twitchy again, I'll damn sure disable him."

Brigid stepped in front of the frightened man, her eyes glinting with a defiant light. "No, you won't do that, either. If you want me to trust you on this, leather your weapon."

Kane barely repressed a curse that leaped to his tongue. But after a second or two, he twisted his wrist and retracted the pistol into its holster. "Satisfied?"

Brigid nodded. "For a few minutes anyway."

The four people entered the elevator, and Kane pushed the button to return them to the main level. He studiously avoided looking in the direction of Philboyd and Brigid. Her defensiveness of the lanky, myopic astrophysicist had reached a stage that seemed almost motherly. He didn't understand what she found so appealing in Philboyd, even if she was drawn to his intellect. He knew, however, that although Philboyd wasn't a man of action, he wasn't a coward, either.

During the nightmarish Moon mission, when Kane was locked in brutal hand-to-hand combat with Maccan, the last of the Tuatha de Danaan, Philboyd and Brigid were facing Enki, the sole survivor of the Annunaki, the legendary Dragon Kings. According to Brigid, Philboyd's courage might have cracked but hadn't completely crumbled, and Brigid had been glad to have a solid bulwark at her side on that terrifying night.

Kane found the notion she might be attracted to the man foolish, but not so foolish he didn't feel a twinge of angry fear that Brigid might prefer the astrophysicist to him. At the moment, the notion seemed not just foolish, but so utterly irrelevant he had no words to describe it.

Sindri eyed Kane superciliously. "I'm a little surprised you're taking such decisive action so quickly, Mr. Kane, particularly under these less than normal circumstances."

A muscle jumped in Kane's jaw. His eyes narrowed, but he said nothing. Sindri continued smoothly, with a studied nonchalance, "After all, even your future counterpart expected you to waste several hours accusing me of contriving an elaborate ruse."

Kane cast his gaze downward. "Did you watch the CD?"

Sindri shook his head. "I didn't have the opportunity, not with all the traveling from here to Colorado and then to China." He smiled slyly. "That Xian Pyramid is quite the place."

Brigid stiffened, alarmed at Sindri's casual admission he knew the location of the imperator's stronghold, but Kane did not react to it. "The story I told myself was very believable," he said to Sindri. "I didn't see any reason to doubt myself. Besides, part of the story I told can be easily verified."

The elevator door slid open on the corridor. Philboyd exited first, with undisguised haste. He demanded, "Are you going to explain what the hell is going on here, Kane? Or is this a coup?"

"Of course I'll explain it," Kane retorted sharply as he, Sindri and Brigid left the elevator. "But I want to do it only once. I need someone to volunteer to gate to Thunder Isle, so word can be gotten to Grant over on New Edo."

"What word?" Brigid asked dourly.

Kane favored her with a grim, level stare. He held up a pair of fingers. "Two words, actually. 'Come a-running.'"

"It's that serious?"

Sindri took it upon himself to answer the question. "Oh, yes," he said somberly. "Oh, yes, indeed. It's *that* serious."

A FEW WEEKS PREVIOUSLY, Grant had announced his intention to reside more or less permanently with Shizuka on the Western Isle of New Edo. The term Western Isles was a catch-all to describe a region in the Cific Ocean of old and new landmasses. Two centuries before, the tectonic shifts triggered by the nukecaust dropped most of California south of the San Andreas Fault into the sea.

During the intervening decades, undersea quakes

raised new volcanic islands. Because the soil was scraped up from the seabed, most of the islands became fertile very quickly, except for the Blight Belt— islands that were originally part of the California coastline but were still irradiated.

New Edo and its companion islet, known as Ikazuchi Kojima, Thunder Isle, were part of the Santa Barbara or Channel Islands. The primary Operation Chronos installation, code-named Redoubt Yankee, had been built on the small island, disguised as a satellite campus of the University of California.

Many of the other Western Isles were overrun by pirates and Asian criminal organizations known as Tongs. The people of New Edo gave these a wide berth but established a friendly relationship with a coastal ville called Port Morninglight. The little island empire traded with them for several years, until it was wiped out by a force of Magistrates dispatched by Baron Cobalt. When Shizuka and a contingent of New Edoan samurai, the Tigers of Heaven, tracked the murderous Mags, their paths intersected with that of Grant, Kane, Brigid and Domi, who were engaged in the same enterprise.

Since initially meeting the female samurai Shizuka and visiting her little island monarchy in the Cific, the concept of relocating only gradually occurred to Grant. Like most of the Cerberus personnel, he was an exile from the baronies and felt he was needed at the redoubt. However, with the influx of people from the Manitius base, Grant reached the conclusion his presence wasn't quite as critical to the work of Cerberus as it had been only a couple of years earlier.

Besides, he had taken no vows or sworn oaths of service to battle the tyranny of the barons. Kane and he were partners of many years standing, true enough, and it was a matter of Mag policy never to desert a partner regardless of the circumstances, but they weren't Mags any longer. Kane had more of a vested interest in seeing the barons overthrown than he did. It was Kane's vengeance trail and vendetta, not his. His primary contribution was to cover Kane's back. But now there were other people who could be trained to perform that function just as well.

But more than that, Grant had realized he was weary of contending with threats, with menaces, with madmen and with weekly doses of violence. He had witnessed many violent deaths, and even been responsible for dozens of them during his Mag days and after.

His first years in exile had been hard and desperate, but they'd been good ones, too. Still and all, at the end of the day he owed Cerberus nothing. He had put in his time, shed his blood, lost his pound of flesh and broken his bones for the cause.

It was no longer enough for him to wish for a glorious death as a payoff. His last brush with mortality resulted in weeks of partial paralysis. Although the condition had been temporary, it proved something he had known for years but never admitted to himself—when death came, it was usually unexpected, swift and almost never glorious.

On a deeper, more visceral level, he was simply emotionally and spiritually drained. He was getting old and feared that he was slowing down, that his reflexes could no longer achieve what his warrior instincts demanded.

Kane understood his old friend's reasoning, even if he felt Grant was somewhat misguided, too intoxicated by Shizuka to think clearly.

Using the Operation Chronos installation on Thunder Isle as a conduit was the only way to reach Grant on New Edo, since the monarchy was within transcomm range of the little islet. A mission a few months before had brought Grant, Kane and Brigid to the installation, a place they assumed had been uninhabited and forgotten since the nuclear holocaust of two centuries before. Only much later did they find out the installation was indeed inhabited by none other than Sindri.

When confronted, the dwarf told them that when he'd first arrived in the facility, he found the temporal dilator's chronon wave guide conformals were activating on wild, random cycles. They either reconstituted trawled subjects from the memory buffer matrix, or snatched new ones from all epochs in history. Thus, specimens of people, animals and plants were randomly trawled from past times.

Sindri managed to get control of the dilator and use it a bit more judiciously. One of the uses to which he put it was to retrieve Domi a microsecond before her death in Area 51. However, his tampering with the technology caused it to become dangerously unstable. With a minimum of tampering from Brigid, the dilator overloaded and reached critical mass, resulting in a violent meltdown of its energy core.

When the radiation in the installation ebbed to a

nonlethal level, Brigid and Lakesh made several visits to the Operation Chronos redoubt, reclaiming what could be salvaged of the technology. There turned out to be a surprising amount of usable equipment. After the arrival of the Moon base scientific staff, a group was assigned to do a complete examination and investigation of the facility, in order to make Thunder Isle a viable alternative to the Cerberus redoubt in Montana.

Back in the operations center, Kane briefly explained to the personnel present that he needed an emissary. Farrell wasn't interested. He was a rangy, middle-aged man who effected a shaved head, a goatee and a gold hoop earring, after watching an old predark vid called *Hells Angels On Wheels.*

Bry, who served as Lakesh's technical lieutenant, declined, as well—very vehemently. His expression and attitude were always ones of consternation, no matter his true mood. Although he and Farrell were studies in physical contrasts, they now shared similar attitudes—both eyed Sindri with a mixture of suspicion and fascination.

Nora Pennick, another émigré from the Manitius base, volunteered for the job. She had been gating back and forth to Thunder Isle fairly frequently for the past three weeks, identifying and cataloging the tech found in the Chronos installation.

Kane always experienced a quiver of surprise when he saw her, since she looked nothing like the woman she'd been when he, Grant and Brigid met in the DEVIL control nexus of the Manitius colony only a month or so before. Then, she was a dirty, undernourished-looking vagabond. Her clothes were ragged and her shoulder-length dark hair was a tangle of uncombed Medusa snarls. Since her arrival in the Cerberus redoubt, she had been sampling the supply of cosmetics left there by the female personnel of the installation before it had been abandoned in the days preceding the nukecaust.

The white bodysuit she wore clung tightly to her trim, small-waisted figure. Her hair was coifed and neatly trimmed. The makeup she had applied had evidently been in fashion before the nukecaust, even though Kane's private opinion was that it made her look like a gaudy slut.

He wrote a brief message on a square of note paper, folded it and handed it to her. Some weeks before, a shortwave radio unit had been installed in the Thunder Isle installation. Although its range was limited, New Edo's matching comm was well within its frequency limit. "When you get Grant on the wire," Kane instructed her, "read it to him word for word."

Nora angled a plucked and darkly penciled eyebrow at him. "Word for word." She spoke with an unmistakable British accent. She and another Britisher, Cleve Randolph, had been part of the DEVIL scientific staff on the Moon. However, Cleve had been killed when he helped Grant steal a Transatmospheric Manta ship.

Unlike some of her colleagues, Nora didn't display a thinly veiled attitude of superiority toward her hosts. Many of the Moon base personnel seemed amused by the Cerberus exiles' ignorance of a number of twentieth-century events and items, but she wasn't one of them. Kane attributed her apparent disinterest in Sindri to her calm and collected British heritage. She didn't appear to even notice the small man, much less the leering examination he gave her.

Turning toward Bry, Kane asked, ''Is the gateway operable?''

Seated at the main ops console, the man lifted his knobby shoulders in a shrug. ''I've completed a level-two diagnostic. Everything from the autosequence scanner to the coordinate lock shows green.''

Kane was a bit surprised by Nora's willingness to undertake a mat-trans jump, since traveling in such a fashion was still new to her. No human being, no matter how thoroughly briefed in advance, could be expected to remain unmoved by a hyperdimensional trip via the quantum interphase mat-trans inducer, colloquially known as a gateway.

After stepping into the armaglass-enclosed chamber, one second a person was there, surrounded by glowing mist, and in the next second, the universe seemed to cave in. Perceptions changed, time jumped and for a heart-stopping instant, the cosmos at large seemed to stand still. Then the traveler was wherever the transmitter had been programmed to materialize him or her. Whatever else, a trip through the gateway was unsettling to the mind, to the nerves and to the soul itself. But as a scientist, Kane supposed Nora Pennick found the experience more stimulating than upsetting.

Kane and Nora walked through the operations center, through the ready room and then entered the free-standing gateway unit. Right above the keypad en-

coding panel, imprinted in faded maroon letters were
the words Entry Absolutely Forbidden to All but B12
Cleared Personnel. Mat-Trans. Even Lakesh didn't
know who the B12 cleared personnel had been, or
what had become of them, though he had opined they
had probably jumped from the installation after the
nukecaust, desperately searching for a place better
than Cerberus and doubtlessly not finding it.

Kane closed the heavy armaglass door behind the
woman. Instantly the lock solenoids caught and triggered the automatic jump initiator. The familiar humming vibration rose, climbing to a high-pitched drone.
The hexagonal metal disks above and below exuded
a shimmering glow that slowly intensified. The fine
mist gathered and climbed from the floor and wafted
down from the ceiling. Tiny crackling static dis-
charges flared in the vapor. Bright flares, like bursts
of distant heat lightning, flashed on the other side of
the armaglass barrier.

Manufactured in the last decades of the twentieth
century from a special compound that plasticized the
properties of steel and glass, armaglass was used as
walls in the jump chambers to confine quantum energy overspills.

Within seconds, the hum climbed in pitch and volume until it sounded like a combination of a runaway
locomotive and a hurricane howl, then it ebbed,
slowly cycling down.

Brigid came to Kane's side and asked, "What was
in the note?"

He smiled thinly. "Basically the same old shit—
world on the brink, millions of lives at stake, death,

destruction and horror right around the corner. The usual."

Brigid sighed. "Doesn't it ever get to be a pain in the ass?"

"What?"

"It seems to me you spend most of your life waiting for someone to come along and try to end it. Isn't that a pain in the ass?"

"You tell me," he countered. "You're a target as much of the time as I am."

She snorted derisively. "Mainly due to my association with you."

Kane snapped, "Do you have a point to make, Baptiste? If so, let's get it out in the open now, not when we're in front of Sindri."

Brigid ran impatient hands through her mane of hair. "You're really enjoying this, aren't you?"

He regarded her with a sideways, slit-eyed stare. "Explain."

Gesturing to the operations room in particular and the redoubt around them in general, Brigid declared, "Taking control, assuming command of Cerberus is something you've wanted to do for a long time."

Brigid spoke without heat, with no hint of accusation underscoring her words. She sounded as if she were commenting on an exceptionally mundane matter. "Ever since we confronted Lakesh about the way he recruited people, you've wanted to completely displace him."

Almost two years before, Brigid, Kane and Grant learned that Lakesh had used his position as a Cobaltville administrator to choose likely prospects to join his underground resistance movement. In the twentieth century Lakesh had been a major player in the conspiracy that led to the nuclear holocaust of 2001.

After his resurrection from cryostasis nearly 150 years later, he became instrumental in establishing the baronial society and served as a trusted member of Baron Cobalt's inner circle. However, all that he'd seen and lived through, and everything he remembered from the past altered Lakesh's alliances.

Instead of remaining a key facilitator of the unification program's aims and goals, Lakesh became its most dangerous adversary. Over the past forty years he'd put his plans to build an active resistance into action and manipulated the political system of the baronies to secretly restore the Cerberus redoubt to full operational capacity. But having a headquarters for a resistance movement meant nothing if there were no resistance fighters.

The only way to find them was through yet more manipulation. Using the genetic records on file in villes, Lakesh selected candidates for his rebellion, but finding them was far easier than recruiting them. With his authority and influence, he set them up, framing them for crimes against their respective villes.

It was a cruel, heartless plan with a barely acceptable risk factor, but Lakesh believed it was the only way to spirit them out of their villes, turn them against the barons and make them feel indebted to him.

To his everlasting regret, Lakesh had never married or fathered children. The closest he came to producing offspring was when he rifled the ville's genetic records to find desirable qualifications in order to build a covert resistance movement against the baronies. He used the barons' own fixation with genetic purity against them.

By his own confession, he was a physicist cast in the role of an archivist, pretending to be a geneticist, manipulating a political system that was still in a state of flux. Kane was one such example of that political and genetic manipulation, and the last thing he felt toward him was fatherly.

After a crisis erupted due to this practice, Lakesh's machinations were exposed. Grant, Kane and Brigid had staged something of a minimutiny over the issue, but nothing had been decisively settled. However, Lakesh was put on notice that his titular position as the redoubt's final authority was extremely weak.

Kane said, "You damn well know I could have dumped Lakesh off the cliff at any time since then and taken over if I wanted to."

Brigid nodded. "Yes, but you would have had to convince Grant to go along with you. Now that he's out of the picture, you don't have much in the way of opposition votes."

In a neutral, flat voice, Kane intoned, "What I'm doing may very well save the entire future from a tyranny worse than anything the barons might impose."

Brigid's lips curved in a disdainful smile. "And how will locking up Lakesh fight the future?"

Kane said, "That's a good question, Baptiste. Suppose we visit DeFore? She might have a couple of answers.''

''Answers to what questions?'' Brigid demanded.

''Mainly,'' Kane replied in a voice pitched low but packed with conviction, ''about whether Lakesh is full of nanites. And if he is, does that make him a traitor or a pawn?''

''Nanites?'' Brigid stared at him in wide-eyed incomprehension for a long moment of silence. Then she husked out, ''Brewster is right. You *are* crazy.''

Taking her by the elbow and guiding her toward the exit, Kane said genially, ''Let's find out together.''

Chapter 3

They found DeFore not in the infirmary, which was her private domain, but seated in the redoubt's cafeteria. Since it was close to dinnertime and shift change, it wasn't too much of a surprise to find her there. However, Kane experienced a moment of queasy discomfort when he saw her dining companion of the evening. Quavell sat across from her, daintily eating from a plate of oatmeal that had two scoops of strawberry ice cream swimming in it.

Quavell was a hybrid, a blending of human and so-called Archon genetic material. She was small, smaller even than Domi, under five feet in height. Her huge, slanting eyes of a clear crystal blue gave Kane a silent appraisal at his and Brigid's approach.

Her eyes dominated a face of chiseled, elfin loveliness. If not for the grave austerity of her expression, she would have been beautiful. White-blond hair the texture of silk threads fell from her domed skull and curled inward at her slender shoulders. Her tiny form was encased in a silvery-gray, skintight bodysuit. It only accentuated the distended condition of her belly and the slenderness of her limbs. The material of the one-piece garment was a synthetic polymer with a high degree of elasticity, and it provided adequate support.

As a hybrid, Quavell required food that was easily digestible for her simplified intestinal tract. Although Lakesh had undertaken a lot of time and trouble to make sure the food lockers and meat freezers of the redoubt were exceptionally well stocked, there was very little in the way of single-cell protein microorganisms hybrids normally ingested. Oatmeal and ice cream were improvisations until a way to manufacture the microorganisms could be perfected. DeFore was testing a synthesization process using equipment recently arrived from the Moon base.

DeFore's eyes widened in surprise when Kane asked, "Mind if we join you?"

In the month and a half since Quavell's arrival at Cerberus, Kane had shown a marked disinclination to be in her company at all, much less share a table with her. The medic nodded toward a pair of empty chairs. "Make yourselves at home."

Before sitting, Kane and Brigid poured themselves cups of coffee at the serving station. One of the few advantages of being an exile in Cerberus was unrestricted access to genuine coffee, not the bitter synthetic gruel that had become the common, sub-par substitute since skydark, the generation-long nuclear winter. Literally tons of freeze-dried packets of the real article were cached in the redoubt's storage areas. There was enough coffee to last the exiles several lifetimes, even with the influx of new personnel.

As Brigid and Kane sat, DeFore eyed them both a little suspiciously and asked, "Where's Sindri?"

Brigid nodded in the general direction of the operations center. "Kane released him. We're letting Bry nursemaid him for a bit."

"Really?" DeFore's eyebrows rose. "And what does Lakesh think about that?"

When Kane didn't respond to the query, Brigid interjected dryly, "Since you already brought him up in conversation, Kane has something to ask you about his medical condition."

DeFore's eyebrows lowered, bracketing a pair of horizontal lines that creased the bridge of her nose. "Your guess is as good as mine."

Brigid and Kane knew the meaning of her oblique reference. The matter of Lakesh's restored youth had been a major topic of speculation for the past few months. Not even Lakesh himself pretended to understand how it had happened. The process he described flew so thoroughly in the face of scientific and medical fact, he might as well have relegated the cause to drinking a magic elixir.

All DeFore really knew was that more than six months earlier she watched Mohandas Lakesh Singh step into the gateway chamber as a hunched-over spindly old man who appeared to be fighting the grave for every hour he remained on the planet.

A day later, the gateway chamber activated and when the door opened, Kane, Brigid Baptiste, Grant and Domi emerged. A well-built stranger wearing the white bodysuit of Cerberus duty personnel followed them. DeFore could only gape in stunned silence at the man's thick, glossy, black hair, his unlined olive complexion and toothy, excited grin. She recognized only the blue eyes and the long, aquiline nose as belonging to the Lakesh she had known for the past five years.

Lakesh attributed the miracle to Sam and his laying on of hands. Even he knew the process was far more complex than that, but he could engage only in fairly futile speculation how it had been accomplished. According to him, Sam simply laid his little hand against his midriff and a tingling warmth seemed to seep from it.

The warmth swiftly became searing heat, like waves of liquid fire rippling through his veins and arteries. His heartbeat picked up in tempo, spread the rhythms through the rest of his body, like a pulsing web of energy that suffused every separate cell and organ.

He described how his body became aflame with a searing pain, the same kind of agony a man would feel when circulation was suddenly restored to a numb limb. His entire metabolism seemed to awaken to furious life from a long slumber, as if it had been jump-started by a powerful battery.

He told them in tones of hushed awe that after the sensation of heat faded, he realized two things more or less simultaneously: he wasn't wearing his glasses but he could see his hand perfectly. And by that perfect vision, he saw the flesh of hand was smooth, the prominent veins of old age having sunk back into firm flesh. Even liver spots faded away as he watched.

Sam claimed he had increased Lakesh's production of two antioxidant enzymes, catalase and superoxide dismutase, and boosted up his alkyglycerol level to the point where the aging process was for all intents and purposes reversed. For the first few weeks following Sam's treatment, his hair continued to darken and more and more of his wrinkles disappeared. But then the entire process reached a certain point and came to a halt. Lakesh estimated he had returned to a physical state approximating his mid-forties.

Lakesh assumed Sam possessed the ability to transfer his biological energy to other organic matter, which in turn stimulated the entire human cellular structure. Beyond that, he could only guess.

Lakesh didn't try to convince DeFore or anyone else that he believed his condition was permanent. He claimed he had no idea how long his vitality would last. Whether it would vanish overnight like the fabulous One Horse Shay and leave him a doddering old scarecrow again, or whether he would simply begin to age normally from that point onward, he couldn't be certain.

However, he told all of them he wasn't about to waste the gift of youth, as transitory as it might be. Nobody knew who One Horse Shay had been or what was so fabulous about him, but DeFore noticed Lakesh surreptitiously eyeing her bosom in a way he had never done before.

Kane suspected that Lakesh was taking full advantage of his restored middle age. The glances he caught Domi and Lakesh exchanging from time to time hinted at that. He was also increasingly assertive and challenging. The confrontational behavior Kane attributed to a higher hormonal level.

Still, Kane was no more inclined to tolerate high-handedness from a middle-aged Lakesh than an elderly one, so their clashes had actually become more frequent.

Kane took a sip of coffee, then said casually, "There might not be any guesswork involved any longer."

Both DeFore and Quavell looked at him quizzically. "No?" queried the medic.

"No. That's what I want you to confirm."

Stiffly, DeFore retorted, "You damn well know I can't discuss a patient's medical condition with anyone other than the patient. I can't violate physician and patient confidentiality unless permission has been given in advance—and in this case it hasn't."

Kane wanted to ask her when she had taken the Hippocratic oath, but he knew she wouldn't appreciate the sarcasm. Reba DeFore had never disguised her antipathy toward him—or rather to what he represented. In her eyes, as a former Magistrate, he was the strutting embodiment of the totalitarianism of the villes, glorying in his baron-sanctioned powers to dispense justice and death. At one time she had believed that due to his Mag conditioning he was psychologically conflicted and therefore couldn't be trusted.

Once, in a private, unguarded moment, DeFore had been driven by frustration to admit that she didn't believe she was really a doctor, not by the predark definition of the term. She described her training as superficial, down and dirty. At best, she felt she fulfilled the functions of what was once known as a general practitioner.

Kane knew he needed the medic on his side, so he dispensed with the old resentments and his tendency toward making snide comments. "A couple of weeks ago," Kane said matter-of-factly, "Lakesh suffered a collapse."

DeFore's lips pursed. "That much is public knowledge. But I'm not obligated to explain why."

Kane nodded as if he expected the answer. Choosing his words carefully, he said, "Doctor, I wouldn't be inquiring if I didn't feel the matter was of utmost importance."

As he had hoped, DeFore reacted with a fleeting, appreciative smile to being addressed by the honorific. "How so?"

"The redoubt's security might be at stake."

"Due to Lakesh?"

"Yes."

She lifted a shoulder in a negligent shrug. "That wouldn't be a new situation."

Kane and Brigid knew DeFore was making a backhanded reference to the occasionally hostile dynamic she shared with Lakesh. Although she was one of the first exiles recruited by him, the two people still disagreed on a wide variety of matters. She had accused him of being overdemanding and high-handed and sometimes she outright distrusted him, particularly after he supplied Balam with the destination lock codes of the redoubt's gateway to bring in Sam.

"Anyway," said DeFore, "before I breach the confidentiality of my patient, you'll have to convince me the circumstances require it."

"That's why we're here." Kane took a deep breath and stated in a neutral tone of voice, "I believe that Lakesh's restored youth is due to the introduction of nanites into his system. Not only did Sam put them there, he's exerting a certain amount of control over them, too.''

DeFore's face molded itself into an expression of shock, but she said nothing as Kane continued, ''I can't even guess at the extent of the control, but I'm not taking any chances. I've confined Lakesh to a holding cell until further notice. How long he stays locked up will be partly determined by what you tell me. So, if you can see fit to sidestep your confidentiality oath just this once to either confirm or deny what I've just said, we can all decide a course of action together.''

During Kane's remarks, even the normally stoic Brigid expressed first surprise, then a deep unease. Due to her many years as an archivist in the Cobaltville Historical Division, Brigid had worked hard at perfecting a poker face. Since archivists were always watched, probably more than anyone else working in the other divisions, she had worked diligently to develop an outward persona of cool calm, unflappable and immutable.

Reba DeFore had no such tradition to which to adhere. Her eyes had become so wide the brown irises were completely surrounded by the whites. Her lips worked, then she sputtered, ''How did you— You couldn't have— How—''

Quavell spoke for the first time since Brigid and Kane sat at the table. Her voice was a musical yet almost childlike lilt despite her claim of being nearly seventy years old. ''I believe the doctor is trying to ascertain who provided you with that information.''

When an answer from Kane wasn't immediately forthcoming, Brigid asked, "It's true, then?" Her tone vibrated with barely repressed tension.

Swallowing hard, DeFore nodded. Pitching her voice to barely above a whisper, even though no one else was present in the cafeteria, she said, "Yes. His entire cellular structure is infested with nanites, from his circulatory system to his glands."

Swiftly she told Kane, Brigid and Quavell how in an effort to find the cause of Lakesh's collapse, she had taken a blood sample and found several different kinds of nanomachines floating within the red blood cells. At first, the nanites had inflicted organic damage on Lakesh, but then repaired it almost as they watched. Lakesh had ominously speculated that Sam had caused the nanites to run briefly amok as a demonstration, a display of power, to show what he could do from his stronghold in Xian, China.

Neither Kane nor Brigid found the possibility of such long-range control out of the realm of probability, since Sam could manipulate the convergence of electromagnetic energies he called the Heart of the World. The Heart existed slightly out of phase with the third dimension, with the human concept of space-time. From its central core extended a web of electromagnetic and geophysical energy that covered the entire planet. Exerting a degree of remote control over tiny machines seemed like a minor accomplishment for someone of Sam's abilities.

DeFore added that trying to flush the nanites from Lakesh's body would not be an efficacious treatment; even a complete blood transfusion and filtering of all of his bodily fluids through dialysis wouldn't work. There were millions of the microscopic machines embedded throughout the soft tissues of his cellular structure.

Brigid pushed her coffee away and husked out, "I didn't make the connection before. The implications—" She bit off the rest of whatever she intended to say, as if it were too horrible to utter.

Kane cast her a sideways glance. Her face was shockingly pale, but he knew what she was feeling and why. To DeFore, he challenged, "You didn't think any of that was worth sharing with us?"

DeFore's lips tightened. "I didn't perceive it as a threat to the redoubt. You apparently feel otherwise, and I'd like to know why. Who told you about the nanites? Domi?"

"Domi?" he repeated. "She knew about them?"

DeFore nodded. "She was there when he collapsed."

Kane shook his head in angry frustration. "No, Domi didn't say a word."

"Then who told you?" DeFore demanded.

Kane pushed his chair back and rose. "That'll have to wait until Grant gets here and we can convene a formal briefing. Until then, consider Lakesh under complete quarantine. Nobody is to go near him, much less touch him."

"Why?"

"It stands to reason," Quavell said calmly, "if the imperator could transfer the devices to Dr. Singh through physical contact, it's possible Dr. Singh may be able to do the same to others."

"For all we know," Brigid declared, "the nanites could have already infected our computer systems and are waiting for a signal from Sam to take them over or destroy them."

A little defensively, DeFore said, "The types of nanites I found inside Lakesh were designed to combine sensors, programs and molecular tools to form systems able to examine and repair individual cells."

"What did you do with the ones you removed from him?" Kane asked.

"They're hermetically sealed," DeFore said, trying to sound reassuring. "I've been studying them when I have the time."

Brigid rose swiftly, standing shoulder to shoulder with Kane. "I'd like to take a look at them."

Chapter 4

It wasn't as if the Cerberus exiles had no prior experience with nanotechnology. Every person in the redoubt had been implanted with biolink subcutaneous transponders based on organic nanotechnology developed two centuries before by Overproject Excalibur. The transponders were composed of nonharmful radioactive chemicals that fit themselves into the human body and allowed the monitoring of heart rates, brain-wave patterns and blood counts. Lakesh had ordered all of the Cerberus redoubt's personnel to be injected with them. The transponders fed information through the Comsat relay satellite when personnel were out in the field.

The signal was relayed to the redoubt by the Comsat, one of the two satellites to which the installation was uplinked. The computer systems recorded every byte of data sent to the Comsat, and directed it down to the redoubt's hidden antenna array. Sophisticated scanning filters combed through the telemetry using special human biological encoding. The digital data stream was then routed to a locational program in order to precisely isolate the team's position in time and space.

However, as Brigid examined the nanites through a microscope, she noted that the dark gray things with bulbous bodies and feebly kicking triple-jointed legs didn't resemble in the slightest the subcutaneous transponders. The nanites' legs swiveled in their sockets, perforating both sides of their torsos.

Brigid straightened from the eyepieces of the microscope and fixed DeFore with a level, unblinking stare, full of unspoken recriminations.

"What?" the medic demanded harshly.

"You should've told us about this immediately, Reba."

DeFore gestured angrily to the microscope, then to the capped, transparent glass tube in Kane's hand. "I just didn't think they were dangerous to anyone but Lakesh."

"I'll admit," Kane said grudgingly as he tapped a fingernail against the tube, "they don't look very threatening."

At first, even on second glance, the transparent cylinder appeared to be empty. Only by holding the tube up to the laboratory's overhead fluorescent lights could he discern the tiny, almost invisible specks on the inner wall of the tube. Even then, they looked like a scattering of dirt particles. They were the nanites found in Lakesh's blood sample. The medic had explained how she used the infirmary's centrifuge to separate them from the plasma.

"I didn't view them as a threat, either," DeFore said.

"But," Brigid interposed grimly, "even repair nanites would have to be connected to a larger computer by means of mechanical data links. The devices pass along information, and the governing computer would pass back general instructions. Lakesh would've realized that."

DeFore nodded a little contritely. "He did. But he also said the machine could repair a body's hardware while neither understanding nor changing its software. In other words, they couldn't control his mind."

"Unless," said Kane, "Sam programmed the damn things to make him say that—or even make him believe it."

The medic sighed as if she had grown very tired of the topic. "Well, it's obvious now the nanites injected into Lakesh's metabolism held it in a state of biostasis. The natural aging process was slowed, maybe even frozen. When they ran wild and damaged tissues on a molecular level, they concentrated their attack on the weakest areas of his body, where the transplant surgeries were performed over fifty years ago."

After Lakesh's resurrection from cryostasis half a century earlier, he had undergone several operations to further prolong his life. His malfunctioning heart had been traded for a healthy one, his glaucoma-afflicted brown eyes exchanged for bright, albeit myopic blue ones, his weak lungs changed out for a strong new pair.

Calcified, arthritic joints in his shoulders and legs were removed and replaced with ones made of polyethylene. None of the reconstructive surgeries or physiological enhancements had been performed out of Samaritan impulses. His life and health had been prolonged so he could serve the Program of Unification and the baronies.

Brigid narrowed her eyes. "Are you telling us Sam is arranging for Lakesh's slow destruction from within?"

DeFore hesitated before replying. "I wouldn't make that kind of extreme diagnosis, that the nanites are eating him away on a molecular level...but they definitely can have an adverse effect on his metabolic functions. Whether it's accidental or part of a program I don't know."

Kane snorted derisively. "I know. I'd say it's pretty safe bet that Sam wouldn't have introduced the damn things into his body without a way to control them."

"Which means," DeFore declared, "he's not the flesh-and-blood entity Lakesh thought he was."

"Exactly." Kane bit out the word. He replaced the tube in a metal clamp attached to the trestle table.

Bitterly Brigid said, "Damn Lakesh and damn all of his secrets."

Neither DeFore nor Kane responded to her contemptuous comment, nor had she expected them to. Despite her great fondness for him, Brigid knew that Lakesh, during his double life as a baronial adviser and insurrectionist, had grown too accustomed to secretiveness to be comfortable sharing much of anything about his personal life.

Sometimes the reticence was understandable, but most often it was enraging. More than once it had been downright dangerous, with dire consequences that had been barely avoided. Even Lakesh himself had shamefacedly admitted that his plans had nearly gotten them all killed—worse than killed—on a number of occasions, often due to his giving them just enough information to plunge them into serious trouble.

Although there were many things Brigid faulted Kane for, she knew at least she could trust him with her life. She was always prepared to defend him if the circumstances warranted. With Lakesh's secretive and almost conspiratorially questionable behavior, Kane—no matter how often she disagreed with him— was the only constant she had in her life.

The suspicion rising to the forefront of her mind troubled her, especially since she didn't know why Lakesh had been silent about the presence of the nanomachines in his blood. Back in Cobaltville, Lakesh had been her mentor. He'd matriculated her and educated her, promoted her to a high-ranking position as an archivist.

But Lakesh had also been the one who had set in motion the events that led to her exile from Cobaltville, driving her away from everything she'd ever known. Her citizenship was stripped from her, and she had been reclassified as an outlander.

She'd always considered herself important to the man, but old doubts that she had never fully examined could no longer be ignored. The way Lakesh had recruited Beth-Li Rouch and attempted to set up his own breeding farm by pairing her off with Kane had been the first indication that Lakesh cared more for the success of his own plans than the feelings of others.

For a moment Brigid considered returning to detention and confronting Lakesh, but she knew she would only be wasting her time. If Lakesh decided he was going to maintain his secrets, then he never said a word about them. Kane seemed to be the only one who could occasionally threaten the truth out of the man.

"What was Lakesh's take on the nanites?" Kane wanted to know.

DeFore shrugged. "He'd been operating under the assumption Sam possessed the ability to transfer his biological energy to other organic matter. His theory was that Sam's energy transfer might have rejuvenated the MHC in the six chromosomal structures, which resulted in turning back the hands of his metabolic clock, persuading the cells to reproduce and repair themselves.

"I told him that if aging was controlled by a sort of biological alarm clock, a kind of genetic switching system and the hands of his clock were turned back, logic suggested they'd start moving in the right direction and the normal fashion again."

"Did he buy it?" Brigid asked.

"I don't know," replied DeFore. "There was no reason for him not to, particularly after I told him different kinds of clocks and watches were designed to run for different lengths of time after being wound—therefore different kinds of bodies were genetically designed to run for different periods. I warned him the mainspring of his body's clock could break at any time, or it could go haywire and he could age ten years in ten seconds. At first that's what I thought might be happening to him."

"Until you found the nanites." Kane wasn't asking

a question; he was making a statement. "Then the entire theory about Sam transferring his own bio-energy into Lakesh went down the toilet."

"Could the nanites really exert some form of control over his mind and his behavior?" Brigid asked.

DeFore frowned musingly. "I doubt it. At least not to any great extent. From the little research I've done on nanotechnology, it appears there are certain kinds of medical treatments beyond the capability of cell repair machines for different reasons—maintaining mental health, for instance.

"Obviously, cell repair nanites would be able to correct some problems, since deranged thinking sometimes has biochemical causes, as if the brain were drugging or poisoning itself. Other mental and emotional problems stem from tissue damage. But most behavior problems have little to do with the health of nerve cells and everything to do with the health of the mind."

"Unless," Kane said, "the nanites function like SQUID implants."

Brigid squinted toward him. "Superconducting quantum interface devices?"

Kane nodded. "Erica van Sloan, Sam's so-called mother, invented them, remember?"

"I'm not liable to forget much of anything, Kane." Brigid's tone was terse. Due to her eidetic memory, everything she read or saw or even heard was impressed indelibly on her mind. She supposed simply possessing an encyclopedic memory made her intellect something of a fraud, at least compared to the staggeringly high IQ of Lakesh.

Although Kane often accused her of using her photographic memory to make herself appear far more knowledgeable than she actually was, she viewed her ability as a valuable resource that had nothing to do with ego.

"Anyway," Brigid went on, "Erica didn't actually invent the SQUIDs. But she refined them to sophisticated levels and pretty much used them as the foundation to make the first fully functioning, large-scale mind-machine interface."

A brilliant predark cyberneticist, Erica van Sloan had perfected the SQUID implants as a way to control the personnel of the Anthill complex. Since the main difficulty in constructing interfaces between mechanical-electric and organic systems was the wiring, Erica herself oversaw the implantation of SQUIDs directly into the subject's brain. They were only one-hundredth of a micron across and drew power from the electromagnetic field generated by the neuronic energy of the brain itself.

DeFore ventured cautiously, "Sam can't really be a machine. I saw him that time, when he and Erica van Sloan gated in here. He looked human enough to me."

A corner of Kane's mouth twitched, either in a grimace or a bleak smile. "So have a lot of monsters we've met over the past few years, Colonel Thrush first and foremost among them."

DeFore scowled at him. "You still haven't told me how you knew about the nanites in the first place, Kane."

"I'd like to know that myself."

Kane turned at the sound of Domi's angry voice as she swept from the dispensary into the laboratory. Eyes snapping crimson sparks, she said, "I just talked to Quavell. What the fuck do you mean by letting that devil dwarf have the run of the place while you lock up Lakesh?"

Kane stood his ground as she strode up to within a foot of him, her bare toes nearly treading on the tips of his shoes. Calmly he said, "At the moment, that devil dwarf doesn't present a threat to us."

"And Lakesh does?" Domi's question was a strident half shriek of outrage and incredulity.

"Yes," Kane answered firmly. "And it's partly due to you by withholding the information about the nanites in Lakesh's body."

Domi thrust her head forward pugnaciously, as if she intended to sink her teeth into the base of Kane's neck. "Little bitty mites in blood? Who cares? They bite him, not us!"

She had reverted to her abbreviated mode of Outland speech as she usually did when under stress. Despite his anger with her, Kane couldn't really blame her for being upset. Only recently had she confided to him about the intimate relationship that had developed between her and Lakesh.

He hadn't spoken about their affair and Domi had revealed very little of her own feelings about it, but Kane had wondered if she was trying to deal with the bitterness she still harbored over her unrequited love for Grant.

Kane guessed Lakesh's reluctance to let anyone know about his relationship with Domi derived mainly from the habit of keeping two centuries' worth of secrets—or the fact that at 250 years old, he might be considered a shade too old for her.

"The problem is," Brigid said, trying to sound soothing, "we don't know if those mites won't end up biting all of us eventually. That's why he's been isolated from the rest of the installation."

Domi didn't even so much as glance in Brigid's direction. Staring directly into Kane's eyes, she hissed fiercely, "Let 'im out!"

"I can't." Kane reached for her shoulders, but Domi evaded his grasp, slapping his hands away.

"You let 'im go," she said between clenched teeth, "or I do it."

Kane's jaw muscles knotted. "No, you won't, Domi. If you try, I'll lock you up, too."

She uttered a hooting, scornful laugh. "Like to see you try!"

Kane took a menacing step toward her, but she stood her ground, not in the least intimidated by him. Her eyes never left his face. Brigid sidled in between them, one hand on Domi's shoulder, the other pressing against Kane's chest.

"Knock it off," she said crossly. "Both of you."

Domi strained against Brigid's restraining arm. "Then tell that full-of-himself bastard to let Lakesh go free and lock up that goddamn dwarf!"

Kane made an obvious attempt to compose himself, forcing himself to relax and inhaling a deep breath. In as unemotional a voice as he could manage, he said, "Domi, you don't know the whole story. Once you do, I'm pretty sure you'll agree with what I've done. But right now you'll have to take my word for it. Once Grant gets here, I'll tell you everything I know—but you'll have to accept that Lakesh is locked up so he won't contaminate Cerberus.''

"Contaminate how?" she demanded.

Before Kane could respond, Bry's voice filtered over the intercom on the laboratory wall. "Grant and Nora are rematerializing.''

Domi exhaled noisily in relief, and some of the anger left her posture and eyes. "Good. Now we can get to the bottom of this."

The trans-comm units were voice activated, and Kane called, "Is Sindri still there?"

"Yeah." Bry's response was dour. "He's still loitering around."

"Get him out of sight. Tell Grant to stay in the ready room."

In a very aggrieved voice, Bry asked, "How do you expect me to do that? Since when has he ever listened to me?"

Wearily Kane said, "I don't know. Tell him we're planning a birthday party and if he comes out he'll spoil the surprise."

"Is it his birthday?" asked Bry.

"Hell, I don't know. Just tell him anything so he'll stay put. For the moment, I need to control the information he gets."

"What information is that?" Bry's tone sounded decidedly confused.

"Bry, goddammit—"

"All right, all right. Will do." Bry paused and

added, in a tone that sounded a bit trepredatious, "Just so you'll know…Shizuka is with him."

At the mention of the name, all the anger returned to Domi's eyes and comportment. In a soft, disgusted voice she said, "Shit."

Chapter 5

Grant and Shizuka were waiting for Kane in the ready room, their stances telegraphing impatience and suspicion. To Kane's considerable surprise and amusement, Grant was attired in the formal samurai dress known as the *kamishimo,* which consisted of wide-legged trousers and a red-and-blue jacket called a *kataginu.* The flaring, stiffened shoulder epaulets only accentuated the massive breadth of the man's shoulders and chest.

Even in the flat-soled sandals, he stood four inches over six feet tall. Gray threaded his short, curly black hair. A gunfighter's mustache swept fiercely around his lips and curved halfway down to his prominent chin, showing jet-black against his coffee-brown complexion. Smiles didn't come easily to him, and as usual his mouth was drawn in a frown, just as his heavy brows were knitted together at the bridge of his nose, casting his dark eyes into deep shadow.

His blunt fingers tapped a nervous ditty on the hilt of the short *wakizashi* sword thrust through a silk sash knotted around his waist.

Before Kane said anything, he cast his gaze around surreptitiously for a glimpse of Sindri. Fortunately, the little man was nowhere in sight. "Well," Kane began, letting a grin spread across his face, "it didn't take you long to go native. Or is it laundry day on New Edo?''

Grant didn't laugh, but Shizuka did, a lovely musical fluting. A slender Japanese woman a couple of inches over five feet in height, Shizuka wore an ankle-length surcoat of blue silk accented by white-and-red embroidery. Beneath it was a pale green billowy *kamishimo*, the uniform of the daimyo's retainer. She carried a *dai-sho* pair of swords in her sash, a long curved *katana* and a *tanto*.

Her tumbles of glossy black hair framed a smoothly sculpted face of extraordinary beauty. Her complexion was a very pale gold with pink roses and ivory for an accent. Beneath a snub nose, her petaled lips were full.

Shizuka's dark brown, almond-shaped eyes held the fierce, proud gleam of a young eagle. Her hair was gathered in a tortoiseshell barrette at her nape, one stray wisp dangling across her cheek.

She started to speak, but Grant growled ''No'' in his lionlike rumble of a voice. ''It was a day like any other—one that began with me waking up and wondering if this would be the day you'd come up with a thin pretext to drag my ass back here.''

Kane's grin faltered at the edge of genuine hostility and accusation in Grant's deep voice. Kane didn't blame him for resenting being yanked unceremoniously from his new life on New Edo, since that life really hadn't had much time to get started. However, he felt the slow flush of anger rising on his neck at the implication he had contrived an emergency in order to summon his friend back to deal with the responsibilities of his old life.

"I don't have a pretext," he stated flatly. "I have a damn good reason. Probably the best damn reason since we left Cobaltville."

Grant seemed unmoved. Crossing his big arms over his chest, he rumbled, "What old sparring partner has come looking for a rematch now?"

Kane understood the reference he made to the circumstances of the last time they embarked on an op, when Grigori Zakat apparently returned from the dead, seeking revenge for a past defeat. That incident was only two weeks in the past, but Grant had brought the situation to Kane's attention, not the other way around. For the sake of diplomacy, Kane decided not to point that out.

"It's not so much an old enemy who has come back," Kane told him, "but one that's been under our noses for quite some time without us knowing it."

Shizuka's delicate eyebrows arched. "What do you mean, Kane-*san*?"

Grant nodded to the Sin Eater strapped to Kane's forearm. "Is that why you're walking around heeled?"

Before Kane could even partially frame a response, Sindri chose that moment to saunter into the anteroom from the operations center. Both Grant and Shizuka stared at him in dumbfounded silence for a long tick of time. Then Grant bellowed, "What the hell—!"

He made a clumsy, fumbling motion to unsheathe his *wakizashi* sword. His motor functions were still impaired due to the residue of the terrible shock that had temporarily paralyzed him less than four weeks before.

Shizuka's sword slid from its lacquered wooden scabbard with lightning speed, the naked steel glittering brightly in the overhead light. The tip touched Sindri's neck and she muttered in low, grim tone, "*Zurui chibi.* I wondered if we would ever meet again."

Kane knew she had said "Sneaky dwarf," and judging by the red spots of anger appearing on Sindri's cheeks, he knew it, too. His face remained impassive even as the razored edge of the sword forced him to tilt his head back. The blades of the Tigers of Heaven were almost supernaturally sharp, able to cleave smoothly even through polycarbonate. Shizuka had once attributed the cutting quality to an old technique of laser-sharpening the edges to only a few molecules of thickness.

"What the fuck is he doing here?" Grant snarled, jamming his sword back into its scabbard. He seemed slightly embarrassed that he had been able to withdraw only a quarter of its length in the time Shizuka had completely unsheathed her own weapon.

"I'd like to know that myself," Shizuka said in a silky soft tone, although her eyes were cold. "I haven't forgotten how this *koitsu* imprisoned me in the Chronos installation, used me as a tool against you. I owe him a bloodletting."

Kane had picked up enough Japanese since meeting the New Edoans to know *koitsu* meant "little rat." He also knew Shizuka referred to the incident some months ago when she and a contingent of samurai arrived on Thunder Isle searching for him, Grant and Brigid. She hadn't found the three friends she sought, but Sindri, who had commandeered the facility, found her.

When the outlanders returned to Thunder Isle a couple of weeks later, Sindri used Shizuka as a hostage and in the process inflicted very superficial cuts on her arms. The regal samurai commander hadn't forgotten either the wounds, or the more serious blow to her pride. Kane was also sure she hadn't forgotten the threat Sindri had levied against New Edo if she refused to cooperate with him during her short imprisonment.

For better or for worse—and New Edo was certainly better than most of the Western Isles—the island was her home. Dangerous, but still hers. Moreover, she considered the well-being of its citizens her responsibility.

A few months before, during an attempted insurrection, the daimyo of New Edo, Lord Takaun, was grievously injured and the former captain of the Tigers, Kiyomasa, was slain. It fell upon Shizuka's slender shoulders to end the rebellion, and she did it in the only way that would satisfy the honor of both factions—by killing the seditionist leader in single combat, literally slicing him in two with her *katana*.

The rebels saw only two options—to continue to press their faltering coup and die to a man, or to swear loyalty to the samurai who had slain their leader. They decided to swear loyalty and live. Ironically, many of them didn't live long after making their oaths, but instead perished repulsing the invaders dispatched by Baron Snakefish. Despite the losses New Edo suffered, Shizuka led her forces to victory over a tactically superior force.

After that, New Edo obeyed her every command, appeased her every whim with a kind of devotion different, yet more powerful than what they would have given a man. Shizuka wasn't viewed as a woman, or even a Tiger of Heaven; she was revered almost as a goddess.

Defiantly Sindri said, "I didn't really harm you then, Captain, I only inconvenienced you. I could have killed you very easily, but I did not. I show myself to you now, in order to prove to you that my intentions are not multilayered."

"In other words," Grant grated, "you're trying to convince us we're not being hustled. Again. We've heard that shit from you before—"

"Yeah," Kane interrupted, "we have. And there's no reason to believe he's sincere this time, either. Frankly, I couldn't give a swampie's ass about whether he's playing us again."

Grant blinked at him in surprise, a bit of the flinty anger softening in his eyes. With a little hiss of annoyance, Shizuka intoned, "I thought this *dani* was dead, killed in the explosion."

Before Sindri could offer a response, Kane said, "I'd hoped much the same thing, but I'm glad now it didn't happen."

Shizuka cast him a puzzled, searching glance, then slowly removed the blade from Sindri's throat, leaving a thin line of blood on the underside of his jaw. "Why is that, Kane-*san?*"

"Because I want the chance to be godfather to your children."

Grant and Shizuka both stared at him as if he had just sprouted donkey ears. Grant inquired mildly, "A little premature, aren't you?"

Kane shrugged. "Not necessarily. From the information given to me, you'll have twins, a boy and girl. The girl will be named Tomei, the boy Kiyomasa."

Shizuka, in the process of resheathing her *katana,* froze in midmotion to gape at Kane with wide, disbelieving eyes. "How could you possibly know something like that?"

"You'll find out when the rest of Cerberus does. I'm ordering an assembly for 1900 hours."

"*You're* ordering?" Grant's expression and tone were rich with suspicion. "Where's Lakesh?"

Kane hesitated a moment before answering. That and Sindri's sly grin didn't help allay Grant's sudden apprehension. His big brown hand closed over the hilt of his sword and he growled, "What the hell is going on here, Kane? Are you and Sindri up to something?"

Sindri's theatrical laugh was full of mock evil. "Do you mean that I've somehow taken over Mr. Kane's mind and turned him and everyone here into my brain-controlled slaves?"

"Oh, shut up, pissant," Grant grunted dismissively. He raked Kane with a penetrating stare. "Did something happen to Lakesh?"

"More or less," Kane said. "He's down in a holding cell. I locked him up."

Grant's reaction was restrained, almost disinterested. "Sounds to me like you've got everything under control."

"I don't," Kane replied flatly. "I need you here, at my side."

"To do what?"

"Just be yourself." Kane offered his hand. "I need you."

At first Grant ignored the proffered hand, then he scowled at it. "What if being myself means that me and Shizuka just gate back out of here?"

Kane said nothing but kept his hand outstretched, waiting patiently. He knew Grant was simply tweaking him. They had been partners for nearly fifteen years, and it was part and parcel of Magistrate conditioning to always back a partner's play.

Grant's deep brown eyes met his. It felt like a very long time, a painfully long time, before the big man reached out and clasped Kane's hand, their mutual grasp reminding them both that whatever their many differences, they shared common goals.

Grant released his friend's hand and opened his mouth to voice a demand, but Kane cut him off with a short, sharp gesture. "Let's wait until after the assembly. I'll answer all the questions I know the answers to."

"What about the questions you *can't* answer, Kane-*san*?" inquired Shizuka.

Kane forced a smile to his face, but it felt and looked stitched-on. "Then all of us will have to work together to find those answers. And it might not be an easy search.''

Sindri snorted. ''That's a very certain thing, Mr. Kane.''

THE CERBERUS REDOUBT HAD an officially designated briefing room on the third level. Big and blue walled, it was equipped with ten rows of theater-type chairs facing a raised speaking dais and a rear-projection screen. It was built to accommodate the majority of the installation's personnel back before the nukecaust when military and scientific advisers visited.

Because the briefings now rarely involved more than a handful of people, they were almost always convened in the more intimate dining hall. The mini-auditorium hadn't been used since Lakesh reactivated the installation, except when the personnel watched old movies on DVD and laser disks found in storage.

Kane wondered if the entire personnel of the redoubt had ever been assembled in the room even during predark days. For that matter, he wondered if he was making a tactical error by ordering the meeting, setting himself up more or less as the installation's leader. But if even a fraction of the tale contained on the disk Sindri had given him was true, then he and everyone else in the redoubt had reached a cross-roads—one path led to extinction and the other to survival. There was no middle road.

He knew it was important that he be able to gauge the personnel's reaction to what they were going to see and hear on the screen, particularly the reactions of the more recent arrivals. During his Mag days, Kane had learned that the sharp edge of peril was always blunted when standing—or in this instance—sitting shoulder to shoulder with a comrade.

Kane also hoped that being in the company of others would help blunt the inevitable sharp edge of disbelief. When he had first seen the contents of the disk, all the skepticism Kane had ever known in his life swarmed over him, like a suffocating blanket of denial, shock and negation. It was like being struck a physical blow. He had found himself sucking in air in great, painful gasps. He couldn't recall the last time his heart had beat so violently within his chest. He had watched it all and believed it, then refused to believe it. Finally, he had no choice but to accept it as fact.

When Kane mounted the stage at 1900 hours with Brigid Baptiste and Grant flanking him, he faced the seventy-plus members of the Cerberus staff who had gathered in the miniauditorium. He experienced a rush of disorientation and a surge of stage fright. Intellectually, he had accepted the fact that the redoubt's population had swelled over the past month, but he hadn't seen everyone assembled in one place until now.

Although the redoubt had been constructed to provide a comfortable home for well over a hundred people and despite the fact there were less than that now, there were currently more people in the facility than had been seen there in the past two centuries.

When he, Grant, Domi and Brigid had arrived at the installation two years before, there had been only a dozen permanent residents. Like them, they were all exiles from the villes, but unlike them, the others had been brought there by Lakesh because of their training and abilities.

The redoubt had suffered casualties over the past couple of years: Adrian and Davis, killed on a mission to Mongolia; Cotta in the Antarctic; and Beth-Li Rouch, killed right within the walls of the installation itself. For a long time, the Cerberus personnel were outnumbered by shadowed corridors, empty rooms and sepulchral silences.

As the three people stood shoulder to shoulder on the stage, all of them heard their names whispered in tones that were almost touched with awe, which was the reaction Kane had hoped for when he asked his friends to join him.

The three of them represented the heroic trinity that had freed the inhabitants of the Moon base from lives of unending terror and offered them an alternative to dying unknown and unmourned on Luna. Kane's status among the Manitius émigrés sprang more from the fact he had faced the fearsome Maccan and imprisoned the crazed Tuatha de Danaan in a stasis chamber than freeing them from a lunar tomb. The mad god had been a symbol of terror among the colonists for generations, and Kane's battle with him was already approaching the level of hero-myth. As far as the Moon base personnel were concerned, that particular accomplishment made him a blend of ninja, demon and rabid wolf.

Kane recalled what Brigid had said to him after Tibetan bandits had bestowed upon him the title of Tsyanis Khan-po, the King of Fear. She had wryly commented, "You're earning quite the reputation in the far corners of the world."

Less than a month after that incident, when Sky Dog's warriors had bestowed upon him the name of Unktomi Shunkaha, or Trickster Wolf, he had realized that he was crossing over the bridge from flesh-and-blood man and entering the realm of legend. He wasn't pleased by the prospect, but he wasn't above exploiting it on this particular occasion.

The sounds of murmuring and shuffling feet faded as Kane stood at the podium and looked out at the faces he recognized and the many he didn't. He saw Wegmann, Auerbach and Banks scattered among the Moon base evacuees. They were all sitting beside women, and Kane repressed a smile.

As more women arrived from the Moon colony, the redoubt's permanent male population was for the first time in their memory in the minority. Bry, Banks, Farrell, Auerbach and even the misanthropic Wegmann had acted at first either like shy schoolboys or Mags in a gaudy house after a long patrol. He spotted Shizuka, DeFore and Quavell sitting together. He looked for Domi, but didn't see her, though he sensed she was nearby. He knew Sindri was lurking in the wings, too.

When silence fell over the room, Kane said without preamble, "I called all of you here because of information I received a couple of hours ago."

The acoustics in the miniauditorium were such he didn't need to use the public-address system. "This is information that has to be acted upon one way or another. It spells out our complete future or complete doom—and for most of you here, they're pretty much the same thing.''

Feet shifted uncomfortably, and there were a couple of self-conscious coughs and mutters. The thought occurred to Kane that there were those in the room who might scoff at his announcements as contrived melodramatics, but he didn't care. ''See for yourselves.''

At a nod from him, Brigid turned a switch on the rear wall to activate the rear-projection screen and play the CD. The overhead lights dimmed. Kane moved aside as Grant and Brigid turned to watch the image forming on the screen.

A face swiftly materialized, building pixel by pixel. The face was that of a man who appeared to be in his late fifties or early sixties. His eyes were his most arresting feature, nearly the same color as the high Western sky at dusk, blue with just a hint of gray. They blazed in a gaunt, bearded face.

The man's face was too harsh and hard to be handsome, even without the long, jagged scar cutting like a lightning bolt from left to right across his features, from hairline to jawline. His dark, silver-stippled hair hung loose past his shoulders, stirred by a touch of the wind. He had the look of fasting, of deep suffering about him.

Kane heard Brigid murmur in horror, ''Oh, my God.''

''What the hell is this?'' Grant blurted in alarm.

The man spoke in a bone-chillingly familiar voice. ''If you're seeing and hearing me, then my plan worked. I don't have any way of knowing who is watching this, so I'll give you a quick back story. My year is 2227, the month is September. I'm recording this outside the good old Cerberus redoubt.''

The man paused and showed the edges of his teeth in a grin. They were slightly discolored. ''As you might've guessed by looking at me, a hell of a lot has happened in the past twenty-seven or so years, not much of it good.''

Grant whirled toward Kane, eyes glinting with a combination of suspicion and fear. ''You expect us to believe that's *you?*''

Kane shushed him by placing a forefinger to his lips, then pointing with it to the screen. ''Don't interrupt me. I have an interesting story to tell.''

Chapter 6

From the screen, Kane announced, "I'll start from the beginning—my beginning, that is. For all of you, that's about a month and two weeks away."

Using clear, concise language, without trying to overdramatize or soft-pedal the future, Kane began relating everything that had happened in the world and to him since the middle months of 2200. He briefly recapped how Sam had appeared virtually out of nowhere to assume leadership of the nine barons.

Sam factionalized the nine barons and in the process brought a new order to the face of the world. The ancient Roman Empire was governed by a senate, but ruled by an emperor, sometimes known as an imperator. This person served as the final arbiter in matters pertaining to government. The baronies acted dependently, unified in name only. The arrival of the imperator changed all that.

During a council of the barons in Front Royal, Baron Cobalt put forth the proposal to establish a central ruling consortium with himself as its leader. But Sam hijacked not only Cobalt's plan but also the title of imperator. A series of battles began, known as the Imperator Wars. The conflict was short-lived and ended with the siege of Cobaltville and the ousting of its baron. Yet peace didn't come with the imposition of imperial rule. Instead, it sparked dozens of smaller wars and a succession of plots and counterplots.

Sam the imperator was fixated on unification, as the barons were, but with a different objective. His stated intent was to end the tyranny of the barons and unify both hybrid and human and build a new Earth. In the months following his appearance, the entire structure of the baronies changed. He made considerable inroads into toppling the old order and enfranchising his forces, although not all the barons supported him.

The general consensus among the Cerberus personnel was that even the barons who withheld their overt support wouldn't undertake organized resistance against him. Even if every one of the baronies united against the imperator, it would require months to prepare any kind of military campaign and they had to do so in secret, or else they would not have access to the medical treatments. And Baron Cobalt, the only hybrid lord who bore Cerberus and the imperator personal malice, was missing, presumed dead. For a short time, an uneasy peace prevailed.

However, Cobalt wasn't dead. No one really knew where he had been, or why he hadn't died when his metabolic treatments were denied. He had been setting the stage for a major, winner-take-all confrontation between the imperator and his allies and the disenfranchised barons.

Major uprisings in several baronies marked the first anniversary of the imperator-inspired rule. Later, out-

law armies of Roamers began moving against baronial operations in the Outlands.

These events proved to be mere diversions. Baron
Cobalt, who had been covertly plotting for months,
infiltrated Area 51 with the forces of several other
barons who didn't care to answer to an imperator.

Cobalt viewed Cerberus as a dangerously unbal-
anced X factor, a wild card that needed to be dealt
out of the equation before Sam could be challenged.
The vengeful baron and his anti-imperial forces did
just that, by essentially neutralizing the redoubt, destroying the majority of its personnel and the advanced tech available to them.

Kane not only told the assembly about what befell
Cerberus and most of its personnel on the day the
combined forces of Barons Cobalt, Samarium, Thulia
and Mande had all converged on the mountain plateau, but the screen also showed them the aftermath.

The scene shifted to an exterior view of the plateau
that sheltered the redoubt. Craters a yard in circumference and nearly twice that deep pocked the surface
of the tarmac. Scattered chunks of asphalt, metal and
other less identifiable objects lay in haphazard patterns.

The gutted shell of a Manta transatmospheric ship
was piled up against the rocky abutment at the base
of the peak. Although the hull was overgrown with
tangled vines, the burned-out wreckage of a Deathbird
could be identified enfolded within the Manta's extended alloyed wings. The rust-edged rotor vanes
thrust up at thirty-degree angles, giving the entire
mass the look of a black windmill sinking into a quag-

mire. An unfamiliar broad-axled assault vehicle Kane referred to as a SPIDE lay on its left side a few yards away.

Along the slope rose triple rows of headstones and grave markers projecting up from the grassy covering. The markers bore only last names, only a few of which could be made out—Domi, Farrell, Falk, Wegmann, DeFore, Quavell. The others were obscured by high grasses and discoloration.

Matter-of-factly, Kane talked about how the battle raged for less than an hour. He described how the plateau had become literally sodden with blood, spilled by defender and attacker alike. He told how for one magnificent moment after Brewster Philboyd crashed the Manta TAV into the Deathbird, the Cerberus warriors swept the plateau clear of black-armored Magistrates. But the Mags regrouped and swarmed into the redoubt.

Kane's voice acquired a tone of pride when he related how the people fought back with anything they could get their hands on. They shot, hacked and stabbed until they themselves were shot, hacked and stabbed. No one gave up, nobody surrendered or begged for mercy, not even the few personnel Kane had once contemptuously dismissed as cowardly "teeks," technical geeks.

On the screen, Kane paused long enough to say, "For all of you out there who I labeled as such, I apologize. You made me proud that day and ashamed of myself."

The scene shifted to the dark interior showing the main corridor beneath great curving ribs of metal that supported the high rock roof. The twenty-foot-wide passageway was clogged by the tons of stone and twisted metal that had fallen from the ceiling.

The next view showed the operations center, or what was left of it. Naked lightbulbs dangled from a network of wires and cords crudely affixed to the high ceiling. The vanadium alloy walls were smeared with scorch marks and perforated with bullet holes. No circuits clicked, no drive units hummed, nor did any indicator lights flash.

All the consoles had been blasted into twisted masses of metal, plastic and broken glass. Every piece of equipment had been shot, smashed and torn. There didn't appear to be a single intact microprocessor within any of the computer casings or chassis.

"I know it looks like shit," Kane commented from the screen, "but it wouldn't look even this good if it weren't for this man."

A figure appeared on the screen, that of a frail old man. His emaciated body was hunched over in a wheelchair. The stamp of years and suffering accentuated the skull-like contours of the old man's face.

Waxy white and deeply seamed, it was the face of a man nearing the conclusion of his life. He wore large dark glasses with heavy rims. What little hair he had was no more than tufts of tangled coppery curls. He wore a patched gray bodysuit that bagged on his scarecrow frame. He appeared to be dozing, his head nodding.

"Hey," Kane's voice called from offscreen. "Give us a smile, tough guy."

The man's head jerked up and he snorted in surprise. Appearing to glare out at the audience, he brayed, "Get that goddamn camera out of my face, Kane!"

"Ladies and gentlemen," Kane's smooth voice said, "you've just met my housemate of the past few years, the lovely and talented Donald Bry."

"Fuck you," the image of Bry snarled. Spittle sprayed from his toothless mouth.

From the audience came gasps and surprisingly, even a muffled but quickly repressed chuckle. Kane heard Bry husk out in a dazed tone, "What happened to him, to me?"

Kane's face appeared on the screen again. "Bry, if you're out there, I'll tell you right now your manners never improved with age. Fortunately, your technical skills did."

Kane went on to describe how there were survivors of the Battle of Cerberus—Grant, Brigid Baptiste, Bry, Lakesh and a handful of Moon base émigrés. They had no choice but to join the imperator in his China stronghold. Even before the smoke had cleared from the Cerberus battlefield, they planned and launched the first counterattacks against the barons that became known as the Consolidation War.

The Consolidation War lasted for nearly five years. Early on, the barons scored a string of impressive victories, occupying several villes with troopers conscripted and recruited from the slums of the fortress cities and Outland pestholes.

According to Kane, atrocities became commonplace wherever baronial armies marched or encamped. He provided visual proof of this. No one in the auditorium was prepared for the scenes of horror that began flashing across the screen, some of them so repulsive that even hardened veterans like Grant and Kane averted their eyes.

They saw living people with the flesh peeled away from their bones, screaming to be allowed to die, Outland settlements completely consumed by flames. There were sickening scenes of black-armored Magistrates laughing at bloody men and women flopping around blindly in the dirt with their heel tendons cut.

However, Baron Cobalt's policy of merciless cruelty was counterproductive. Instead of breaking the spirit of the conquered outlanders, it only fired resistance, particularly when the people knew there was a viable alternative to baronial rule. Many of the hybrids who shared the Archon-derived DNA of the barons joined imperial forces, although most of them made very poor soldiers due to their physical fragility.

To offset this manpower deficit, Sam and Lakesh saw to the creation of genetically engineered warriors, the Pischacas, named after the demon warriors of Hindu myth. They augmented the imperial armies. On the screen appeared creatures that only remotely resembled humans. Greasy, greenish-gray skin sagged around their massive frames, loose and thickly knobbed, with fist-sized warts. The clots of raised, callused flesh gave them half-formed appearances, as if they were sculpted out of modeling clay by an amateur.

The hairless, simian faces of the Pischacas were broader from side to side than their heads were deep from front to back. Their mouths were straight horizontal gashes, with almost no trace of lips. Their deep-set eyes were yellow, with hazel irises and tiny pupils, like black beads.

Part of Kane's duties was to lead troops of the Pischacas into the Outlands and recruit the people there, if not making them official soldiers in Sam's armed forces, at least convincing them to become guerrilla fighters. Those who refused to take sides were neutralized.

By harnessing the energies of the Heart of the World, Sam implemented a long-range strategy that eventually culminated in the systematic and utter destruction of everything baronial. Over the course of the war, the entire system of baronial rule withered from within and without. More and more Outland territories split away from the direct influence of the barons. By the time the imperator claimed those territories, the baronies lacked their former strength-in-unity that had once enabled them to hold firm against all threats.

The end, when it came, was swift. All the barons were killed, either in battle or executed. The Consolidated Confederation of States was formed shortly thereafter. Victory, although absolute, wasn't celebrated for very long due to the revolts of the Pischacas. They were created to wage war against baronial forces. With those forces defeated, they then turned on their creators.

The Consolidation War was won by the sheer determination of the newly formed Consolidated Confederation of States. By war's end the armies of the barons were not only broken and scattered to the four winds, but the entire feudal system of god-kings was also dismantled.

Thus America was united again. But soon afterward there were rumblings of new threats, new menaces to the hard-won peace, first and foremost among them the Nirodha movement.

"According to what Lakesh told me," the image of Kane declared, "Nirodha is a Sanskrit term meaning complete destruction, or the utter cessation of existence. It's nihilism in its purest form...nothing from nothing and into nothing."

Kane described the Nirodha as having roots that took seed in India before the Consolidation War. It had been the remnants of a loose affiliation of fanatics that emerged fifteen hundred years earlier from the steamy jungles of India to loot and pillage everything from settlements to merchant ships. It adhered to the cataclysmic teachings of a thirteenth-century prophet known as Scorpia Prime.

Its most public incarnation had been in late twentieth century Japan, surfacing as a doomsday cult known as the Aum Shinrikyo. That particular version was a heavily financed movement that infiltrated almost every aspect of Japanese life. They were rumored to have been intimately involved in the development of doomsday weapons to hasten Armageddon. The nuclear holocaust of 2001 was a fulfillment of their prophecy, but it had not gone far enough, since humanity as a species survived.

In the two centuries following the nukecaust, the cult slowly revived. The movement regained its former strength during the chaos and carnage of the Consolidation War. It fell under the control of a female Sikh militarist who took the title of Scorpia Prime. No one knew where the title originated, other than the obvious fact the name translated as Royal Scorpion or Scorpion Queen.

Kane held up an elaborate helmet that looked to be crafted out of burnished silver and fashioned to resemble the body of a great scorpion. "This is what she wore, a symbol of her office. Whether it was a crown or a disguise or both, I never found out."

The helmet's gleaming mandibles swept down to form a mask over the wearer's eyes. The foreclaws and pincers curved along the sides, resembling the jaw guards of ancient Roman helmets. The stinger-tipped tail curved up over the ridged crown of the headpiece like a crest.

"The philosophy of the Nirodha," explained Kane, "was to bring about the Tandava, the Dance of Shiva, the destruction of all creation. As Shiva dances, he brings about the time of Pralya, the destruction of the universe. Everything disintegrates into nothing-ness...even the ego is consumed and everyone is rendered pure and without spiritual blemish."

The Kane on the screen took a deep breath and said in a rush, "I know they don't sound like much of a threat, but the Nirodha extended their claws out of the jungles of Assam to hook onto like-minded fanatics here in America.

"In the early days, the Nirodha's set policy was to destroy as they moved in. The Scorpia Prime intended to impress upon the Consolidated Confederation of States that our country would be in shambles if anyone resisted their movement. So, of course, we went looking for them. But before we did, we tried to get on with our lives the best way we could.''

On the screen flashed a series of candid shots, of people familiar and unfamiliar laughing, at work and at play. There was an extensive sequence shot on the palace grounds of New Edo, where Shizuka cradled identical dark-haired babies in her arms. Both infants seemed to stare at the audience with solemn, shoe-button eyes. Grant and Brigid fawned over the twin babies. Their dark golden skins and firm-chinned features unmistakably marked Grant as the father.

The scene shifted to different views of Brigid, looking heartachingly, hauntingly beautiful in a white diaphanous gown, a garland of bright flowers binding her ringleted hair. The Kane who stood beside her looked little different than the Kane who stood upon the stage, except he wore an anachronistic but formal-looking black-and-white suit.

Dressed in elaborate Japanese finery, Shizuka and Grant stood on either side of the couple. Behind them, a waterfall poured into a foaming, crystal-clear pool. A fine mist drifted around the people, the droplets of water reflecting sunlight like powdered diamonds. It was obviously a wedding ceremony.

Standing on the podium and watching the sequence for a second time, Kane didn't so much as glance toward Brigid. He figured she was probably as stunned as he had been when he first saw it.

The next sequence was a long, high-angle view of a reception, with people gathered by long tables and dancing. Two of the dancing people were Kane and

Brigid. As the camera followed them, it panned past some of the guests in attendance. The scene paused briefly on a black-haired, sultry and very voluptuous woman wearing a sheer dress stretched taut across her sculptured body. Her eyes were masked by dark glasses, but Kane, Grant and Brigid all recognized Erica van Sloan. The expression on her face as she watched Brigid and Kane was inscrutable.

"In the long run," Kane's grim voice-over declared, "trying to get on with our lives was a mistake. It gave the Nirodha the opportunity to grow in strength and influence. By the time we took the fight to them, it was almost too late."

The scene shifted back to Kane's bearded face. He stared out at the audience, not speaking or moving for a long moment. When he spoke again, his voice was a hoarse, harsh whisper, like the grate of chipped pottery. "I won't go into detail about what happened when we penetrated the Scorpia Prime's stronghold in Assam. I'm not withholding information because I'm afraid of altering the timeline—hell, if I cared about that, you wouldn't be seeing or hearing me in the first place. It's just too damn painful for me to talk about even twenty-four years later."

Chapter 7

Everyone in the miniauditorium watched in rapt silence as, on the screen, Kane traced the scar cutting across his face with a trembling forefinger. "And I don't mean the kind of pain associated with this. I've got a hell of a lot more of them under my clothes. No, we may have succeeded in overthrowing the Scorpia Prime and breaking the Nirodha's power, but we paid for the victory with our dearest blood."

Kane's eyes grew wet. In a strained, snuffling tone he said, "Excuse me," and his right hand swelled in size as he reached toward the camera. The image broke up in a series of jagged lines and pixel-shot snow.

When the visual returned, Kane's bearded, haggard face looked as if it were chiseled from granite, his eyes dry and gimlet hard. "All right," he declared flatly. "I won't dance around the subject. Bry, Grant and myself were seriously wounded during the op. Bry ended up as a cripple. Grant was shot three times and stabbed at least twice. Brigid and Shizuka were killed, murdered and mutilated before our eyes. We both lost our wives that day."

"*No.*" The single word issued from Grant's lips as a whispered groan of anguish. Kane glanced toward him. The big man, never one to register much emotion other than irritation, was for once profoundly affected. His eyes glistened with moisture.

On the screen, Kane swallowed hard. ''Our bodies eventually healed and our lives went on, after a fashion, but we never really recovered. Grant ended up assuming the daimyo's position on New Edo, sharing it with his children, Tomei and Kiyomasa. At the point I'm recording this, I haven't seen or spoken to him in nearly ten years. We had a disagreement about the best use for the Operation Chronos tech on Thunder Isle.

''Lakesh married Erica van Sloan and they produced a daughter, Tanvirah. Sam turned all of his attention into reshaping first the CCS and then the world at large.''

Kane described how Sam developed a method of insuring that menaces from within the body politic, like the Nirodha fifth-columnists, would be neutralized in the future. The imperator ordered that every citizen of the CCS be required to receive SQUID implants. During the last couple years of the Consolidation War, the implants were mandatory for new recruits. Now, even infants born within the direct sphere of influence of the CCS cities were implanted with the devices.

By the time Sam instituted this policy, the Consolidated Confederation of States was completely entrenched as the form of government, far more securely rooted than the god-king system practiced by the barons. With every citizen now linked by the neuronic energy of the SQUIDs, old and new human alike living in harmony, Sam announced his intention to build a new world—an adaptive Earth, he called it. He described it as a world where everyone had an important niche to fill. Therefore, they would be able to adapt to any changes or new set of circumstances that might arise, confident they could deal with them efficiently.

Now, twenty-plus years after the fact, the citizenry of the CCS were so accustomed to obeying the edicts of imperial law that any question, much less opposition, was unthinkable. From babyhood they were indoctrinated to serve the universal good of imperial law.

It was a world of peace, of modern cities that were connected by monorail tunnels, where hellzones had been remade into Eden-like parks. Ruins of old nuke-scarred cities were torn down and playgrounds were built in their place. On the screen flashed images of beautiful buildings, some tall and elegant, others with austere lines and many windows.

Human and hybrids, once bitter enemies, one perceiving the other much like the Neanderthal had looked at the Cro-Magnon, now coexisted, even intermarried. They had adapted as Sam had wished. He envisioned transforming Earth into a garden of beauty and knowledge, but only if the planet's inhabitants could adapt to his vision.

"I never adapted," Kane declared grimly. "In fact, I began to suspect that Sam's vision was a false one, the result of interfering with timelines, of deliberately triggering temporal distortions, alternate event horizons and probability wave dysfunctions. So I started looking for and found—at least to my personal satisfaction—several incidents in my past but your future, that met my criteria of temporal fault lines.''

The screen displayed the Cerberus mat-trans unit. An access plate was missing from the elevated platform, exposing the confusing circuit network of the emitter array. From the aperture stretched a webwork of fiber-optic cabling, terminating in a control console spanning the far wall.

The console was crescent shaped, surrounding a single operator's chair in the center. It bristled with thousands of tiny electrodes and complexities of naked circuitry, leading to a switchboard containing relays and readout screens. Below the console rested a small square generator bolted to a wheeled palette.

Jutting above the inner horseshoe curve of the console, attached to a stanchion, revolved a model of Earth. The diameter was around three feet. The contoured surface showed rivers, lakes and oceans in blue, forests in various shades of green, deserts in beige and light gray for mountain ranges. Cities were rendered in pale yellow. The carefully detailed surface was mostly beige.

Kane's voice announced, ''This is what is known as a Sloan Spatiotemporal Dissociator, an early prototype of what eventually became the Operation Chronos temporal dilator. It was designed by Erica, back in the twentieth century when she was still working for Overproject Whisper's time-travel division. Bry and myself have been working to reconstruct it for the last ten years. We've refined it from the original specs, using the gateway unit as the basic channeling conduit to pierce the quantum field.

"No, I don't intend to go back in time to the fault line I described and try to repair it myself. That would trigger a double-occupancy paradox. Nobody can co-exist at any point in the past where they already existed. A temporal fault line will then be created, knocking causality on its ass. So my present self and my past self can't coexist...or at least I don't think they can. And I don't want to take the chance of undoing all of our work."

The scene panned rapidly away from the jump chamber and stopped on the wheelchair-bound Bry, who glared at the camera. "Explain what we have in mind," Kane's voice urged.

With an exasperated scowl, Bry said, "For a time-travel mission of this sort to have any chance of success, we'll require a subject who was completely out of the chronon stream during the last two and a half decades...someone who didn't contribute to the temporal fracture lines.

"So, instead of either Kane or myself going back in time, we'll use the dissociator to *pull* someone out of nontime, zero time. For the past twenty-eight years, he's been in the Operation Chronos memory buffer matrix, reduced to digital information. He's been outside space-time for all those decades, frozen for nearly thirty years in a noncorporeal holding pattern."

"The subject we're discussing," Kane's voice said, "is Sindri. What I have in mind is to retrieve him from the matrix and then dispatch him down the chronon stream with this record. If he arrives, you'll have the opportunity to repair the major temporal fault lines at the fracture point. One of them is to keep

Baron Cobalt from returning to power and enlisting the aid of the other barons to attack Cerberus.

"The second fracture point is in India, when the Nirodha movement rises out of Assam. It was starting to form even in your time period. It'll be up to you which fault line, which temporal breach you want to repair."

The camera switched back to a view of Kane again, as he stood in front of the console. "But all of it depends on whether we can retrieve Sindri from the memory matrix. To do so means I have to gate to Thunder Isle and steal the data cards from the dilator's main processor, get out without Grant finding and executing me. I might mention that Grant instituted a death penalty for anyone found snooping around Redoubt Yankee on Thunder Isle. Even Sam obeys it."

Kane shrugged. "Grant's only had to implement it a couple of times, I think. If I get back alive and whole, I can only hope to God the data cards are compatible with the dissociator. Who knows? This may be the most stupendously unworkable idea in the entire history of stupendously unworkable ideas. Stay tuned."

The scene faded. When it returned, a head-and-shoulders view of Kane filled the screen. He wore a black shadowsuit, and though the background was blurred, the setting was obviously his quarters. The impression was that quite a bit of time had elapsed since the last recording.

Pitching his voice low, as if he were afraid of being overheard, he said, "Apparently our idea isn't quite as stupendously unworkable as I thought. The Cerberus redoubt is now playing host to none other than Tanvirah Singh, Erica and Lakesh's daughter. Although she claimed she came here to enlist my help in stopping a new Nirodha uprising, I'm pretty damn sure her mom and dad and maybe even Sam himself are afraid of what our dissociator might accomplish.

"That's a confirmation that me and Bry are on the right track, but the only way to make sure is to go to Thunder Isle and recover the last bit of hardware we need to finish out Sindri's retrieval circuit."

Kane grinned wolfishly. "More later."

The image dissolved, then a new one appeared a moment later. Once more it was a head-and-shoulders view of Kane. His bearded face was split by a jubilant smile and his eyes shone brightly. "I've just gotten back from Thunder Isle," he declared proudly. "Grant cooperated with me—finally. He allowed me to take the temporal dilator's memory cards."

Kane leaned toward the lens, his face growing large on the screen. He squinted, as if he were trying to see into the past. "Grant, if you're watching this—thank you. You had a lot to forgive and even though it took you ten years, you forgave me at last."

He sat back in the chair. "But you let me have more than the memory cards…you helped me crystallize theories and suspicions I've had for many years, and I'm going to put them into words for all of you to chew on. When Sam and Erica finally realized none of us in Cerberus were going to join them willingly in their war to overthrow the barons, they decided to reduce our options. They purposefully allowed Baron Cobalt to return and take over again.''

Kane heard Grant mutter something indistinct, as the implications sank in. The digital copy of his future self continued, ''There was no way Cobalt could have secretly enlisted the backing of the other barons and managed to grab back the reins of power without help from some quarter. I always suspected Sam had something to do with it. How else could Cobalt and the other barons know Cerberus was occupied?''

The on-screen Kane shrugged. ''It's possible Sam could have pretended to negotiate terms with Cobalt, knowing in advance he couldn't be trusted. If that happened, Sam would have essentially financed his own war of attrition.

''As for the Nirodha movement, at this point in your time period, they're just a small rag-ass sect of fanatics controlling an isolated part of Assam. In the near future, they'll receive a special kind of assistance in order to expand their field of operations and sphere of influence and gain new recruits. The practice of Tantric sex worship never died out completely in India…that was a powerful tool and inducement to join up.

''And thus the shit continued to be stirred up, with the Pischaca revolts and the Nirodha exporting their terrorism. A society built on war and threats of war is usually too distracted to question itself. With those goddamn SQUIDs linking his mind to everybody else's, Sam pretty much owns humanity. He's accomplished in one generation what the barons tried to do for ninety years…unifying the world under one whip, like a team of horses.''

Kane paused to inhale a long breath. He exhaled it and tilted his head toward the camera. "For me, for Bry, for Grant, it's been twenty-seven years of suffering through wars, hardships, strife, personal loss and recently, faulty plumbing. I grew old and gray while Erica, Lakesh and Sam retained their youth…and the three of them stay together, linked by the SQUID implants while everyone and everything that meant anything to me was taken away, so they could build the world the imperator wanted. His adaptive Earth. This is my last chance to keep it from happening."

Kane pushed his chair back from the camera. "I already turned the data cards over to Bry, and we'll be making the retrieval attempt shortly. Before we do, I need to locate Tanvirah, because I don't trust her to be out of my sight when we power up the dissociator. I don't know if she's here as a pawn of Sam or if the reason she gave actually has some truth to it, but at this juncture I can't take the chance."

The scene faded and almost instantly returned, the screen once again displaying a medium close-up of Kane. "It worked," he announced. "Sindri came through alive and whole and apparently as nasty as he was when I—you—last saw him. I've already briefed him on what Bry and I hope to accomplish by injecting him into your time period. He's agreed to it, but then I haven't given him many options."

He paused to smile, but it looked a little forced. "I hope this works, but if it does, I won't know it. I won't be here to think about it. But if it does work, do me and yourself a favor even though you won't like hearing this—'' He took a deep breath, then declared in a rush, ''The next time you're alone with Brigid, stop acting like an idiot and tell her how you—''

There was a distant sound from offscreen, like the bursting of a wet paper bag. Kane turned to his right, his face registering surprise and consternation. Then the screen went dark. No other image flickered across it. The people assembled in the auditorium didn't speak or so much as cough.

When the lights came back up, Kane walked to the center of the stage. Gravely he surveyed the stunned faces in the auditorium he knew and the many he didn't. He couldn't bear to look at either Grant or Brigid. ''We just saw a glimpse of the future, one that begins in about a month. It starts with the assault on Cerberus, and we already know how that ends.''

There was stir, a shuffling of feet, a creak of chairs and fearful murmuring. Kane sensed Brigid moving up behind him. It took a great deal of effort not to look at her. He couldn't think of anything relevant or comforting he could say to her or the assembled people. For those who couldn't deal with what they had just seen and heard, nothing he could say would change their reactions.

''I'm expecting Sindri to fill out the rest of the picture for me,'' Kane said quietly. ''But regardless, we have two options, two paths to follow that might avert the future. You're free to make your own choices. I've already made mine.''

Then he turned and left the stage, passing Brigid, Grant and Sindri on his way. He beckoned to the little man with a forefinger. ''Come with me.''

Chapter 8

Lakesh lost all track of time while waiting in the cell. The overhead neon strip always burned bright, unlike the lights on the upper levels, which could be adjusted to simulate daytime and sunset.

He had tired quickly of shouting through the heavy door and of pounding on it. All he had accomplished was to make his vocal cords and his hands sore. For a little while he tried to distract himself by pacing around the cell, measuring it off, even though he knew its dimensions.

Although Lakesh hadn't taken a hand in actually designing the Cerberus redoubt, he had often looked over the construction specs and blueprints while it was being built, back when the Totality Concept's Overproject Whisper still shared space with Overproject Excalibur in the Archuleta Mesa.

Constructed in the mid-1990s, no expense had been spared to make Redoubt Bravo, the seat of Project Cerberus, a masterpiece of concealment and impenetrability. The researches to which Project Cerberus and its personnel had been devoted were locating and traveling hyperdimensional pathways through the quantum stream. Once that had been accomplished, the redoubt became, from the end of one millennium to the beginning of another, a manufacturing facility.

The quantum interphase mat-trans inducers, known colloquially as "gateways," were built in modular form and shipped to other redoubts.

The thirty-acre, three-level installation had come through the nukecaust with its operating systems and radiation shielding in good condition. When Lakesh had reactivated the installation some thirty years before, the repairs he made had been minor, primarily cosmetic in nature. Over a period of time, he had added an elaborate system of heat-sensing warning devices, night-vision vid cameras and motion-trigger alarms to the plateau surrounding it. He had been forced to work in secret and completely alone, so the upgrades took several years to complete. However, the location of the redoubt in Montana's Bitterroot Range had kept his work from being discovered.

In the generations since the nukecaust, a sinister mythology had been ascribed to the mountains, with their mysteriously shadowed forests and hell-deep, dangerous ravines. The wilderness area was virtually unpopulated. The nearest settlement was nearly a hundred miles away in the flatlands, and it consisted of a small band of Native Americans, Sioux and Cheyenne.

Planted within rocky clefts of the mountain peak and concealed by camouflage netting were the uplinks with an orbiting Vela-class reconnaissance satellite, and a Comsat. It could be safely assumed that no one or nothing could approach Cerberus undetected by land or by air—not that anyone was expected to make the attempt, particularly overland. However, there had been a recent exception when Quavell arrived.

The road leading down from Cerberus to the foothills was little more than a cracked and twisted asphalt ribbon, skirting yawning chasms and cliffs. Acres of the mountainsides had collapsed during the nuke-triggered earthquakes nearly two centuries earlier.

It was almost impossible for anyone to reach the plateau by foot or by vehicle; therefore, Lakesh had seen to it that the facility was listed as irretrievably unsalvageable on all ville records. Although official designations of all Totality Concept–related redoubts were based on the phonetic alphabet, almost no one stationed in the installation referred to it as Bravo. The mixture of civilian scientists and military personnel simply called it Cerberus. It had been Lakesh's home far longer than he cared to acknowledge.

Sitting in a corner, hugging his knees, Lakesh examined the door. It was a single slab of unprepossessing steel. It bore a peephole but no other opening, not even a Judas window.

As the word *Judas* popped into his head, Lakesh fought back a surge of guilt. It wasn't an emotion he was used to grappling with, and certainly not one he enjoyed. Nevertheless, the guilt was neither neurotic nor misplaced. Sometimes he felt that he and his scientific colleagues should have been locked up, if not in a dungeon then in a madhouse.

He and other twentieth-century scientists had willingly traded in their human heritage for a shockscape of planet-wide ruins. After all, they had been selected to survive in order to reshape humankind in a new image, and if that meant planning the eventual extinction of the old humans, then that was simply part of summoning the future. The Totality Concept would insure that the future would be a glorious one, wherein the most eldritch workings of the universe would be like an open book.

All of the scientists and military officials involved in the Totality Concept endeavors were too fixated on reaching short-term goals, making quotas and earning bonuses, to devote much thought to the workings of the universe, or even where the basic components to build the first mat-trans unit had come from. Lakesh included himself in this number, although he hadn't been so much fixated as blinded to the vast sea of disastrous consequences that could result from the Totality Concept's myriad divisions.

As it was, he had lived daily with the fear that he would anger Grant or Kane over some matter or another and they would expose his biggest secret—of how and why there were any exiles in Cerberus in the first place. He doubted that was the reason he had been confined to detention.

And perhaps this was the most fitting way to end it, he thought bitterly. The long career of a scientist, an exiled insurrectionist, a master planner and schemer—it was all distilled down to one man sitting in loneliness, waiting and almost wanting someone else to decide his fate. He knew he couldn't expect gratitude from anyone he had manipulated into joining his cause.

Because of learning to think several steps ahead, Lakesh was unaccustomed to being caught flatfooted by circumstances. His imprisonment was all very puzzling—and very upsetting because it was so puzzling. Lakesh had no idea what had motivated Kane to exchange him for Sindri as the cell's occupant.

He dredged through his memory, sifted among recent events, looking for a single incident no matter how trivial, that might have angered Kane. He couldn't find one, but then Kane hadn't seemed really angry. Beneath his no-nonsense "get the job done" demeanor he had displayed while locking him up, Lakesh had sensed a very real fear. He supposed Kane's reaction might be connected to Sindri's enigmatic reference to Colonel Thrush, but even that didn't strike him as particularly reasonable.

Sindri had proved himself to be a liar and trickster on numerous occasions, but how he could have heard about Thrush was beyond even Lakesh's ability to speculate. Then again, the ingenious dwarf had once sent him, via the mat-trans unit, his signature walking stick. The theatrical gesture told him Sindri was still alive and could overcome the gateway security locks. Therefore, there wasn't much beyond the reach of an intellect who could accomplish such a feat.

Lakesh sighed wearily. There were too many conjectures and memories crowding in. Gazing moodily at the wire-encased light strip on the ceiling, Lakesh knew the motivation for imprisoning him was somehow connected to Sindri's arrival. He had no doubt the little man had traveled the chronon stream, since he was somewhat familiar with Operation Chronos due to his occupation of Redoubt Yankee on Thunder Isle.

"Lakesh!"

Domi's voice, as faint and as muffled as it was by the thickness of the door, nevertheless galvanized Lakesh into struggling to his feet and rushing across the cell. "Yes, I'm here, darlingest one."

"You all right? Bastard didn't hurt you?"

"No, of course not," he said reassuringly. "Unless you count confusion as being hurtful, then I'm in a great deal of pain."

Domi didn't respond immediately. He was on the verge of calling out to her when he heard distantly, at the edge of audibility, the electronic beep-beep of the lock keys being pressed.

"Don't know combination," she spit in frustration. "Sorry."

"I'll be released sooner or later. Somebody will have to bring me food—I hope." He paused, then asked, "Darlingest one, do you have any idea of what's going on?"

"Only a little," she admitted. "Kane called a big meeting for everybody in the place. Attendance is mandatory."

Lakesh forced a chuckle, even though his mind wheeled with conjecture and fearful speculation. "Except for you?"

A little self-consciously, she answered, "Peeked in a few minutes ago. Kane was showing a movie."

Lakesh felt his eyebrows crawling toward his hairline. "A movie?" he echoed incredulously. "What kind of movie?"

"Not a movie," Domi corrected herself curtly. "It was that disk Sindri gave Kane."

"What was on it?"

Domi was so quiet for so long, Lakesh wondered if she hadn't heard him or had walked away. When she did reply, her voice was pitched so low, Lakesh had to strain to hear her, putting his ear to the door. "It was supposed to be made by Kane in the future. He sent it back with Sindri to warn us."

Tension coiling in the pit of his stomach, Lakesh asked querulously, "Warn us about what specifically?"

"Warn us—" Domi broke off, then blurted in desperation with a sob catching at the back of her throat, "Oh, Lakesh—got to get you out! Afraid they kill you because of those bugs in your blood!"

The fear that washed over Lakesh was so overwhelming his knees grew watery and his temples began throbbing. He took a stumbling step away from the door. "Nanites," he said mechanically.

"Nanites," Domi confirmed, the quaver in her voice chilling his blood. "Kane knew about them, talked to DeFore, then me! Thinks you're threat to redoubt, to the future! Thinks you slave to imperator!"

"How—?" Lakesh coughed, then asked loudly, "How did Kane find out about the nanites? Not from you?"

"No!" Domi's response was sharp and even a little accusatory. "He knew about them already. Think Sindri told him."

Lakesh raised his hands before his eyes and inspected them, not in the least ashamed by the sudden tremor causing the fingers to tremble violently. He hoped the shivering was due to tension-induced adrenaline flooding his system, not the nanites attacking his cells again, but he couldn't be sure.

"Lakesh? I can get gren and blow door out…me and you then escape." Domi's tone carried a plaintive, worried note. "We can use interphaser, go someplace they can't follow."

Lakesh felt tears sting his eyes. Throat constricted, he managed to say, "Thank you, darlingest one. But such an overreaction isn't necessary. I'll face up to this crisis, not flee from it."

"I'll face it with you, too. They have to kill both of us."

Lakesh wheeled around, eyes blinded by unshed tears. He went to the far wall and leaned his head against its padded surface. Domi's fatalistic yet self-confident proclamation of loyalty nearly had him weeping. He had been fond of Domi since the day they first met, and over the past couple of years that affection had grown to love.

He hadn't been able to demonstrate his feelings for her until six months or so, when he regained his youth. It was still a source of joy to him that Domi reciprocated his feelings and had no inhibitions about expressing them, regardless of the bitterness she still harbored over her unrequited love for Grant. In any event, he had broken a fifty-year streak of celibacy with her and they repeated the actions of that first delirious night whenever the opportunity arose.

Yet he had felt compelled to keep his relationship with Domi a secret, and he wasn't sure why. At first he tried to convince himself it was concern over raising Grant's ire, but he knew that was simply a feeble excuse. With Grant's heart more or less pledged to Shizuka, the big man was too preoccupied with his attempts to make a new life with her to give more than cursory attention to the more covert—and personal—activities among the redoubt personnel.

At first Lakesh figured his reticence to allow his affair with Domi to become common knowledge derived mainly from the habit of keeping two centuries' worth of secrets. Domi had recently accused him of being ashamed of their relationship, despite his trying to prove to her that wasn't the case at all. Now, with her promise to stand by his side in the face of adversity, he suddenly realized the true reasons he had kept their relationship a secret—he feared she would be swept up in the same karmic backlash that had at long last caught up to him.

Lakesh returned to the door, leaning against it. In a voice packed with urgency and desperation, he said, "Domi, darlingest one—I beg you not to interfere in anything that might happen. Do not put yourself at odds with Kane or anyone who supports him in this course of action. Do you understand me? This is a situation I have earned and deserve."

Suddenly the door opened, swinging outward, and Lakesh stumbled literally into Kane's arms. The man instantly recoiled, pushing him back into the cell. He glimpsed Brigid pensively standing in the corridor behind him. Domi stood off to one side, giving Kane an up-from-under glower of pure venom. He effected not to notice.

"I don't know what you've earned, old man," Kane said, reverting to his habitual form of address to Lakesh, ''but I think you deserve to know what's going on. I'm going to release you under the condition you promise not to touch anyone or anything on our way out.''

Lakesh's belly turned a cold flip-flop. ''Our way out? To where? A place of execution?''

Kane shrugged. ''That's sort of up to you.''

Chapter 9

As Lakesh marched along the corridor, flanked by Kane and Brigid, a comment Grant had made to him long ago kept echoing in his mind. "I think they'll lynch you."

Grant's bleak opinion had been voiced on the occasion of learning Lakesh's method of enlisting new recruits. He had challenged Grant's anger by asking if he thought his fellow exiles would vote him out of office if they knew the truth.

Lakesh smiled sourly at the recollection. Grant had spoken partly in jest, but a nugget of truth gleamed there. At the time, Lakesh had entertained himself with a fanciful vision of the Cerberus exiles marching on his quarters, waving torches and pitchforks, hauling him to a makeshift gallows out on the mountain plateau.

Now the image didn't seem quite so fanciful, particularly since neither Brigid nor Kane seemed inclined to answer any questions he put to them. Only Domi trailing along in the passageway behind them, cursing periodically under her breath, gave him any comfort. He tried to convince himself he wouldn't be summarily executed before her eyes—or at least not until a hearing or trial of some sort had been convened.

The passageway ended at the massive sec door. The multiton vanadium panels opened and closed in an accordion-like fashion. It was so heavy, the door took several minutes to seal and unseal, so it was usually left partially open, with two of the thick panels folded aside. The door was controlled by a keypad and lever on the right-hand wall.

Lakesh glanced at the illustration of the slavering black-and-tan hound painted on the wall beneath the controls. Three snarling heads grew out of a single corded neck. One of the enlisted men with artistic aspirations had rendered the image of a three-headed hellhound. Rather than attempt even a vaguely realistic representation, he used indelible paints to create a trio of snarling heads sprouting out of an exaggeratedly muscled neck. The neck was bound by a spiked collar, and the three pairs of jaws gaped wide open, blood and fire gushing between great fangs. The eyes were solid crimson orbs. Beneath the image, written in exaggerated, Gothic script was a single word: Cerberus.

Lakesh paused before squeezing through the door. He glanced back at Kane, only slightly reassured by the fact he was no longer armed. ''We're going out there?''

Kane's lips twisted as if he tasted something sour. ''What do you think? Get moving.''

Inhaling a deep breath, stiffening his spine and squaring his shoulders, Lakesh sidled through the opening and onto the plateau. The touch of the wind was cool, with just a hint of the past winter's frigidity underlying it. The constellations wheeled overhead, burning frostily in the vast, blue-black canopy of the night sky. They glittered there like powdered diamonds sprinkled by the diffident hand of creation. The light provided by a half moon struck silver highlights from the scraps of the chain-link fence that once enclosed the perimeter.

At the far edge of the plateau yawned an abyss. There was nothing at its bottom to see, even had he been able to pierce the deep dark. It plunged straight down a thousand feet or more to a streambed where the rusted-out carcasses of several vehicles lay. They were probably submerged by the torrent of meltwater rushing down from the mountain peaks during the spring thaw.

To his mild surprise but great unease he saw Grant, Shizuka, Quavell, Bry and Sindri assembled at the center of the plateau. The moonlight sculpted Sindri's face with sinister shadows. The black shadowsuit he wore blended with the surrounding murk so his head seemed to float disembodied in the air.

Lakesh's eyes traveled to Grant, and despite the situation, he couldn't help but smile at the big man's mode of dress. His smile faltered and faded when he glanced at Shizuka. Her raven's-wing hair framed the chill beauty of her face, and her almond-shaped eyes gazed at him, glinting with dark, accusing flame.

Lakesh surveyed all the silently staring people with an appraising, neutral glance, then asked sardonically, ''Is this the end of all my noble thoughts, deeds and sacrifices?''

''We'd have to credit you with them first,'' Kane retorted with icy sarcasm.

Lakesh frowned at him. "What's going on? If you intend to throw me off the cliff, then by all means get on with it."

Brigid said earnestly, "We brought you out here for two reasons, Lakesh. First is because of the nanites infesting your body."

Lakesh knotted his fists and snapped angrily, "Damn the woman. So much for patient-and-physician confidentiality."

"Reba didn't tell us about the nanites," Kane interjected, nodding toward Sindri. "He did. Reba only confirmed it."

Lakesh gazed with slitted eyes at Sindri. "Indeed? And who told you?"

A cold, ironic smile tugged the corners of Sindri's mobile mouth. "You did. So did your wife and daughter."

Sindri's calm words stunned Lakesh into speechlessness for a long moment, long enough for Brigid to say, "We don't know the extent of Sam's control over the nanites or if they can leave your body and infect other organic or inorganic material. We brought you out here, away from our electronics, so if Sam by some chance is listening in, he won't command the nanites to jump into the computers."

"The second reason," Kane said, "is simply so we can all talk privately, away from the new personnel. Sindri has a great deal more to tell us about the future. From what he's said already, we're the ones—the core group of Cerberus—who can best effect the changes, to keep the future from coming to pass."

"How so?" Domi demanded, coming to Lakesh's side.

"We'll be the ones to decide and implement a course of action," Grant rumbled.

Lakesh's voice shook when he asked, "What are you talking about?"

"The future," Kane replied grimly. "And a way to avert it. We may all die in the attempt, but at least we'll die as free as we possibly can be—and if we succeed, we may save the world from suffering any kind of tyranny, baronial or imperial."

In a terse voice, using unadorned language, Kane provided Lakesh with an overview of the history his future self had related. When he was done, the man looked more than shaken; he appeared to be profoundly shocked, almost sickened by what he had heard. Sweat glistened on his forehead.

"That's the way it's going to be," Kane said flatly. "More or less."

"But," Lakesh said in a faltering voice, "it can be stopped?"

"According to what Sindri says, it can. If we're lucky and if you cooperate, we can keep the Great Plan from coming to fruition."

Domi's eyes narrowed. "The great what?"

Lakesh looked from Kane's face to Sindri's. "Tell me," he said hoarsely, a sudden terror tingling his nerves. "Tell me what I can do."

Sindri glanced expectantly toward Kane. "Shall I?"

Kane gestured to Sindri. "It's your show."

ALTHOUGH SINDRI ENJOYED being the center of attention, this time he didn't indulge his taste for the theatric or the melodramatic—or at the very least, he refrained from making it too intolerable.

He skipped over the back story about Sam, since everyone present was familiar with how, some six months before, a mysterious figure calling himself the imperator appeared and set himself up as overlord of all the villes, with the barons subservient to him. That bit of news was surprising enough, but it quickly turned shocking when they found out that none other than Balam, whom they had thought was gone forever, supported the imperator, who liked to be called Sam.

Sam not only claimed to carry the DNA of Erica van Sloan and Enlil, the last of the Annunaki, but he also restored Lakesh's youth in order to swing him to his side.

None of the Cerberus exiles was disturbed by the concept of an entity bearing the blended genetic material of three races. However, the powers he appeared to wield and his autocratic attitude were frightening. Sam hadn't come right out and threatened the lives of those in Cerberus if they didn't join his cause, but he hadn't needed to. The inference that he could do so if they turned down Sam's offer certainly hadn't been subtle.

On the face of it, what Sam offered was exceptionally tempting and even logical. Rather than have Lakesh and his Cerberus warriors continue to wage their uncoordinated guerrilla war on the barons, Sam wanted those resources under his dominion, where they would be given direction and focus.

By allying with the imperator, Lakesh and his people would be protected and he would have a voice in the implementation of a new order. There would be no more need to hide, and the Cerberus exiles wouldn't bear the stigma of being outlanders any longer.

Therefore Sam's proposal made perfect sense—and that was what made all of them so suspicious.

According to what Sindri had learned in the future, that suspicion was well-founded. In the political backwash of the Consolidation War and Nirodha conflict in Asia, the standard of living for the population at large dropped off. Most of the individual governments in Europe fell, and almost all of Asia came under a worldwide military dictatorship formed by imperial forces.

The fledgling economy of Sam's Consolidated Confederation of States was thrown into turmoil. The new government groaned under the weight of countless unskilled unemployables who had to be fed, clothed and housed at the expense of the states. The corrupting influences of state-supplied SQUID implants kept the idle from rioting and committing crimes, true enough, but it also deadened them to truth and individual initiative, blinding them with a cloak of illusory beauty.

No one knew or cared any longer about the difference between freedom and cushioned slavery. Behind the facade of well-being created by the SQUIDs, the culture seethed with indolence and ugliness, but it was all part of the long-range program Sam called the Great Plan.

Ambition, even the Olympian aspirations of an imperator, had to accept the limitations of reality. It required much time and greater effort to control the wild, mad human beings who infested the planet. Even twenty-seven years hence there were still people scattered throughout the Outlands who refused to become part of the imperial society and therefore hadn't been subjected to the SQUID implants. Although the advent of the imperator had changed the old caste system, those who didn't submit willingly to Sam's authority were threats to the Great Plan.

The sheer enormity of the Great Plan was enough to intimidate anyone. But Sam's ideals governed his life, and those ideals were focused on one goal—to dominate everyone, to control every destructive urge, to eliminate waste, to unify, to establish the law of pitiless logic and cold reason wherever humanity could be found. The only way the species could survive was by the domination of it.

However, the neuronic energy provided by the SQUIDs channeled through the Heart of the World didn't allow the imperator to read or directly control minds. It did, however, permit him to give and receive impressions, ideas and visualizations. From these various stimuli, Sam possessed the ability to extrapolate from a handful of known facts and to predict the logical sequence of events. It was truly a talent, not necessarily a learned skill that relied solely on cerebration.

To gauge and evaluate and to extrapolate a conclusion that was so probable as to be almost certain, was more than precognition. It was a given. He had blended technology to augment his own natural psionic abilities.

Definitely, Sam employed nanotechnology to maintain his health. The ill, the old and the injured all suffered from misarranged patterns of molecules, whether misarranged by invading viruses, passing time or genetics. Sam's nanotechnology rearranged and corrected cells at a molecular level.

Therefore, in the eyes of many, that one single ability made Sam as close to a genuine messiah as was ever born in the history of the world. He made no real claim of divinity. He didn't need to, inasmuch as he set out to earn the title of messiah by deed, not by word.

An aspect of those deeds involved doing away with those who didn't share his vision or his lofty goals of a unified world, of an adaptive Earth. His control of the SQUID implants helped that along, too.

The implants kept the population of old and new humans in check by numbing the drive to procreate. It was a cleaner way to exterminate the useless eaters than pogroms and mass executions, but just as effective. Sam foresaw that the population would be slashed from millions to mere manageable thousands in less than a decade. And those thousands would be slaves adapted to meet various needs.

Even the hybrids who in the future coexisted peacefully with humanity were at risk. No matter that they were not completely Homo sapiens, they sprang from essentially the same roots and were humankind transformed. Therefore, they were still a continuation of the race. Hybrid females and human males had been pairing off, and the past two decades had seen a rise in mixed-breed offspring, children bearing the best qualities of old and new human.

The world may not have been as violent and brutal as before, but it was far from being the utopia Sam had described. It was a comfortable prison, but a prison nonetheless.

But Sam had built more than a prison for the human soul—he had constructed a window that would reach into the past or the future and inject matter throughout the chronon stream whenever and wherever he wanted.

Sam called it the microcosm, and he described it as that which arose from a conjunction of two laws of physics. The first had to do with the changes in the mass of a particle as it approached the speed of light. Through his work with the Heart of the World, he determined that measurements of particles that had been raced up to close to the speed of light showed a strong and rapidly rising increase in their mass—so much so that it seemed as if it would always be impossible to supply enough energy to bring the particle finally to that ultimate speed.

The second factor that occurred to him was at almost the opposite end of the research spectrum, the concept of absolute zero in temperature. It was known that the temperature of an object was the product of the relative speed of its molecules. As a body heated up, its molecules moved farther apart from one another and moved faster.

At absolute zero, the molecules would lose all motion and come to a dead stop. Such a stop would presumably cause all the molecules to come together to form one mass without internal motion. The final phase of the Great Plan was to combine both operations.

To attempt to have a particle of matter reach both the speed of light and absolute zero simultaneously was a challenge. But he suspected that by combining the molecular speed-up with ultra-low-temperature physics, he would reach his goal—even though conventional physics stated he could never attain it.

But Sam did attain it, and found an interesting quality about the speed of light and the absolute zero of temperature—both were apparently boundaries of our universe. Both were part of the restraining walls of our particular continuum.

In achieving his goal, Sam pierced the restraining walls of the continuum and the Heart of the World became a true independent space-time unit, free from the constraints of the quantum field, yet still connected to it. That was why he feared Kane's temporal manipulations. He worried his own experiments might cause chronon ripples that could impact negatively on his ambitions to topple the entire principle of causality, that causes precede effects. Once the microcosm was created, it negated temporal paradoxes and Sam was free to inject whatever matter he chose into the chronon and spatial continuum.

The matter he chose was a mutated plague virus, a deadly pathogen that could decimate population centers and empires, monarchies and democracies. The survivors of the plague would be struck down by an enervating weakness. Resentments and jealousies between nations that were once allies would be exacerbated, since none of them could extend aid to the other. A savior would be sought, and Sam would be there with his treatments.

By the time Sam's Great Plan reached the pinnacle of its success, not only would he have everyone in this future time period neuronically linked by the SQUIDs, but also he would have accomplished it throughout the past. Everyone who was ever born, or who might be born, would be his servant.

Of course, no one would ever realize it, because after the temporal manipulation ripples faded, the whole of humanity's history would have always been determined by Sam. He would wield infinite power over a finite existence, an eternity stamped with the impression of his consciousness.

"UNLESS, OF COURSE," Sindri said in conclusion, "you stop him. And I presume all of you will at the very least want to take a shot at it. That's the kind of work you do here, isn't it?"

"We've certainly tried to stop you often enough, pissant," Grant rumbled, but his tone was distracted, as if he made the comment out of habit alone.

"And Thrush." Brigid's voice was a rustling whisper. "You mentioned him."

Sindri shrugged. "Actually, it was Mr. Kane—the Mr. Kane twenty-seven years hence—who told me that the imperator's true identity was Colonel C. W.

Thrush. He was very insistent I convey that message to all of you. They were literally his last words.''

He arched quizzical eyebrows at Lakesh. ''I presume that name means something?''

Lakesh stared at Sindri, wide- and wild-eyed as if he were seeing him for the first time. Then he took two faltering back steps and fell to his knees, burying his face in his hands.

In an agonized groan, Lakesh said, ''Thrush…I'm a slave to Colonel Thrush…and I've betrayed all of you to him.''

Chapter 10

The baronial oligarchy that ruled postskydark America shared very little in the way of cultural legends and almost nothing that corresponded to spiritual beliefs. They worshiped no pantheon of deities, made no pilgrimages to holy sites. There were no versions of Mount Olympus, Jerusalem or Mecca.

The one possible exception was Front Royal. The barons didn't hold Front Royal in any kind of awe, and they certainly didn't sanctify it, but the ville occupied a significant place in their common history. The ville in Virginia was the birthplace of the Program of Unification, the undertaking that consolidated power in the baronies and returned a measure of order to the brutal and chaotic land.

Almost a century earlier, the Council of Front Royal met for the first time. The ten most powerful barons, those who had survived territorial wars and clawed out stable enclaves of civilization in the Deathlands, convened to discuss their admitted strengths and definite weaknesses. All of them had been summoned to the ville in the foothills of the Shens by a mysterious, black-clad emissary who went by the sinisterly simple name of Thrush.

Front Royal was chosen for the historic summit because it the was the most influential and democratically governed ville on the eastern seaboard. Its current baron had expressed his desire to decisively end the reign of blood and anarchy. Front Royal was probably the most powerful of the baronies, despite the fact it never made raids into other territories or enslaved its people. The ville was well-known and envied for its high standard of living, despite the fact the baron's home and seat of government resembled a medieval fortress.

Long-ago siege damage had been repaired to the keep, restoring its former appearance of forbidding majesty. The weathered bricks and blocks were clean of vines and lichens. The main building, the castle, rose above the walls in a defiant thrust of chiseled stone, flying buttresses, stained-glass windows and forged steel.

The ville was enclosed by walls nearly half a mile in circumference and fifty feet tall, offering flat buttresses of impregnable fortifications. The walls in turn were surrounded by a river with only a single bridge that crossed it into a central cobblestone plaza.

Despite the setting, or because of it, the ten barons met with the diplomatic envoy who outlined all the rewards that would be theirs if they put aside their differences, concentrated on their commonalties and united. Barons had united before, observing trade agreements and nonaggression pacts. What Thrush proposed was different. A new form of government would be institutionalized in the baronies, and all the villes would be standardized according to preexisting specifications.

The barons would be provided with all the materials needed to achieve these goals, including a vast treasure trove of long-lost predark technology, as pristine as the day it was manufactured. Thrush wove a thoroughly spellbinding tale of a vast vault designed to protect everything stored in it from the ravages of time.

Not just a few boxes of ammo, he hastened to point out, or a couple of crates of guns or the odd wag, but literally tons of matériel—advanced weaponry, electronic equipment saved from electromagnetic pulses, even aircraft. All of it was in perfect operating condition. No longer would the individual barons be forced to cobble together electrical generators with spit and baling wire or waste time with long periods of trial and error to figure out how to repair rusty engines. Moreover, they would be participating in a grand, radically new kind of social engineering.

Although intrigued and galvanized by the morsels of bait, the barons harbored doubts that such items still existed. They knew all about the Continuity of Government stockpiles, and they also knew most of them had been looted years before. Only the baron of Front Royal accepted Thrush's words at face value, having ventured into just such vaults more than once and barely escaped with his life.

When asked about the social engineering plan, Thrush argued that humans were too intrinsically destructive to be allowed free will any longer. The ruined planet was mute, utterly damning testimony to the philosophy of individual choice and freedom. The old predark system of smoldering desperation and unchecked societal chaos that burned out in a final nuclear conflagration was inferior in every way to the society the barons could build.

The barons quickly understood they weren't being offered an option as much as being given an ultimatum. Essentially, they were told if they didn't endorse the doctrine of unification, the same power that had turned the world into a nuke-scoured hellscape more than a century before would devastate it again.

The tough and cynical barons weren't easily intimidated or impressed by promises with threats attached. They challenged Thrush to bring forth this so-called power, so they might see it with their own eyes. For all intents and purposes, they sneered in Thrush's calm, pale face.

Much to the surprise and unease of the ten assembled barons, Thrush rose to their challenge and introduced the representative of the Archon Directorate. Thrush referred to him as Balam. The Archon was strange, unsettling in appearance, but no more so than some of the strains of human mutants skulking through the Deathlands. The small, slight-framed, big-skulled and -eyed creature didn't look even as fearsome as an infant stickie.

But even the dullest of the barons in attendance couldn't deny he radiated a disquieting aura, an eerie sense of otherworldliness. Without preamble or social fripperies, Balam addressed them, speaking to them without opening his mouth, imparting the same message at the same time into all of their minds. His black, fathomless eyes held all of theirs captive, peering deep, deep through them into the roots of their souls.

We are old, they were told. *When your race was wild and bloody and young, we were already ancient. Your tribe has passed, and we are invincible. All of the achievements of man are dust, they are forgotten.*

We stand, we know, we are. We stalked above man ere we raised him from the ape. Long was the earth ours and now we have reclaimed it. We shall still reign when man is reduced to the ape again. We stand, we know, we are.

At the same time, images crowded into their minds, glimpses of a history hidden from humanity for aeons.

They learned how the entirety of human development was inextricably intertwined with the activities of the entities called Archons. Balam showed them how modern humankind was bioengineered millennia ago, and how his race had maintained a covert dominance over humankind ever since. Always the Archons subtly—and sometimes not so subtly—influenced human affairs. The Archons' standard operating procedure was to establish a privileged ruling class dependent upon them, which in turn controlled the masses for them. Throughout history, their manipulation of governments and religions was all-pervasive.

Their goal was the unification of the world under their control, with all nonessential and nonproductive humans eliminated. Now, over a hundred years after the nukecaust, the seeds planted long ago were ready to bear fruit.

Balam's telepathic speech and the images he conveyed were more than rhetoric, less than a threat. It was the scornful, prideful doctrine of a race so old that the most ancient civilizations on Earth were only a yesterday beside it. The underlying psychological message of the address was intended to stimulate panic, fear and despair. You cannot win, the barons were told. We are undefeatable, bow to the inevitable. Surrender.

The barons attending the inaugural council of Front Royal, after two days of discussion, agreed to the Archon Directorate's terms—except for the baron of Front Royal. He perceived the program as nothing more than tyranny with a new face. He had spent much of his adult life opposing the tyrants who sprang up like malign tumors in the aftermath of skydark. He had no intention of participating in a plan that would institutionalize despotism.

The baron of Front Royal raised a revolt, and those who rallied to his cause were known as baron blasters. Even former adversaries made common cause to oppose an inhuman enemy. The early years of the unification program were very violent and bloody and launched an entire cycle of legends and myths. The band of wolfsheads led by Front Royal's baron were revered as folk heroes, the subject of ballads and tall tales.

Eventually, although the original projected timetable was skewed by several years, the united baronies were established, through propaganda and sheer naked force. Unity Through Action was the rallying cry that had spread across the Deathlands by word of mouth and proof of deed. The long-forgotten trust in any form of government was slowly reawakened, generations after the survivors of the nuclear war had lived through the deadly legacy of politics and the suicidal decisions made by elected officials.

The leaders of the powerful baronies offered a solution to the constant states of worry and fear—join the unification program and never worry or fear or think again. Humanity was responsible for the arrival of Judgment Day, and it had to accept that responsibility, before a truly utopian age could be ushered in.

All humankind had to do to earn this utopia was to follow the rules, be obedient and be fed and clothed. And accept the new order without question. Surrender.

For most of the men and women who lived in the villes and the surrounding territories, this was enough, more than enough. Long-sought-after dreams of peace and safety had at least been transformed into reality. Of course, fleeting dreams of personal freedom were lost in the exchange, but such abstract aspirations were nothing but childish illusions.

Over the following four generations, order was indeed restored to America and the barons themselves represented the new order as well as a new form of humanity. Only the barons themselves knew how different they were, not only from their human progenitors from whom they inherited their names and territories, but also from the humans they ruled.

A major aspect of the unification program was improving the breed. This was accomplished through bioengineering, employing advances in genetics made in the years leading up to the nukecaust. The primary link between the baronial oligarchy and the Archons was the incorporation of their genetic material into offspring of the barons. Thus was created the hybrid dynasty, a revival of the ancient god-king system that deified monarchs as semidivine.

Furthermore, the Archons saw to it that the barons would have at hand, in vitro, genetic samples of the best of the best of humanity. In the vernacular of the time, it was known as purity control. Only the best of the best were allowed full ville citizenship. The caste distinctions were based primarily on eugenics. Everyone selected to live in the villes, to serve in the divisions, met a strict set of genetic criteria, one established before the nukecaust.

The in vitro egg cells were developed to embryos. Through ectogenesis techniques, fetal development outside of the body eliminated the role of the mother until after birth. The ancient social patterns that connected mother, father and child were broken. That break was crucial in order for the unification program to succeed to its final level.

The existence of the family as a unit of procreation and therefore as a social unit had to be eliminated. Everyone who enjoyed full ville citizenship was the direct descendant of that undertaking.

Of course, the gene pools of the individual barons derived from combinations of superior human DNA and Archon—or so they believed. That belief kept them from wondering too deeply why, if they were so superior, they suffered from so many physical ailments.

Like Balam, they were slightly built, with oversized craniums and large light-sensitive eyes. The tissue of their hybridized brains was of the same visceral matter as the human brain, but the fifteen million neurons that formed the basic wiring operated a bit differently in the processing of information. The brains of the barons could absorb and process information with exceptional speed, and their cognitive abilities were little short of supernatural.

Almost from the moment the barons emerged from the incubation chambers, they possessed IQs so far beyond the range of standard tests as to render them meaningless. They mastered language in a matter of weeks, speaking in whole sentences. All of Nature's design flaws in the human brain were corrected, modified and improved, specifically in the hypothalamus, which regulated the complex biochemical systems of the body.

They could control all autonomous functions of their brains and bodies, even to the manufacture and release of chemicals and hormones. They could speed or slow their heartbeats, increase and decrease the amount of adrenaline in their bloodstreams.

They possessed complete control over that mysterious portion of the brain known as the limbic system, a portion that predark scientists referred to as the "god module," which possessed great reserves of electromagnetic power and strength.

But since they were bred for brilliance, all barons had emotional limitations placed upon their enormous intellects. They were captives of their shared Archon hive-mind heritage, a remorseless mind-set that didn't carry with it the simple comprehension of the importance to humans of individual liberty.

Visceral emotions didn't play a large part in the

psychologies of the so-called new humans. Even their bursts of passion were of the most rudimentary kind. When they experienced emotions, they only did so in moments of stress, and then so intensely they were almost consumed by them.

Although the tissue of their hybridized brains was of the same organic matter as the human brain, the millions of neurons operated differently in the processing of information. Their thought processes were very structured, extremely linear. There were variations among them, of course. A few of the barons were gifted psionically, able to tap into flashes of clairvoyant insight during periods of meditation or to invade a mind telepathically. All in all, they were as intellectually superior to humankind as the Cro-Magnon was to the Neanderthal.

But they paid a heavy price for their superior abilities. Physically they were fragile, their autoimmune systems at the mercy of infections and diseases that had little effect on the primitive humans they ruled. Nor could they reproduce by intercourse. The nine barons were the product of in vitro fertilization, as would be their offspring and all hybrids.

Therefore the barons lived insulated, isolated lives, cloaking themselves in theatrical trappings that not only added to their semidivine mystique, but also protected them from contamination—both psychological and physical.

Once a year, the oligarchy traveled to an installation beneath Archuleta Mesa in Dulce, New Mexico, for medical treatments. If not for the Directorate, the vast installation within and beneath the Archuleta

Mesa, on the border of New Mexico and Colorado, would not have been built.

If not for the Totality Concept's Overproject Excalibur and its three subdivisions, the barons would not have existed in the first place or continued to do so. During the annual visits to the mesa, they received fresh transfusions of blood and a regimen of biochemical genetic therapy designed to strengthen their autoimmune systems, which granted them another year of life and power. They also were recipients of organ transplants if necessary.

Although all the hybrids were extremely long-lived, cellular and metabolic deterioration was part and parcel of what they were—hybrids of human and Archon DNA. And even though they were a biological bridge between two races, the barons weren't precisely sure of the reasons behind the hybridization program.

They knew the Archons had been a dying race, on the verge of extinction before the nukecaust. They also knew the nukecaust itself to have been a major component of their program. After the masses of humanity had been culled, the herd thinned, then the hybrids would inherit the earth, carrying out the agenda of the Archon Directorate. All of the barons believed that they acted as the plenipotentiaries of the Archons and therefore, they were the intermediaries between gods and Man.

But the barons weren't so blinded by arrogance that the irony was lost on them—in order to rule humans, they were dependent on the biological material they provided.

Just as the barons had traveled once a year to the underground facility in New Mexico, they also met once a year at Front Royal to discuss matters of state—or at least that had been the custom for nearly a century. The oligarchy of nine barons almost never had face-to-face exchanges except at the yearly councils. Occasionally, an emergency demanded a special summit.

The last such emergency council had been several months before, shortly after the destruction of the Archuleta Mesa facility. Now another council was about to be convened, but this one was very different, since it excluded all but two of the oligarchy and had been called, not by a fellow baron, but by Erica van Sloan—the imperial mother herself.

Chapter 11

In Erica van Sloan's world there was a place, a definition and a purpose for everything and she had spent the better part of the past forty years placing everything, from people to objects, in their proper categories. She had decided to make cybernetic science her profession because she was attracted to the geometric order and pristine immutability of applied statistics. The lesser educated or the jealous might have called her tendencies anal retentive or obsessive compulsive.

After her resurrection from cryostasis more than four decades before, Erica had served as an adviser to the baronial oligarchy in general, rather than to an individual baron. Like a handful of other predarkers, Erica van Sloan had been revived when the Program of Unification reached a certain stage of development.

Erica wasn't assigned to any one barony for an extended period of time. She was given quarters in Front Royal and from there she traveled from ville to ville, setting up computer systems, training personnel in their operation and the troubleshooting procedures. The systems, although in pristine condition, were not state-of-the-art, certainly not by the standards of the late twentieth century.

None of the mainframes employed the advanced biochip features that would have been commonplace

had the nuclear megacull not occurred. Most of the
software, hardware and support systems were fairly
basic, not much more complicated than the personal
home computers in wide use before the nukecaust.

Erica had always suspected that the truly advanced
predark tech was deliberately withheld so the new baronial society wouldn't become as dependent on technology as the old one. She didn't disagree with the
principles behind the suppression, but she couldn't
deny it made her job more difficult. But, when distilled down to its essence, her job consisted primarily
of pigeonholing and compartmentalizing.

She never had been able to find the right mental
pigeonhole for Front Royal, since its form followed
neither function nor aesthetics. That the barons preferred to maintain the keep's quaint, medieval architecture, in lieu of redesigning it to resemble the Ad-
ministrative Monoliths in the villes didn't make it
more defensible. However, as one of the concessions
to modern times, powerful halogen spotlights were
mounted both on the walls and atop the turrets. Projecting from each corner of the walls were Vulcan-
Phalanx gun towers, the heavy-caliber weapons ready
and waiting to fend off any sort of attack, not that
there had been any kind of major assault in living
memory.

Front Royal was occupied only by a skeleton maintenance staff and a garrison consisting of twenty soldiers. It wasn't a ville in the conventional sense, but
more of a neutral zone, a place where the barons
could meet on equal terms for their annual council.

The main hall of the keep was immense. Its heavy-beamed ceiling and waxed, oak-paneled walls always danced with the light of a hundred false electric candles in the wrought-iron chandelier.

The floor was of polished marble in swirling patterns. At the far end was a hearth big enough to comfortably sleep four barons and two of the security staff. A yard-long electric log always glowed there.

As far as she knew, none of the barons objected to the installation of a mat-trans unit within a shielded cubicle complete with stripped-down control room, on the opposite side of the main hall. Erica didn't think the six-sided elevated chamber with its sky-blue armaglass walls added or detracted from the Old World feel of the big room. It simply stood there, at the far end of the control room, like an ugly conversation piece.

Sitting in the main hall and facing the control room, she nearly jumped out of her chair when she heard the characteristic high-pitched drone from the emitter array within the platform. The sound was an electronic synthesis between a hurricane howl and bee-swarm hum, dropping down to inaudibility as the mat-trans cycled through a materialization.

The noise was nerve-racking, but she didn't bother trying to make out the two vague shapes shifting into corporeality on the other side of the translucent armaglass shielding. She knew the identity of at least one of the people. Erica also knew she was undertaking a sizable risk by greeting the arrivals alone, dressed as she was. But she followed the imperator's will and she understood he had his reasons for ordering her to wear the Shakti priestess raiment—what there was of it.

Erica van Sloan was clad in a white, floor-length shift composed of about five percent loosely woven linen. Silver bracelets, a jeweled bangle and a pair of sandals made up another five percent of the ensemble. The other ninety percent was all her, but she didn't really mind.

She was tall and long-limbed, with a flawless, honey-hued complexion. Her long, straight hair, swept back from a high forehead and pronounced widow's peak, hung in a thick braid down the middle of her back. It was so black as to be blue when the light caught it. The large eyes above high, regal cheekbones looked almost the same shade of indigo, but glints of violet swam in them. The mark of an aristocrat showed in her delicate features, with the arch of brows and her thin-bridged nose. Her eyelids glistened with narrow stripes of crimson and silver.

When she heard footfalls, Erica rose, noting absently how her full breasts swayed beneath their thin covering. She knew the sexual effect would be wasted on one of the visitors, but she halfway hoped the other man would show arousal at the sight of her barely concealed charms. As a newly appointed Shakti priestess, it was only fitting that her body would be one of sinuous perfection. At least, that was what Sam had told her when he imparted the information about the Nirodha movement. During that same meeting, he had imbued her with more of his bioenergy, and the gray streak in her hair almost immediately darkened. She had been secretly preening ever since.

Two figures entered the main hall from the mat-trans control room. There was a formal council room adjacent to the main hall, holding a conference table twelve feet in diameter. The walls, ceiling and floors of the huge, sprawling chamber were sheathed with slick, slightly reflective vanadium alloy. Not only was the shielding for security purposes, but it also provided protection just in case a Roamer fired a LAW rocket at the keep.

Erica had decided not to convene the meeting in the conference room, inasmuch as the primary topic of the discussion was located elsewhere in the fortress. She worked hard to keep her face composed, despite the surge of anxiety the sight of Baron Cobalt evoked within her, even though he was physically no different than his fellow barons.

All of the barons were so similar in appearance they might have been born from the same mother and father. In many ways, they had been. Their builds were small, slender and gracile. Their faces were uniformly sharp with finely complexioned skin stretched tight over prominent shelves of cheekbones.

The craniums were very high and smooth, the ears small and set low on the head. Their back-slanting eyes were large, shadowed by sweeping supraorbital ridges. Only hair, eye color and slight differences in height differentiated the barons from one another.

Even their expressions were markedly alike—a vast pride, a diffident superiority, authority and even ruthlessness. They were the barons, and as such, they were the avatars of the new humans who would inherit the earth.

The last time Erica had seen Cobalt, he wore the ceremonial garb of the baronial oligarchy—flowing, bell-sleeved robes of gold brocade, and a tall, conical crested headpiece, ringed by nine rows of tiny pearls. No one, not even the humans who had advised them for years like Erica van Sloan, knew from whence the tradition of ceremonial attire sprang. She always presumed the design had something to do with Archon culture, whatever that might be.

Baron Thulia's adviser, a man named Bakshmi, had told her in an unguarded moment that there was an uncomfortable similarity between the barons' ceremonial garb and that of Tibetan high lamas. If indeed the entities called Archons had influenced humanity since the dawn of time, then it stood to reason they had interacted with Tibetans.

As he approached, Erica saw that Baron Cobalt wasn't wearing ceremonial garb. In fact, his mode of dress was even more unusual, so startling for a baron that Erica found herself staring, shocked into speechlessness. Faded blue denim overalls swallowed the baron's slender figure, making him look almost as if he were wearing a barrel. The elephantine legs of the pants had been hacked off crudely, and the cuffs were frayed and uneven, accentuating the fact he wore battered and discolored moccasins soled with old tire treads.

Although all the hybrids were slight of build, the baron looked thin to the point of starvation. His almost poreless skin was stretched drum-tight over protuberant facial bones, all sharp angles of cheeks, brow and chin. His elongated skull tapered from a high, round, completely bald skull down to a pointed chin.

Deep lines marred the face and scored the high forehead. Below it large, slanting golden-brown eyes stared out from deep sockets. The thin slash of the mouth showed barely repressed pain, and the tiny nostrils in the fine, thin nose flared with a soul-deep anger. His untrimmed fingernails were caked with dirt down to the cuticle. He had the look of living in desolate places, burned by the sun, scourged by blowing sands.

Erica was so taken aback by Cobalt's wasted appearance, she didn't realize for a moment that the tall figure looming beside him was not a man, as she had first assumed, but a hulking woman. Erica guessed her height at six foot three and her weight in the vicinity of 250 pounds.

The giantess's wiry dark blond hair was cut exceptionally short. She wore a one-piece zippered coverall that looked very old, judging by its threadbare elbows and knees and the patches sewn onto it in places. When she got a good look at Erica, her mouth gaped open, revealing tobacco-stained teeth. Her features were so coarse it was impossible to gauge her age, but Erica didn't care one way or the other.

Baron Cobalt stared, too, but Erica could easily guess why. The last time he had seen her, nearly a year ago in this very room, she had been a seam-faced cripple. She knew it was difficult even for so regimented a mind as a hybrid's to reconcile the memory of a withered old hag hunched over in a wheelchair with the reality of the tall, vibrant, superbly built beauty standing before him now. She had difficulty accepting it even now herself.

By now, Erica realized Cobalt had learned how the imperator had not only restored her youth, but also put life back in her legs again. Sam had also given her a purpose beyond acting as an adviser to the baronial oligarchy. She dedicated her life to building a new, productive society on the framework of the ville system.

As a cyberneticist, she applied those same mechanical principles to management and organizational theory. Just as everything that occurred in the universe could be analyzed according to cause-and-effect chains, the chains themselves could be used to build organizational models.

Now, months after the end of the so-called Imperator War, a new model was being constructed. Erica had rebuilt Cobaltville so it would serve as the template for all the others. She was positive the baron had heard about that, too, and hated her for it.

"You are Erica van Sloan?" Cobalt challenged, the rich, musical tones of his voice sounding harsh, as if he had been gargling with gravel. "Former adviser to the oligarchy, now the self-proclaimed imperial mother?"

Erica nodded coldly, formally, but said, "I am not the self-proclaimed imperial mother. The imperator made that claim himself, and I saw no reason to question him. Neither did anyone else."

Cobalt waved the objection away impatiently. "You've changed considerably since we last met."

"As have you. But, apparently, not for the better."

His face flushed with barely suppressed anger. "Is there some reason you are dressed like a maharajah's houri other than to show me you are unarmed?"

Erica didn't respond to the question. She impaled the big woman with a frigid, inquisitive stare. "Who is this?"

"Her name is Mary Lou McSween," Cobalt replied. "I call her Mare. She is my servant."

Erica flicked a contemptuous glance up and down the woman's broad frame and then stared challengingly into her coarse-featured face. She felt only a little better when the woman averted her gaze. "She looks more like your strong-arm, Cobalt. Quite a comedown from being protected by the baronial guardsmen, isn't it?"

"You should know, Sloan." The baron's retort was soft, but his tone was underscored by a hatred so strong and venomous Erica wouldn't have been surprised had he spit at her. His eyes seethed with fury.

"That I do," she replied calmly. "What I don't know is how you survived without access to the medical treatments. By my calculations, you should have been dead at least a month ago."

A thin smile touched Cobalt's lips, and he cast a sly glance up toward the woman called Mare, who smiled back at him with undisguised adoration. Erica felt her stomach spasm in nausea. Still, she took a secret, gloating satisfaction in the knowledge that for the first time in his artificially prolonged life, Cobalt was forced to achieve short-term goals—like living through the end of a day.

"Perhaps I *am* dead," he replied. "And what you

see before you is only a ghost, a shade of the Baron Cobalt you once so faithfully advised, then so viciously betrayed. Perhaps I am his spirit, summoned to curse you and hound you to your own grave.''

''Or,'' Erica said, unperturbed, ''it's more likely you found a secondary source of treatments. It certainly couldn't have been the Archuleta Mesa facility.''

Cobalt nodded. ''In that we are in total agreement. The Dulce installation is completely destroyed. We of the oligarchy should have removed the entire biological and genetic processing center from the place after the first…incident.''

Cobalt intoned ''incident'' in a sarcastic drawl. Erica was familiar with the event to which he referred, and ''incident'' was a woefully understated description.

More then two years earlier, a pair of renegade Magistrates and a turncoat archivist from Cobaltville invaded the medical facility beneath the mesa during the baron's annual treatment. Kane, Grant and Brigid Baptiste wreaked much havoc and left the installation littered with the bodies of many hybrids. At the time only Baron Cobalt was undergoing the process, and he, as well as the other barons, realized the invasion was not sheer happenstance.

Inasmuch as Baron Cobalt had been assaulted by Kane, his fellow barons agreed to help him find the criminals. For the first few months following the Archuleta Mesa incursion, it was as if Kane, Baptiste and Grant had vanished off the face of the earth.

Then reports of sightings came in from all over.

The obvious conclusion was they were using the forbidden mat-trans units to jump from sealed redoubt to sealed redoubt. A cooperative undertaking among the nine barons to inspect all of the installations in their territories resulted only in false trails—and violent attacks on two barons.

When Baron Sharpe was personally investigating a redoubt near the ruins of Washington, D.C., he was severely wounded. By his description, his assailant could have only been Kane.

The next, and truly horrifying incident, was the assassination of Baron Ragnar in his own bed. Although intel reports from Ragnarville identified a woman as the culprit—possibly the insurrectionist historian, Baptiste—Kane and Grant's names figured prominently.

And because their names figured so prominently, they became figures of inspiration to the disenfranchised, to the outlander. Their acts of terrorism triggered sporadic rebellions in the Outlands. The uprisings were not organized uprisings, but their frequency was of a kind not seen in more than ninety years, since the days of the baron blasters.

Barely a year later came the event that not only threatened the barons' authority, but also their very survival. The medical facility beneath the mesa, which the barons depended upon to stay alive, was virtually destroyed. According to the intelligence reports, the unbelievably destructive chain reaction had been triggered by the crash of an aircraft.

The crash breached the magnetic field container of a fusion generator in the hangar. The result had been akin to unleashing the energy of the Sun itself inside an enclosed sports arena. Although much of the kinetic force and heat were channeled upward and out through the hangar doors, a scorching, smashing wave of destruction swept through the installation. If not for the series of vanadium blast bulkheads, the entire mesa could have come tumbling down.

Cobalt shook his head as if trying to drive the memories from his head. "How did your people succeed in locating me?"

Erica smiled a thin, superior smile. "The imperator can find whomever he wishes."

Cobalt didn't refute her statement, but the glint in his eyes and the set of his mouth called her a liar. He said quietly, "The most important question is, why have I been summoned here under terms of truce instead of being hunted down and killed outright?"

Erica's smile widened. "The task of turning an enemy into an ally is difficult enough without turning a living creature into a dead one. The imperator needs you…my lord baron."

Chapter 12

Mammoth Mare McSween had lived the entirety of her twenty-five years on the raw edges of the Outlands frontier, and for the most part she fraternized only with others of the same background and breeding—or lack thereof. There was never any question the people she knew were imperfect, physically, mentally and otherwise.

Outlanders, or anyone who chose to live outside baronial society or had that fate chosen for them, were of a breed different from those who were born within the walls of the nine villes. Birthed into a brutal, wild world, they were accustomed to balancing themselves on the line of death. Grim necessity had taught them the skills to survive, even thrive in the postnuke environment. They may have been the great-great-great-grandchildren of civilized men and women, but they had no choice but to embrace lives of semibarbarism.

They were tough and vicious and cared little about abstract concepts of beauty or morality or even comfort. Few lived beyond forty, and those who did rarely managed to make it without losing parts of themselves. Mare grew accustomed to seeing men and women with missing eyes, ears and limbs. Therefore, perfection was not just an unreachable ideal; it was beyond imagining.

But the woman whom her lover lord had addressed as Erica van Sloan was as perfect a human being as Mare had ever dreamed existed. Other than her pliant body, Sloan's voice was as rich and vibrant as a musical instrument.

In some ways, the woman's eyes reminded Mare of her lover baron's—she could verbalize thoughts with her eyes and a simple quirk of the corner of her mouth. Of course, Baron Cobalt planted images in her mind, even channeled her thoughts into directions he convinced her they should go. That was different from the kind of communication Sloan's eyes imparted.

Mare once again surreptitiously swept her gaze across Erica van Sloan's stunning figure, made all the more provocative by the gauzy quality of her garb and the way her full breasts strained against the crisscrossing strips of linen. She had never been attracted to another female before, but then her mother, Big Ma McSween, was about the only other woman she had ever known. On the other hand, she had never been particularly attracted to most of the men she had known, either. The internal quiverings of attraction she experienced when looking upon Sloan's body confused her, but aroused her nevertheless.

"Come with me, please." Erica van Sloan turned smartly on a heel and strode with an aristocratic gait toward a door on the far side of the main hall. Mare felt her throat tighten as she watched the sensuous twitch of her buttocks beneath the diaphanous gown.

Although Mare wanted to follow her instantly, she waited until Baron Cobalt took his first step after the woman. She began marching along at his side, remembering his harsh remonstrance not to gawk at their surroundings. It was very difficult not to stop and stare with her mouth agape.

Just as Mare had never seen a woman like Sloan, she had never seen a place like the fortress of Front Royal, either. But it felt as if she had been living in the epicenter of an explosion of wonders, of miracles, marvels and terrors for the past month or so—ever since the night of the chem storm.

She didn't question it too much. Mare's philosophy, handed down to her from Big Ma, was always to follow the path of least resistance. Although Mammoth Mare fancied herself a champion salvager, she didn't like to take risks, therefore, she suffered through one lean time after another.

Looting the abandoned ruins of predark villes was not only an Outland tradition, but it was also Mammoth Mare's family business. Her mother, her mother's father and his father before him had made a career from ferreting out and plundering the secret stockpiles the predark government had hidden in anticipation of a nation-wide catastrophe.

Most of the early survivors of the nukecaust had been scavengers. They really had no choice. They banded together, found predark wags and recruited men and women strong enough to defend their armored vehicles. They raided villes of the dead where the radiation had finally weakened enough to allow limited egress. They traded among the few settlements, swapping equipment for supplies, supplies for gas, gas for ammo, and the ammo they used to blast the hell out of whatever muties or competitors stood in the way of their scavenging.

Finding a well-stocked redoubt, one of the many underground military installations seemingly scattered all over the nuke-ravaged face of America, assured a trader wealth and security, presupposing he or she didn't intersect with the trajectory of a bullet that had his or her name on it.

But it was tougher and tougher to find untouched stockpiles. The tougher the going got, the more most of her crew got themselves going, leaving her operation for greener pastures—not that there were many pastures, green or otherwise, around the Big Smoke Valley she used as winter quarters.

Mammoth Mare's crew didn't have a centralized or permanent headquarters. They had to be able to travel with the trade, as nomadic as any group that made its living from mobility. New markets often opened up when other scavenger groups made new strikes digging through rubble down into the predark villes, and supplies had to be gotten to the other scavengers that joined them, as well as transport arranged for all the things they found. A permanent location would have been detrimental to profit.

Although Mare's mother, Big Ma, had discovered some fine hauls in the past—crates of blasters, of ammunition, even clothes—by the time she died after meeting up with a bullet with her name on it, most of the easy pickings and higher-quality items had become as rare as a smiling Magistrate.

In the southwestern Outlands—New Mexico, Arizona, Nevada—small, impoverished settlements were

isolated by hundreds of square miles of barren wasteland. Although they were prey for marauders, Mammoth Mare didn't care to turn her mother's operation
into that of a wolf pack. Her reluctance had little to
do with morals or ethics. Most of the outlanders who
lived in the settlements rarely agreed to give up their
possessions without a fight—even if they were possessions they would have had difficulty giving away.

As far as Mare was concerned, it wasn't worth risk-
ing life and limb to raze a settlement to the ground
and then find out all they had were some old boots
and maybe some home-forged black-powder firearms.

So, when one of her crew brought word that there
was a brisk, burgeoning trade in human beings out
around the Timpahute Mountains, Mare began to seriously consider expanding the focus of her operation.
Humans were legitimate commodities, and though
there was no longer a thriving market for slave labor,
due in the main to the Magistrates, people were easier
to find than useable engine parts.

Mare wasn't very comfortable with the concept of
trading in human flesh, but there was nobody in her
crew she felt intimate enough with to share her
doubts. They were all men, and thus they couldn't be
trusted. Her mother had told her many times that the
female chief of a scavenger crew couldn't afford to
get lonely or vulnerable. "You get too close to one
of them slag-jackers," she had said, "and some night
he slits your throat and takes what's yours."

Big Ma had a very low opinion of men, although
Mare figured it had to have been fairly high at one
time; otherwise she would have never been born. She

often wished for a mate, so she could have a child herself, but most of the men in her crew had spent their lives scrounging around the edges of hellzones and hot spots. Her mother had warned that such men could shoot nothing but strange, twisted seed that produced offspring fit only to be drowned as soon as they drew their first breath.

Therefore, the female of the species was vastly superior, and it did no good to wish for companionship. Mare never sought it out, but she couldn't help but admit to herself she wished she had, if not a faithful lover, then a man she could relax around. She had resigned herself to realizing that such was an unattainable dream, despite the fact women were at premium in her part of the country.

Although she had been christened Mary Lou, somewhere in her teens the Mammoth Mare sobriquet had been applied to her, probably after she topped six feet tall and began weighing in at two hundred plus pounds. Once that name became common, few men cared to spend much time in her company. Becoming known as Mammoth Mare's consort wasn't exactly a high ambition. So she concentrated on business.

As lean as the times were, Mare was inclined to discount the rumors of a trade in human beings when they reached her through a couple of her scouts. Since they were thirdhand reports she dismissed them altogether.

When she was a child, she had heard similar stories of cannibals running wild in the deserts, eating everybody and anybody they saw. She assumed the people-trade tale was nothing but an updated version of that old fable with the cannies now buying human meat from intermediaries instead of tracking it down themselves. But the bizarre rumors persisted, and she seriously considered sending out a scouting party to ascertain their validity.

Before Mare could do so, one of her scavengers, a little rodent of a man named Squint, sauntered into the camp and began yapping in his characteristic staccato, full-auto fashion about the profitable trade in humans conducted out in the old dry basin of Groom Lake.

Squint claimed that a band of people was living in a collection of shanties near old 376 just outside of Big Creek. He assured her they weren't any kind of mutie but were genuine, bona-fide human beings, about as healthy as could be expected, so they definitely weren't Dregs.

Dregs were the outlanders shunned even by other outlanders. One of the legacies of the nukecaust was a fixation on genetic purity. Ville doctrines revolved around purity control, and an important aspect of the unification program had been the extermination of all human deviates, particularly muties.

Dregs weren't muties, although they had been classified as such, a hundred or so years before, saddled with the label of scabbies. Therefore they hadn't been spared the genocidal purges that virtually exterminated all the mutie strains except for a few isolated pockets in dark territories. The Dregs were diseased, genetically ruined humans who had lived too long near hellzones and rad hot spots. They were the lepers of the postskydark world.

Squint's story sounded convincing, although he couldn't offer much in the way of intelligence regarding the identity of who the people buyers were or what they wanted the merchandise for. Mare decided that wasn't important, so the next morning she had the crew climb aboard one of her two wags and went in search of the merchandise.

Her converted dump truck was about the only thing of any great value she owned, so she maintained the vehicle as best she could, spending a lot of time and jack to keep it in good condition. People could still be found with the skills to repair the vehicles, but making tires and finding fuel was a lot more difficult. Gasoline that even remotely approached the quality of predark supplies was almost nonexistent anywhere but the villes.

There were a few crude processing plants down along the Gulf Coast of Texas, a few more in Oklahoma, but the product certainly wasn't cheap and just as certainly it was barely acceptable as fuel. For her part, Mare had preferred to deal with a fuel trader calling himself Lindstrohm.

The merchandise was exactly where Squint had claimed it would be. Mare and her crew captured the people and transported them to the Groom Lake basin—only to find, to her commingled terror and horror, that the buyers were Magistrates. And where there were Magistrates, there were bound to be barons. Before the Mags could do more than look over her captives, the entire transaction came to an explosive, utterly final halt, when two terrifying aircraft screamed out of the sky.

Neither she nor any of her crew had ever seen anything like the aircraft that skimmed across the sky at eye-blurring speeds, and apparently the Magistrates hadn't, either, judging by their panicked reactions. The two ships swiftly destroyed the Mag's wag, a Sandcat, blew up a ground gun emplacement and just as effortlessly shot down three Deathbirds.

Mare watched the airborne assault from beneath her truck in the company of her terror-stricken crew. What they witnessed was so out of the realm of their experience, they almost couldn't comprehend any of it. They had been conditioned to believe in the invincibility of the Mags and their ordnance.

When the two ships landed, Mare couldn't help but remember old folk tales told around campfires about sky-monsters, giant bats that haunted the ruins of nuke-scorched cities. Two men in skintight black outfits disembarked from the aircraft, and only then did Mare and her scavenger crew dimly begin to understand what was happening and why.

The men in black were armed with Sin Eaters, the official blasters of Magistrates. They disarmed Mare and her gang and told her grimly they had no sympathy for them. One of the Sin Eater–toting apparitions, a huge black man said to her, "You were going to sell your fellow human beings like they were cattle, so they could be harvested—their blood drained, their bodies cut open, their guts unwound, all their organs, glands and even bone marrow removed and processed. All to keep the barons alive."

In a voice so thick with barely repressed fury it was a guttural growl, he went on to say how the barons needed "human blood and guts to survive, so they set up a processing center here in Groom Lake."

The men in black turned the truck over to their captives, and after it had been driven away they returned to their aircraft, but not before telling her, "The barons can have *you* if they want."

Before the sky-ships took off, Mare killed Squint, but the other members of her crew overpowered her and then cast her out. Mare had no choice but to walk alone, having been deserted once and for all by the male sex. Not only had they abandoned her, but also they took her beloved Mossberg rifle with them.

As she walked across the hellishly rugged terrain, she spied at least half a dozen Deathbirds cutting search patterns across the sky. She knew they were looking for her crew, so she didn't mind that they had left her. Most of them had stayed together and offered easy targets for the Mags.

Night fell and she tramped through a gully trail that became rockier and more treacherous with every step as it wound through steep ravines. The detonation of thunder boomed in the distance and billowing clouds massed above the jagged peaks of hills, less than a couple of miles away. The underside of the clouds bore a sickly green tinge, undershot by a salmon pink.

Fingers of fear stroked the base of her spine at the prospect of being trapped out in the open by a chem storm. Such storms were dangerous partly because of their intensity, but mainly because of the acids, heavy metals and other chemical compounds that fell with the rain.

In the immediate aftermath of the nukecaust, chem

GET FREE BOOKS and a FREE GIFT WHEN YOU PLAY THE...

Lucky 7

SLOT MACHINE GAME!

Just scratch off the silver box with a coin. Then check below to see the gifts you get!

YES! I have scratched off the silver box. Please send me the 2 free Gold Eagle® books and gift for which I qualify. I understand I am under no obligation to purchase any books, as explained on the back of this card.

366 ADL DRSG

166 ADL DRSF

FIRST NAME	LAST NAME

ADDRESS

APT.#	CITY

STATE/PROV.	ZIP/POSTAL CODE

7 7 7	Worth TWO FREE BOOKS plus a BONUS Mystery Gift!
♪ ♪ ♪	Worth TWO FREE BOOKS!
♣ ♣ ♣	Worth ONE FREE BOOK!
♫ ♫ ♪	TRY AGAIN!

(MB-01/03)

DETACH AND MAIL CARD TODAY!

The Gold Eagle Reader Service™ — Here's how it works:

storms could strip flesh from bone in less than a minute. As the environment recovered, the passage of time diluted the potency of chem storms, but the lethal acid rain could still melt flesh from the bones during long exposure.

Fortunately, chem storms were no longer as frequent as they had been even a century before, but the peculiar geothermals of hellzones seemed to attract them. Although fewer hellzones existed now, there were still a number of places where the geological or meteorological effects of the nuking prevented a full recovery. The passage of time couldn't completely cleanse the zones of hideous, invisible plagues.

Mare quickened her pace, even though the footing was uncertain. There was another flash of lightning, so close Mare felt her body hair tingle and stand up. The thunderclap followed almost immediately. She smelled the sharp sting of acid in the air and knew the storm would be a bad one.

Then, when lightning flashed again, she saw the dark mouth of a cave only a few yards ahead of her. Mare quickened her pace but she didn't immediately enter. Cupping her eyes, she peered into the shapeless darkness. She sniffed the air, but didn't detect the musky scent of an animal.

Then, from the blackness ahead of her, she heard a voice, taut with fear but sounding old and tired. "So, you've found me at last."

She heard the scuff of shambling feet. From the shadows limped a gaunt, man-shaped figure with unusually long arms. He appeared to be naked, his body covered with leaking sores and discolored lesions.

The man's face was in dark shadow, but Mare was able to glimpse a long, narrow visage and a round, hairless skull that seemed just a bit too large.

In a hoarse voice, but with a steel edge to it, the man declared, "I was Baron Cobalt. And I command you to do one of two things—help me live or help me die."

Mare had heard about the barons her entire life, of course. Even though she lived far from his ville, she had even heard tales of Baron Cobalt. He was reputed to be the most cunning, the most treacherous and vicious of the nine.

She had always pictured him as a bearded giant in armor, a roaring berserk tyrant lopping off the heads of all who displeased with an ax. The black man's ominous parting words about the barons having her if they wanted echoed within the walls of her skull, but even she was surprised by her lack of true fear.

She had never envisioned Cobalt or any of the barons as small-boned, fragile creatures covered with sores and smeared with their own waste. Mare actually contemplated killing the foul-smelling slagger who seemed more mutie than man. He had told her to help him die or help him live, and it seemed far easier to do the former. She picked up a rock to crush his oversized cranium. She contemplated murdering him for all of five seconds.

Then Baron Cobalt turned and looked at her. His huge eyes seemed to leap from his head and enter Mare's mind, seemed to completely fill the confines of her skull. Staring transfixed, she heard a faint, agonized cry and distantly, she knew it had been torn from her own lips. An unreasoning, undiluted terror filled her, as if her consciousness were an empty cup.

Then it was as though she were tumbling headlong down a black tunnel, and a thousand images flashed by in kaleidoscopic flickers. She glimpsed tall, round towers of white stone and with a sense of shock, Mare realized she was looking at a barony, a fortress city, as if from a great height. She knew it was Cobaltville and the massive white tower stretching up from the center of the walled ville was the Admin Monolith.

She saw fireballs blooming from the impact of high-explosive shells, punching deep, smoking craters in the walls and in the white facade of the Monolith. Masonry tumbled down. Mare saw wheeled artillery pieces, flame and smoke belching from their bores.

In a series of staggered visions, she saw the siege of Cobaltville from different perspectives. Cobaltville's armed defense was holed up in dugouts and trenches outside the bunkers, waiting wearily for the artillery barrage to lift—waiting and wondering whether they would be able to stem the attack, or even if they should make the attempt. All of them wore the black armor of Magistrates.

The close-packed troops of the enemy suddenly poured up from the riverfront. Across the grassy fields they swept, moving as though they were pushed forward by a wind from hell. They rushed upon the barricade, and the first burst from the mini-gun emplacements threw the ranks back in bloody confusion. But the inexorable rush from the attackers in the rear vanguard pushed them forward. The troopers regrouped and blastermen split to either side, forming a wedge flanking their comrades. Though a hail of high-velocity rounds struck them and knocked them down, they kept coming, trampling their dead or dying comrades.

Then the images faded, but Mare felt Cobalt's emotions—terror, rage and an almost suffocating sense of betrayal. His eyes still held her mind captive, peering deep into it, down through the roots of her soul. She felt her memories being rifled, examined, weighed and judged.

When he was done, Baron Cobalt's eyes seemed to recede, pulling away from her mind. She found herself kneeling before him, with the hot sting of fresh tears on her cheeks. She understood with a terrible sense of finality how utterly empty her life as a scavenger had been. It had no purpose, no direction and it barely qualified as existing, much less living. She had gone on eating, breathing and scavenging strictly through unthinking force of habit.

Baron Cobalt gazed down at her, and he looked very sad. "We are kindred spirits, you and I." He spoke softly. "We have lost everything that filled our lives. Now we are empty vessels, and we must fill ourselves with a purpose. This can be done together, but you must help me live."

His voice rolled and vibrated through her head, like the echoes of a gong. The sound of it made her hungry to hear more, and the only way to hear more was to swear fealty to Baron Cobalt, to give him her undying loyalty. He explained the nature of what he needed to live and gave her detailed instructions to follow in order to sustain his life. She listened carefully and questioned nothing.

In the weeks that followed, Mare submitted to Baron Cobalt's wishes, whims and commands, carrying them out wordlessly and efficiently. He transmitted his wishes directly into her mind, as if he were showing her pictures. The picture the baron had been transmitting for the past few minutes was slightly disturbing, but the notion of refusal never occurred to her.

If her lover, her lord, wished Mare to wrap Erica van Sloan's braided hair around the slender column of her neck, thrust her knee into the small of her back and then garrote the beautiful woman to death, then she would do so without question.

All she waited for was the whim to become a command, and the beautiful dark-haired, violet-eyed woman, the mother of the hated imperator, would die.

Chapter 13

Rolling his eyes heavenward, Kane groaned, "Oh, for the love of—" He prodded Lakesh's backside with the toe of a shoe. "Turn off the waterworks and get up. We don't have time for this."

Lips peeled back from her teeth in a snarl, almost spitting in a feline fury, Domi lunged forward and pushed Kane backward. "Get away from him!"

Lakesh reached up and grabbed her by the wrist. "This is all my fault," he said in a husky whisper. "I should have…" His voice trailed off as he struggled to swallow down a sob.

Domi dropped to her knees beside him and put her arms around his shoulders protectively. She glared up at Kane defiantly, silently daring him to touch Lakesh again.

"You should have killed Sam when you had the chance," Grant grunted, "instead of letting him give you a youth treatment."

Quavell raised a brow arch. "What makes you think Dr. Singh had the chance to kill him? And if he did, would he have been able to do so?"

"We were all there with Sam, too," Domi snapped. "We coulda tried to kill him, but we didn't."

Brigid said sympathetically, "You're absolutely right, Domi. We can't blame Lakesh."

Tears shone on Lakesh's cheeks as he lifted his head to look at her. "No," he said, voice thick with self-loathing, "Grant is right. I sold myself to Sam much like Faust traded his soul to Mephistopheles in exchange for an illusion of youth. But my crime is worse than Faust's, because I sold out all of you along with myself."

Quavell sighed. "Dr. Singh, I think you are suffering from a terrible self-deception, if not a delusion. Or perhaps you simply enjoy playing the martyr."

"*Shup!*" Domi cried fiercely. In her anger, she reverted to the Outland mode of speech and combined *shut* and *up.* "You don't know what you talking about!"

"I know he is trying to retreat from responsibility." Quavell's soft voice carried no heat or edge of accusation, but Kane found himself staring at her in surprise. The hybrid had maintained such a low profile in the weeks since she arrived at the redoubt, her calm words now were as attention-getting as if she were in the throes of a hysterical fit.

"You know shit," Domi half shrieked. "You not even human—"

She bit back the rest of whatever she had to say, but Quavell nodded as if in understanding. "But we share similar interests, do we not? We are kin in spirit. Our bonds are finer and stronger than bonds of blood. Except I will not abandon myself to hate and violence." She touched her swollen belly. "Nor will my child."

Lakesh's face twisted as if he were in great pain. Then, slowly, he pushed himself to his feet, filled his lungs slowly and then emptied them in a prolonged sigh. He turned toward Bry. "Have you detected any ELINT signals indicating movement among the barons who oppose Sam?"

Lakesh made an oblique reference to the Comsat eavesdropping system. Several months before, Lakesh and Bry had created a communications scanner with ville radio frequencies and channels, involving the redoubt's satellite uplinks. They hadn't heard much about the reaction of the rank-and-file ville citizen to the rule of the imperator—most probably knew very little about it, but they had picked up signals confirming Quavell's report of civil unrest in some of the baronies.

Bry shook his head. "The electronic intelligence I've patched into is basically flat-line. Nothing unusual has been transmitted from any of the villes or the outposts for the past couple of weeks. Not since the op to the Antarctic, anyhow."

"There really wouldn't be," Grant stated. "The sea water level has pretty much gone back to normal." He glanced quizzically at Shizuka. "Right?"

Shizuka nodded. "Yes. There has been no further flooding on any of the New Edo island chain."

Less than three weeks earlier, Grant, Brigid, Kane and Brewster Philboyd had traveled to the continent of Antarctica to prevent Grigori Zakat's scheme to cause the great ice sheet to slip into the ocean.

"So," Bry continued, "if Baron Cobalt is making a move to regroup or reach out to other barons so he can lead a resistance force against Sam, he's doing it very covertly."

"Or," Quavell interjected, "he has yet to implement any plans he might have made. In his present circumstances, survival might be all he can focus his attention upon. Even if he received a full complement of medical treatments before the siege of Cobaltville, he would be in dire need of boosters by now. And the question of where he has been hiding for the past six months is still unanswered."

Lakesh sighed dolefully. "There are many questions, and not just about Baron Cobalt, that have yet to be answered." He fixed Kane with a direct stare. "Regardless of the information imparted by your future self, it doesn't seem as if the baron is in any kind of position to accomplish what you—he—alleges he accomplishes in such a short time."

Brigid said, "The only other possibility is that everything we've been told has been part of a ruse." She flicked her penetrating green gaze toward Sindri. "An elaborate plan to get inside Cerberus and gain our confidence."

For a moment Sindri seemed unaware of both Brigid's stare or the implications of her statement. Then he glanced up at her, forehead furrowed in consternation. "I can assure you, Miss Brigid—assure all of you—that everything I've told you is the truth. I don't have any ulterior motives in all of this."

"Which in and of itself is enough to make me suspicious as hell," Grant growled. "You and Sam would work pretty fucking well together."

Sindri sighed. "Mr. Grant, despite your justifiable dislike of me, if I was truly in cahoots with the imperator, engaged in a joint plan against Cerberus, this is not the way I would put my end of it into action. As a trained tactician, you should agree that there are far and away too many elements left to random chance—first and foremost that you or Mr. Kane could have simply shot my fair young ass dead as soon as you saw me step out of the gateway unit.''

Grant said nothing, nor did his scowl lift, but it was apparent he found himself in grudging agreement with Sindri's argument.

''Besides,'' put in Bry, ''if anybody should fall under suspicion of working with the imperator, it would be Lakesh. He sent Sam our gateway coordinates, remember? He allowed him to gate right into the redoubt.''

Domi glared at Bry, but Lakesh asked calmly, ''What do you propose to do with me now that it's been established I compromised Cerberus security?''

Kane chuckled suddenly, surprising everyone. ''Don't be so melodramatic, old man. What we propose to do is have you contribute to an overall strategy.''

He swept his glance across the faces of everyone assembled out on the plateau. ''It's a strategy everyone needs to contribute something to. Especially you, Sindri. You're the only eyewitness we have who can offer firsthand intel.''

Sindri grinned up at him. ''Mr. Grant's suspicions to the contrary, I have every intention of helping in whatever way I can. The imperator's adaptive Earth is not my idea of a viable future. It doesn't seem like any fun at all.''

''My idea of a viable future,'' said Shizuka coldly,

"is one where that conniving dwarf has been tossed over a cliff."

"Please," Lakesh said with a feeble attempt at a smile. "We don't need to revive the fine old sport of dwarf tossing."

When his comment elicited only blank looks, he cleared his throat and announced brusquely, "First things first, then. The story of the Nirodha movement in Assam, led by the Scorpia Prime, isn't as foolish as it seems on the surface. Throughout the centuries, that land was victimized by mystery-cult Tantrism sects, worshipers of sex and death. In fact, some of my ancestors fought battles to contain it."

"But why Assam?" Bry asked. "I looked it up in the GPS database a few minutes ago. If the Indian subcontinent has an ass, Assam would be it."

"According to Hindu myth," replied Lakesh a little stiffly, apparently not impressed by Bry's flight into punnery, "when the great god Vishnu dismembered the body of Shiva's consort, Shakti, her *yoni,* her sexual organs, fell to Earth there, in a district known as Golapura. Later legends state that a secret temple to venerate Shakti and her totem, the scorpion, was built there on the exact spot."

Lakesh paused to take a breath. "However, matters of myth can be attended to later. At the moment, we need to reach a quorum about who we are really contending with—Sam or Colonel C. W. Thrush."

"Does it really matter?" Brigid asked.

"Perhaps not," Lakesh answered. "But if Sam is the living storage vessel for the Thrush program, it's possible he has yet to fully download all the algorithmic data.''

"Thrush program?'' Sindri echoed in confusion.

No one responded to his query. Kane said, "I hadn't thought of that. You mean Sam might not realize he's Colonel Thrush yet?''

"It's possible," Quavell declared.

All eyes turned toward her. Grant demanded, "What makes you say that?''

Quavell made a diffident gesture with one exceptionally long-fingered hand. Anyone who had dealt with hybrids for any length of time knew it was their equivalent of a shrug. "From what I read of your encounters with the Thrush entity, it's well within the realm of possibility that the complete Thrush ID is suspended in a form of a memory buffer.''

"That has a certain logic to it," Brigid said thoughtfully. "If what Sindri said about Sam and his SQUID network in the future is true, then it's apparent his brain was wet-wired to act as a CPU. Right at the moment, that process might be ongoing. Therefore the Thrush identity may be compressed, not fully downloaded into his brain.''

Bry said slowly, "And that might mean Sam isn't as formidable as he—and we—think he is.''

Dryly, with undisguised sarcasm, Sindri stated, "It might help me make more of an overall contribution to a strategy, if I knew who the hell Thrush really is.''

"Or what he is," Shizuka interjected. She cast her dark gaze toward Grant. "You mentioned him in passing, but I never really formed a good idea of who or what he was."

"That's because none of us really know." Grant's tone was grim.

"I do," declared Kane confidently. "If there's such a thing in the universe as a pure, personified aristocracy of evil, then Thrush is heir to the throne."

GRANT, KANE and Brigid all retained exceptionally unpleasant memories of their first meetings with Colonel C. W. Thrush. Even Domi had her own tale to tell of how she saw Thrush execute Adolf Hitler on April 30, 1945.

Nearly two years before, Lakesh had embarked on the most audacious and desperate plan in a double lifetime filled with scheming. He had constructed a small device on the same scientific principle as the mat-trans inducers, what he called an interphaser. Designed to interact with naturally occurring quantum vortices, the interphaser opened dimensional rifts much like the gateways, but instead of the rifts being pathways through linear space, Lakesh had envisioned them as a method to travel through the gaps in normal space-time.

However, the interphaser hadn't functioned according to its design, and due to interference caused by Lord Strongbow's similar device, the so-called Singularity, its dilated temporal energy had sent Kane, Brigid, Domi and Grant on a short, disembodied trip into the past. The unforeseen temporal dilation swept them to four focal points in history. As invisible spectators, all of them had witnessed Thrush's involvement in past events that affected the future and ultimately led to the nukecaust.

Domi saw Thrush, uniformed as an SS colonel, kill Hitler in an underground bunker in the Reich Chancellery, instead of spiriting him to safety as the führer had apparently been promised.

Brigid had watched Thrush, in the persona of an American intelligence agent, issue the orders to cover up the Roswell Incident in 1947.

Kane had witnessed Thrush's involvement in the assassination of President John F. Kennedy in 1963, in the guise of the black-clad "Umbrella Man."

On January 19, 2001, Grant observed Thrush personally setting the timer on the nuclear warhead concealed within the Russian embassy. The warhead detonated twenty-four hours later, triggering the global apocalypse known to later generations as the nukecaust.

According to Lakesh, he had seen Thrush in the Overproject Whisper testing facility, back in the 1990s, where he claimed to be a colonel in the Air Force.

In each time period, Colonel Thrush had sensed their disembodied presence, and he had even told Grant his name was derived from a poem by T. S. Elliot, a verse that asked, "Shall we follow the deception of the thrush into our first world?"

Thrush had always looked the same in each time period, despite adding minor disguises and cosmetic changes to his features. His high-boned face was very pale, with sharp cheekbones and a jutting chin. His ears were very small and delicately shaped, nestled close to the hairless skull. His inhumanly large, curved eyes had no pupils, only obsidian irises with a bare hint of white at the corners. Those eyes always struck Kane as less organs of vision than apertures leading to the fathomless ends of the universe.

Brigid had described Thrush as a prototypical MIB, a Man In Black, those sinister figures associated with the conspiracy theories of the twentieth century, whether they dealt with UFOs or political unrest.

Despite the disembodied trips to the past, Lakesh tried to duplicate the accidental dilation effect by turning the Cerberus gateway unit into a time machine. Although the interphaser had been lost, its memory disk had been retrieved, and Lakesh used the data recorded on it to write the Omega Path program.

Two centuries before, during development of the mat-trans gateways, the Cerberus researchers observed a number of side effects. On occasion, traversing the quantum pathways resulted in minor temporal anomalies, such as arriving at a destination three seconds before the jump initiator was actually engaged.

Lakesh found that time couldn't be measured or accurately perceived in the quantum stream. Hypothetically, constant jumpers might find themselves physically rejuvenated, with the toll of time erased if enough ''backward time'' was accumulated in their metabolisms. Conversely, jumpers might find themselves prematurely aged if the quantum stream pushed them further into the future with each journey. From these temporal anomalies Operation Chronos had the starting point, using the gateway technology, to develop time travel.

Without access to the specs and data of Operation Chronos, Lakesh could not duplicate what they had done, so he determined to circumvent it. He saw to the creation of the Omega Path program and linked it with the mat-trans gateway.

The concept was sound—to dispatch Kane and Brigid back through time to a point only a month before the nukecaust, so they could hopefully trigger an alternate event horizon and thus avert the apocalypse.

The Omega Path had worked, at least insofar as translating them into a past temporal plane, but they came to learn it was not their world's past, but another, almost identical to it. Any actions they undertook had no bearing whatsoever on their world's present and future.

Kane and Brigid learned the shunting to a parallel timeline was not accidental, but an intentional act performed by Colonel Thrush himself. Thrush claimed versions of him existed in all times to prevent his interference in human history being undone and the nukecaust averted.

Brigid considered him to be a faux human, a fake, and that appellation proved to be more than a guess during their final confrontation on a Manhattan rooftop on New Year's Eve, 2000. Thrush had described himself not as a fake human, or even an individual, but "A program. My body is mortal…the program will simply animate another like me."

Kane had believed him to be an Archon agent, a chrononaut dispatched by the Directorate to prevent their machinations in time from being undone. However, Thrush had never actually admitted to working for the Archons.

Later, upon researching the database, Brigid learned that mysterious figures who fit Thrush's general physical description and methods popped up everywhere throughout the past, usually in times of strife or at a crossroads in human history.

From the era of the Roman Empire, to the UFO phenomena of the twentieth century, sinister Men In Black appeared, influenced events or important people, then vanished. It was tempting to dismiss such reports as paranoid fantasies, but the database contained stories from all over the world and from all times about the MIB.

All of the Cerberus warriors soon discovered that Thrush had not restricted that interaction with humanity to only a single plane of existence. Somehow he, or manifestations of himself, bridged all the vibrational barriers between alternate realties, the so-called Lost Earths. Neither Brigid nor Lakesh had a clear idea of how he accomplished this, except he used the Black Stone as a focal point in all of the parallel realities. The stone had been known by many names, by many peoples of civilizations both primitive and advanced—Lucifer's Stone, the Kala, the Kaa'ba, the Chintamani Stone, the Shining Trapezohedron.

Always it had been associated with the concept of a key that unlocked either the door to enlightenment or madness. It had served as the spiritual centerpiece of the race they had known as the Archons, even after it had been fragmented and the facets scattered from one end of the earth to the other.

According to Balam, the Black Stone was far more than a calculating device that extrapolated outcomes from actions. Balam had said, ''It brings into existence those outcomes.''

Balam had referred to the stone as a channel to sidereal space, where many tangential points of reality lay adjacent to one another, the parallel casements of the universe, a multitude of realities coexisting with their own. But there was commonality linking Thrush to all of the casements, and they learned of it during the final confrontation with the entity in a parallel casement aboard the huge, transdimensional ship he called ''the Hub.''

Grant, Kane and Brigid discovered that the entity they knew as C. W. Thrush had begun his facade of life as the envoy of the Archons, charged with the task of arranging probabilities so humanity would be unified and therefore safeguard the essence of the Archons.

But the task was really a program, and Thrush interpreted it as accomplishing his objective by any means necessary. Always he sought out those whose monomania for power was pathological. The Third Reich, the military, the intelligence services.

They were the easiest to manipulate, because their paranoia and obsessions blinded them to what Thrush was actually planning—complete domination of the human race. He had said once ''Few conspiracies succeed unless the keynote is simplicity. Even then they succeed because humans overlook obvious dangers such as a blind man could see. That is why human history is such a morass of inconsistencies."

But Thrush was more than an artificial life-form or a program—his existence was linked with that of the Chintamani Stone. The relic was his anchor, and his life force was more than cybernetic or extraterrestrial. It was not just unhuman; it was antihuman. He was a blending of machine, human and Annunaki.

More than five hundred thousand years before, the reptilian Annunaki, the Dragon Kings of legend, had claimed Earth, all of its natural resources and its inhabitants as their own. The Annunaki had arrived on Earth when humankind was still in a protoform of development. They viewed Earth as a vast treasure trove of natural resources, upon which their technology depended. As labor was their scarcest commodity, the Annunaki set about redesigning Earth's primitive inhabitants into models of maximized potential.

The civilizations that had arisen in Mesopotamia had been greatly influenced by the Annunaki. They had built a base on the moon and even used its system of caverns as a necropolis for their dead. They, along with the more human-appearing Tuatha de Danaan, were one of the root races of the Archons.

Due to his linkage with the Chintamani Stone, Thrush was a subjective property, a creation of the minds of the Archons. He existed only because those who interacted with him believed he did. He absorbed and transmitted to the Archons emotional states of the people he came in contact with, which gave the Archons an idea of how best to proceed with their own plans.

Kane hadn't really accepted that assessment of Thrush's existence and purpose, since he found it difficult to hate a creature that did not truly live. It was only during his final confrontation with Thrush aboard the Hub that he realized the absolutely soul-deep hatred he felt toward the creature. He saw him not as a Man In Black, but as what he really was, an ancient evil thing that crept among the primordial grasses, apart from human life, but watching it with eyes of cold wisdom, laughing its silent laugh of superiority, giving nothing but bitterness.

He had the name of a bird and the appearance of a man, but his brain was that of the serpent. Kane had been overwhelmed with a hate-fueled mad rage to crush what passed for life out of him. And even though Thrush disappeared along with the Hub, Kane had never completely believed the entity was gone forever.

Intermittently over the past two years, Kane had jerked awake from slumber, sweat-drenched and shaking, as his sleeping mind dredged up with terrifying clarity the words Thrush had once psionically impressed into his memory: "You will know my presence in your own casement soon enough. By then, I hope you will have resigned yourself to what cannot be changed. Do not fight anymore. There is no use in it."

The sharp shiver of a chill wind slicing over the plateau emphasized the profound stillness at the summit of the mountain. Brigid involuntarily hugged herself, and her eyes locked on Kane's.

''What do we do now?'' she asked, trying to keep her teeth from chattering.

Kane turned toward the sec door. ''What Thrush warned us not to do…we fight.''

Chapter 14

"I know what you're thinking, Baron." Erica van Sloan's rich, vibrant voice echoed inside the vaulted stairwell, but the mockery underscoring her words wasn't distorted.

She led the way down the stairs, one hand lightly caressing the banister. Dim light was shed by electric lamps set in niches on the wall.

"What might that be?" Cobalt demanded, doing his best to sound scornful.

Erica indicated Mare with a backward jerk of her head. The big woman lumbered down the steps several yards behind Cobalt, despite the width of the stairwell. "You're thinking how easy it would be to order your strong-arm to kill me right here and now."

"And why," he asked in a silky soft whisper, "would that be a bad idea for anyone but you?"

Erica laughed. Even though neither Cobalt nor Mare could see her face, they heard the note of cruel triumph in the sound. "At best, my death would be a temporary victory for you, a Pyrrhic bit of vengeance. But the reality of the situation is you would forevermore lose any opportunity to regain your power—in fact, you will lose the opportunity to gain more power than you ever dreamed was within your grasp."

As they reached the foot of the stairs, Cobalt uttered a spitting sound of disdain. "And who offers me this opportunity? You?"

"I do." The melodic voice jerked Cobalt's head around. A man of medium height but exceptionally lean build stood in an open doorway to his right. He was dressed in an impeccably tailored white linen suit, but he exuded as ominous a flair as if he were dressed in funeral black.

His head was long, and his face high planed with prominent cheek and brow bones. The chin was small but sharp. His hair was a lusterless silvery gray and looked very thin, even sparse in some places, but it swept across his high forehead and left temple in a dramatic style.

His ears were very small and delicately shaped, nestled close to the skull. A pair of dark, curve-lensed sunglasses masked his eyes. His thin lips were creased in a smile. The color of his hair, the shape of his head and the way he smiled made Baron Cobalt's belly slip sideways with the cold shock of recognition.

"I always knew Baron Cobalt had far more expansive ambitions than simply ruling the nine baronies," the man said. "Or did I presume too much?"

His voice was wonderfully musical, like the pealing of a crystal bell. Cobalt realized he was manipulating the timbre and pitch so the vibrations of his voice would resonate sympathetically to the inner ear and stimulate the neuroenergy system. It was a trick he himself had practiced many times in his eighty years of life, most recently to control Mary Lou McSween.

Even though he struggled to maintain a relaxed

posture and demeanor, wild thoughts tumbled through Baron Cobalt's head. "*You* are the imperator? You?"

The young man smiled. "Don't sound so shocked, my lord baron. Granted, I've changed a bit since we last saw each other, but not that much. Have I?" He paused and added with a chuckle lurking at the back of his throat, "Perhaps 'evolved' would be a more appropriate term."

Baron Cobalt didn't respond, assuming Sam's comments to be rhetorical. When he had first met the imperator, a little over half a year before, he looked like a boy about seven years of age. His face was cherubic, his skin was smooth, alabaster in hue, and his thick hair was pure warm silver, framing his full-cheeked face like the edges of a summertime cloud. His big eyes seemed to shift with all colors like the dawn sky. They were old in his childish face, wise and sad in their wisdom.

Baron Cobalt had no idea of the color of his eyes now, nor of the relative sadness contained within them. He had no doubt of the depth of wisdom in them, however.

"You arrived at an opportune time, Lord Baron," Sam continued.

"And what time is that?" Cobalt didn't move, although he was aware of Mare moving up close behind him, either in a silent display of protectiveness or to seek out his comforting energy in the face of such strangeness projected by the man in the white.

Erica van Sloan stepped toward Sam, smiling at him fondly. "The lord baron is understandably suspicious, Sam."

Sam chuckled lowly. "By nature, rather. If barons weren't suspicious to the point of paranoia, then they wouldn't be barons."

Baron Cobalt stiffened. "You didn't summon me here to insult me or my kind."

Crossing his arms over his chest, Sam replied, "Indeed not. You have a unique potential that I wish to consult you about, to tap into."

Baron Cobalt knew his face registered surprise, but he couldn't help himself. Sam gave him a sense of complete confidence. His tone, his words, the way he held his body, his very presence seemed to soothe him, make him feel bizarrely secure.

"What potential is that?"

Sam inclined his head backward, through the open door. "I'll demonstrate first what I have in mind, an opening component of what I have begun to call the Great Plan."

Cobalt hesitated, and Erica laughed disdainfully. "Do you think we lured you here just so we could assassinate you in the basement of Front Royal?"

Face flushing with embarrassment, Baron Cobalt stepped purposefully toward the door, feeling thoroughly inferior in his dirty overalls and makeshift footwear. He experienced a moment's mad impulse to dry-wash his dirty hands on the man's spotless white blazer.

To Cobalt's mild surprise, Sam permitted not just him, but Mare to stride past him. He even nodded deferentially to Mare. "Just go forward," he directed.

They walked down a narrow passageway with undecorated walls of dented and patched plaster. A faint odor of mildew was in the air. Passing an open door, Cobalt glimpsed a collection of buckets, mops and other cleaning supplies. The imperator was allowing him to tour parts of the fortress he had never before visited, or cared to know existed. He glanced over his shoulder, preparing to make a snide remark to Erica van Sloan, but he saw she wasn't with them.

"Where is your mother?" he demanded, his survival instincts flaring.

"She's gone to join the theater troupe," Sam replied blandly. "She's directing our first full dress rehearsal."

"What?" The word burst from Cobalt's lips as a bleat of complete bewilderment.

Sam laughed. "You'll see what I mean soon enough. Hopefully you'll find the rehearsal very illuminating…and stimulating. More so than feeding on the fluids of Mary Lou, at any rate."

Cobalt rocked to a halt, whirling on Sam, his eyes narrowing, face contorting in rage. "You overstep!"

All the gentle good humor fled from Sam's voice and bearing. "And you forget where you are and who I am, Lord Baron."

He turned his dark-lensed gaze toward Mare. "Roll up your sleeve, please."

Although the pitch and volume of his voice hadn't changed, it was obvious the imperator had not made a request that could be politely refused. Without hesitation, Mare unbuttoned the cuff of her sleeve and began folding it upward.

"You do not obey him!" Baron Cobalt's exclamation was a squawk of outrage. Mare started to turn toward him, but then she felt a warm blanket settle over her mind. A whimper of fright escaped her lips when she realized she was powerless to stop herself from continuing to tug up the sleeve of her coverall to just above her bicep.

Raw, ugly, half-healed slashes, most of them inflicted by a razor, ran in series of horizontal lines up her arm, from midwrist to elbow. Some had scabbed over completely, while others were still fresh enough to glisten dully with blood.

Sam stated matter-of-factly, "Baron, I know you received a full regimen of genetic therapies and medical treatments shortly before Cobaltville was overthrown. I also know you used the mat-trans unit in the Admin Monolith to transport yourself and a few supplies to a hidden gateway unit, right outside of Groom Lake. The unit was one of the modular models developed by Mohandas Lakesh Singh, more than two centuries ago.

"It was installed in the cave just in case an emergency arose in Area 51 and high-ranking military officers and visiting dignitaries could be evacuated quickly. You thought you were the only one who was aware of the unit's existence, much less its location, were you not?"

Glowering, Cobalt said nothing, waiting for the imperator to continue.

"You managed to carry some food, some water with you, but even by strict rationing, they didn't last very long. Away from your insulated, sterile environment, you began to sicken long before the time limit of your last metabolic treatments had been reached. You despaired, knowing you were dying.

"Then—" Sam nodded toward Mare, still standing motionless with her bare arm displayed "—Mary Lou found you. You realized this poor creature's mind was easy to manipulate, even for you in your weakened condition. She was desperate for love, both to receive it and to give it. You took advantage of that yearning by feeding on her blood. She even allowed you to suckle during her menstrual cycle. What she was able to provide wasn't enough to restore you, but she kept you alive...after a fashion. Your relationship with her has nothing to do with love. It is that of the parasite and the host."

Cobalt said nothing for a long moment, but his lips quivered tremulously, as if he were trying to keep from bursting into tears. Sam knew he was struggling to tamp down his mounting humiliation. He knew dignity was the key to any human's confidence and his resistance.

It was far more extreme with one of the barons, since by their way of thinking, they represented the final phase of human evolution. They created wholesale, planned alterations in living organisms and were empowered to control not only their environment, but also the evolution of other species. They wholeheartedly believed the pinnacle of evolutionary achievement was themselves.

Sam knew that as long as Cobalt felt he was still a baron with rights, privileges and deserving of worship, then he would be difficult to persuade to join any cause but his own.

"Why," Cobalt breathed out, "are you telling me this?"

Sam's dark gaze was unflinching. "There is more I can tell you, much, much more. But it can wait until you and I reach an accord."

Sam nodded toward Mare, who instantly rolled down her sleeve, her face a blank mask. Suddenly, floating down the corridor came the steady sound of drumming and a babble of voices.

Sam gestured in the direction of the noise. "The curtain rises."

The corridor stretched beneath a linteled stone arch and led into a chamber shaped like a perfect cube. Glowing electric candles set in sconces on the high, vaulted walls cast a steady yellowish illumination. The four people stood in a cramped aisle between a guardrail and a triple row of theater-type seats.

The aisle overlooked a square pit, a smaller cube within the larger, even though it appeared to be fifty feet by fifty across. The top of the pit was surrounded on all four sides by glass panels. As they approached it, Cobalt realized the panels were actually one-way mirrors, reflective on the other side. The walls plunging downward were sheer. Cobalt guessed it was about a twenty-foot drop to the floor below.

What appeared to be a temple stage set occupied the entire area. Stone pillars were carved to represent every conceivable sexual joining of male and female, male and male, female and female. The set was illuminated by flaming braziers that threw a shimmering veil of color over the people milling about below. Torches sputtered at equidistant points around the chapel, the wooden columns thrust into wall sconces of sand. The glow of the torches was dimmed by shifting planes of hot, acrid smoke.

In the center of the columns rose a high, wide altar of perfectly round stone that was a fleshy pink in color. It was roseate granite, but polished and burnished to such a smooth luminosity that it appeared to be alive. A naked man lay spread-eagled atop it.

Dark complexioned and black of hair and eye, he was bound to the altar by canvas restraints crisscrossing his chest and leather shackles around his wrists and ankles. A strap of leather over his forehead pressed the back of his skull against the stone. His wide eyes gleamed with sheer, abject terror. The man's hair-covered chest rose and fell in spasmodic jerks. Veins stood out in stark relief on his neck as he strained against the restraints.

"What is this?" Cobalt demanded, looking down into the pit. "A theater?"

Sam nodded. "More or less. However, most of the people involved in our little drama aren't aware it's an act. As far as they know, they are in the temple of Shakti."

"What people?"

Sam made a downward, sweeping gesture. From the murky shadows among the columns stepped a number of men and women, some of them carrying brass panniers of dried, smoldering plants. Others carried hide-covered drums that they beat steadily with their hands. All of them wore billowy robes of red and black, the colors divided sharply down the middle of the garments. After a swift head count, Cobalt estimated there were perhaps two dozen of them.

The atmosphere in the temple was one of electric eroticism. The robed men and women formed and reformed in excited clusters, their conversations all revolving around the same subject, the same obsession: Scorpia. They ignored the man on the altar.

They pounded the drums with their fists, setting a hypnotic rhythm. Strings and bells and cymbals clashed and whined deafeningly. The musicians shouted words in a singsong chant, but Baron Cobalt didn't understand anything that was said.

As a woman passed a pannier over the bound man, a cloud of greenish-yellow cloying smoke poured from it, collecting in a cloud above him. Even through the glass panels, Cobalt's nostrils recoiled from the opiated stench filling the temple.

When the vapor thinned, he saw Erica van Sloan standing on the far side of the temple. She held a loop of slender gold chain in both hands, and it trailed away into the shadows behind her. As one, all of the robed celebrants dropped to their knees, but they didn't bow their heads.

Erica strode to the altar and came to a halt, regarding the kneeling congregation silently for a long moment. In a loud, clear voice, she began speaking in a lyrical, almost singsong language. Anticipating Baron Cobalt's question, Sam said, "It is a dialect of Hindi, spoken by natives of a region of Assam, in India. Do you wish me to translate?"

Cobalt nodded. "Please."

As if by rote, Sam intoned, "'The enemies of divine annihilation gather in the darkness…they would continue to ravage the earth by burning away the green from our jungles, turning flower to ash, our clean water to poison!'''

The assembled horde howled in approval. Erica stopped speaking as they shouted and cried out their praise. Sam murmured, ''A tad on the purple-prose side, I must admit, but I have to keep the audience in mind.''

Cobalt gave him a curious glance. ''You wrote her lines?''

Sam smiled nervously, almost abashed. ''Guilty. I also choreographed the entire ritual. It was more difficult than it looks.''

Erica began speaking again, telling the people of the new glory that would come to them all. She told them they were the children of a new age of humankind. Their concerted effort and dedication within the framework of the Great Plan would bring bounty beyond their imaginings to all their houses.

As she went on, her voice climbed in intensity and emphasis rather than volume, carrying her words, Sam's words, directly to the individual members of the congregation.

''She's a fine actor, isn't she?'' Sam asked, glancing at both Mare and Cobalt, seeking their agreement.

Mare said nothing but Cobalt murmured, ''She is very multitalented. More than I ever suspected.''

Erica announced loudly, ''Tonight we seal our pact to serve Shiva, to bring about the Pralya, the destruction of the universe. As a scorpion stings itself to death in the hot sun, we shall see to it that humanity does the same! The moment of our triumph is upon us.''

She gestured to the man bound to the altar, struggling against his bonds. "As we possess him, so do we possess the secret steps to the Tandava, the dance of destruction. We will mingle this man's two life forces as a consecration of our pact! Tonight, Shakti strides among us!"

Erica began pulling on the chain, wrapping its delicate lengths around her right forearm. A shape shifted in the smoky gloom on the far side of the temple set. It was a naked woman's body, small and lithe, holding the end of the golden chain in her right hand. Her skin was smooth and of a marble whiteness, but with a faint olive undertone. Her small breasts were firm, her belly flat and tautly muscled, but the face wasn't human.

It required a few seconds for Baron Cobalt to realize the woman wore an elaborate helmet. It was apparently crafted out of burnished silver and fashioned to resemble the body of a great scorpion. He also recognized her body type—all hybrid women were slender like that, small breasted and narrow waisted.

From the crowd a chant arose, a babble of confusing voices, but one word finally became identifiable: "Scor-pay-*ah*! Scor-pay-*ah*! Scor-pay-*ah*!"

"Who is that?" Baron Cobalt snapped.

"You knew her as Baron Beausoleil."

"One of my own kind, participating in this absurd street theater?"

"Absurd it may be," Sam said mildly. "That is a matter of taste. However, Baron Beausoleil is no longer one of your kind. She is one of mine."

Chapter 15

The cymbals clashed, the pipes skirled and the drums throbbed. Beausoleil began to dance around the man on the altar, moving her hands and arms in ritualistic, intertwining angles and arcs. Steel gleamed in both of her hands. Her thumbs were tipped with curving tips of metal, like talons—or the stingers of scorpions.

Erica, her strident voice a counterpoint to the musical accompaniment, cried out, "As we possess this man, so do we possess the secret steps to the Tandava, the Dance of Shiva. He came here to destroy us, to prevent us from fulfilling our pact with Shiva. So we will mingle this man's two life forces as a consecration of our pact! Tonight, Shakti strides among us!"

As Cobalt watched Beausoleil, Sam, in quiet academic tones, described the sacred dances of Shiva, the divine creator and destroyer who haunted graveyards as the lord of ghosts. First, Beausoleil danced the part of one of Shiva's wives, Kali, who feasted on sacrifices of human blood. At that point, the masked woman swept her right thumb down across the man's torso, the steel stinger inflicting a crimson-welling incision from his chest to his pelvis. The man jerked and cried out.

Beausoleil, as the Scorpia Prime, continued to dance around the altar stone with consummate grace and erotic abandon, beginning Shakti's dance of divine lust to the pulsing beat of the drums. In slow motion, Beausoleil swirled around the man, inflicting a dozen superficial wounds on his torso, then smearing the blood that welled from them into artful designs.

Erica then stepped to the edge of the altar and, swaying her hips in time to the music, she used the palms of her hands to spread the man's blood over his upper body and over his face. Her movements were slow and languorous. The prisoner shuddered at her touch, eyes rolling in animalistic panic. When his entire torso from the neck down glistened with a thin film of blood, Erica stepped away.

Beausoleil moved around the altar again, stepping with a lithe grace to the man and laying her delicate hands on him, caressed him slowly and even lovingly.

Her hands made slow sweeps over and around and down his body. She bent her helmeted head and kissed his lips. The prisoner stopped shuddering, but his limbs still shook, but it was due to building sexual arousal. By degrees, as Beausoleil caressed him, the man's penis engorged, enlarged and finally jutted out and up in full erection.

Beausoleil began stroking his member with her fist, bending her head over it, licking and laving with her tongue. The prisoner's body twitched and his hips began a thrusting motion.

Beausoleil climbed onto the altar, straddling the man's pelvis, and she slowly began lowering herself onto his erection. There was a moment's tension as of resistance, then she slid down onto him completely.

She moved up and down and from side to side, twisting all of her body from her thighs up to her shoulders.

Erica reached out and lifted away the scorpion headpiece to reveal a woman's face that appeared to be no more than twenty years of age, but her big eyes, dark as if they had been cut from onyx, bespoke an almost ancient wisdom. Cobalt knew that Baron Beausoleil was probably his age.

She reached up behind her and unpinned her hair. It fell in a silky stream down to the base of her spine, like a flow of frozen obsidian. The ends were cut off as square and as straight as a ruled line. Equally straight-cut bangs bisected her high forehead, falling almost to the delicate brow arches above her eyes.

She had the long, pointed hybrid face that a poetically minded man might have tried to describe as elfin with its high, angular cheekbones. Her lips were fairly wide, curving naturally upward so that she always seemed to be on the point of smiling—or sneering—even when her face was in repose. Still her beauty had the fascination of being an unhuman beauty but close enough to humanity's ideal to arouse the man trapped beneath and between her thighs.

She tossed her arms about in intricate, semaphore-like motions as she rode the prisoner steadily. Cobalt noted with a quiver of nausea that Beausoleil seemed to be turning from a baron into an animal, and then into something that wasn't even flesh and blood, only divine lust disguised.

When she reached her shuddering peak, Beausoleil arched her back and lifted both arms upward—then she drove them down again, the taloned tips slashing across the prisoner's throat, severing both the carotid artery and jugular vein at the same time. Crimson sprayed out in thick jets, splattering her belly in artless speckled patterns. The man shook violently, spasmodically beneath her.

As he expired and orgasmed simultaneously, Beausoleil threw her head back and shrieked, *"Avatara Shiva!"*

Sam provided the translation in an uninflected tone: "'Incarnation of Shiva.'"

The announcement and the sacrifice triggered a mad, howling explosion among the celebrants. The men and women clutched at one another wildly, ripping at their robes and clawing at one another's flesh in a mad variety of sexual joinings. They cried out, "Shakti! Shakti!"

From the braziers gushed thick columns of smoke. Peering through the billowing clouds with slitted eyes, Cobalt glimpsed Erica van Sloan helping Beausoleil to climb off the twitching prisoner and they both rushed into the shadows at the far end of the temple. The lust-drunk celebrants didn't see them go.

"Well," Sam said cheerfully, turning away from the observation panel, "what do you think of my little model?"

Cobalt shrugged, absently noting that Mare, though she still stood motionless and expressionless, was perspiring heavily. "I suppose it's all very colorful, exploiting as it does coarse human nature and its attraction to theater. Bread and circuses, I've heard it called. But what purpose does it serve?"

"Purposes, plural," Sam smoothly corrected him. He brushed a strand of silver hair back from his forehead. "First and foremost is the revival of the cult of the mother goddess, personified by Shakti. It's a very powerful draw for desperate and poverty-stricken peoples of all lands, since it taps into mythic archetypes dating back to the Stone Age."

Cobalt shook his head as if in pity. "The old humanity, ruled by myth and superstition."

Sam smiled thinly. "I don't think you fully understand. In this cult, there is a mixture of sex and mystery and the promise of salvation by indulging the baser aspects of human nature."

"I understand perfectly," Cobalt said coldly. "One of the easiest ways to control humanity is to allow it full rein to wallow in its animal instincts. But unfortunately, that usually leads to widespread devastation. That's the reason the barons were created, to act as governors to human's more atavistic behaviors."

Sam snorted through delicate nostrils. "Kindly don't expect me to be impressed by baronial dogma and propaganda. Widespread devastation didn't occur in Assam, where the Nirodha movement, the cult of Shakti, originated. For the past few months I've been marshaling all the distaff Tantric cultists into a formidable force that will establish my permanent influence on the Indian subcontinent."

"I still fail to see how manufacturing a movement like that would advance your objectives."

Sam sighed, as if he found Cobalt too dense to bear. "What makes you think you know what my objectives are? The Nirodha movement is nothing but misdirection, an elaborate piece of sleight of hand.''

"So this is a fake religion?''

"Not so much fake as a revival, a consolidation of a number of old cults to give the disaffected a focus around which to rally. Although it might take a bit longer for the Shakti sect to establish a foothold here, I will give it an inducement.''

"Such as?''

"A war,'' Sam declared. "A war between the barons loyal to me and those who seek to overthrow me.''

Cobalt seemed dumbfounded. "What I just witnessed was only a deception?''

"All war is based on deception, on misdirection and misinformation. As Sun Tzu said, 'Use deception when you have not the power to win in open battle.'''

Cobalt had no quick rejoinder. Instead, he gnawed nervously on his lower lip. Confusion wasn't an emotion any of the hybrids, particularly the barons, dealt with easily. Sam recalled all of the barons' bewildered reactions when they came to the realization the Archon Directorate didn't exist, and then when they first met him, when he was introduced to them by Balam.

Sam easily imagined the thoughts careening and colliding within the oversized craniums of the barons. For the entirety of their artificially prolonged lives, the barons believed they served the will of the Archons—or they convinced themselves they were the Directorate's servants and therefore any action they undertook to safeguard their positions as the overlords of humankind was justified.

But their probing intelligence needed proof, and without it, doubt inevitably ate away the belief structure. Although none of the barons spoke of it, they had ceased to subscribe to the belief in the Archons. In which case, they were no longer content with their roles as the plenipotentiaries of a higher, grander authority.

They had reached this conclusion tentatively, by degrees over a period of time. When they finally did, they were as absolutely certain of it as they had been certain of the existence of the Archon Directorate.

At length, Baron Cobalt demanded, "Who are you trying to deceive?"

"Look down into the temple," suggested Sam. "What do you see?"

Cobalt glanced through the glass, then shrugged. "Other than a lot of rutting apelings, vapor for the most part. Smoke."

"Mist, actually a spray. The worshipers of Shakti are now carriers for a virulent viral pathogen. They have been infected harmlessly, but when I return them to Assam and expose them to the second component of the binary compound of the formula, their very breath becomes deadly."

Cobalt regarded him silently, skeptically.

"Genetically tailored diseases are not new," Sam continued quietly. "They are a completely vicious method of waging war. Utterly ruthless. And what I have in mind is no exception. My pathogen attacks corn, wheat, rice—every grain crop and thus every form of livestock, because they can't live without the grasses. The people down below are my prototypes.

They themselves will spread the plague that will eventually kill them through famine.''

''What is its chemical composition?'' Cobalt inquired.

Sam put a thumb and forefinger to his lips and mimed turning a key. ''My lips are sealed. However, I call it Attila's Mount.''

''Attila?'' echoed Cobalt dourly. ''Why choose that name?''

''It's very appropriate, inasmuch as an old proverb stated that no grass grew where Attila's horse trod.''

''Is it harmful to humans?''

Sam turned toward Mare, at the same time producing a metal cylinder from a coat pocket. ''Mary Lou, if I might bother you to roll up your sleeve again...''

Mare obediently did as he said, standing there with her bare right forearm thrust out. The cylinder in Sam's hand was topped by a spray pump, and he pushed it down with a thumb. A yellowish mist puffed out and wetted Mare's flesh near the crook of her elbow.

''When it's in pure liquid form, my compound has an exceptionally adverse reaction with all organic substances.'' Sam spoke very matter-of-factly. ''And it works very, very fast.''

''How fast?'' Cobalt asked.

Mare suddenly gasped in pain and clasped her arm. She doubled over. ''It hurts!''

''Of course it does,'' said Sam. ''Inside of a minute, the Attila's Mount compound will penetrate all of your epidermal layers and then sink into the bone itself. It will attack and poison the marrow. You'll be dead inside of another minute, and shortly thereafter the affected flesh will turn brown and fall off the bone.''

"Is there a counteragent?" Cobalt demanded.

Sam smiled sadly. "Yes. But unfortunately, there's no way I can reach it in time to do her any good. Nice meeting you, Mary Lou.''

Mare stared at Cobalt with beseeching eyes. "It *hurts!* Worse than anything I ever felt!"

Falling to her knees, holding a hand over her arm, she reached for Cobalt, who moved back a few steps. "My lord! My love!"

Mare's body swayed, trembled and then went into convulsions. Her eyes remained wide and staring but they no had vision. Her mouth gaped, her lips writhed, but no words came out, only a croak of agony and terror. She toppled sideways, her body spasming as her lungs ceased their function.

"As you can see," Sam stated, "Attila's Mount is pretty potent stuff, if I say so myself.''

Cobalt shook his head in disgust. "You're mad.''

"Hardly. I'm just not limited by two- or even three-dimensional thinking. I can easily perceive the glory of the final result, despite a few bad points of the process. But most plans are that way, and since the magnitude of my plan is so great, the bad points seem very bad indeed. Conversely, the final result is even more glorious.''

Cobalt ran a hand over his hairless pate. "Why cause a famine?''

"Why would you think? If you're seeking followers, first you empty their bellies in order to empty their minds. It's the old axiom of, If you can feed them, you can lead them.''

"Logical. You starve your potential followers first. Most of the people in the Outlands are desperate, waiting for a leader, for a cause.''

"Exactly,'' Sam replied approvingly. "As you fill their empty bellies, you can then fill their minds with whatever you wish. No concept, no idea, no belief seems too absurd or repulsive as long as they eat. You will witness this firsthand once you join me.''

"Why would I join you? To fight with you against the barons who seek to displace you?''

Sam grinned bleakly. "No, actually, I want you to lead the barons against me.''

Due to their size and shape, it was virtually impossible for a hybrid's eyes to widen, but Cobalt managed to pull it off. Incredulous, he cried, "There are no barons willing to attack you! They fear you will prevent them access to the metabolic treatments since your forces control Area 51.''

"True,'' Sam conceded. "But if the barons, like the natives of Assam, have the proper rallying point, the correct motivator, they might consider such action would be in their best interests. They might take the risk.''

"And who would serve as this rallying point?'' Cobalt asked suspiciously.

"You, of course. You're something of a legend among your fellow barons, you know. Your audacity, your courage, your unregenerate treachery are admired at the same time they are despised.''

Cobalt shook his head, his lips twisting as if he

tasted something exceptionally bitter. "You have summoned me here to mock me, to make sport of me. I have nothing with which to draw followers, nothing to gain anyone's support, much less a baron's. You took it all away from me. All I have is—" he hooked a thumb toward Mare "—is her. And as you so candidly pointed out, she played host to my parasite. Now that she is dead, I no longer even qualify as a parasite. That is the role you have cast me into."

Sam laughed. "Apparently, I'm not making myself clear, Lord Baron. I will supply you with everything you need to stage a war of attrition. Men, matériel, state-of-the-art ordnance, some things you don't even know exist."

Cobalt leaned forward, his stance telegraphing his sudden hunger and desperation. He closed a hand around Sam's forearm. The imperator permitted the touch.

"You would do this?" Cobalt hissed between his teeth. "You *can* do this?"

"Of course I can," Sam answered with a sage nod. "There are, however, a couple of conditions to the offer I just made."

Cobalt withdrew his hand, his face locked in a mask of angry disappointment. He mumbled, "I should have known."

"Don't be so quick to ascribe to me your own treacherous tendencies," Sam admonished. "The first condition is that you agree I will ultimately be the victor in the rebellion you stage. You will, when I tell you to do so, end your hostilities and announce that you and I have reached an accord and are now fast allies.''

Cobalt nodded, facial muscles relaxing with relief. ''I understand. And the second condition?''

Sam paused a moment before answering, a lazy smile tugging at the corners of his mouth. ''Once the war begins, your first target will not be a military one, nor one of the baronies that support me. It will be a place situated in the Bitterroot Range in Montana.''

Cobalt blinked at Sam in puzzled surprise. ''But there's nothing of strategic value. Except—''

Comprehension suddenly glinted in the baron's eyes. As if dredging his memory, he said in a pondering tone, ''There's a place called Cerberus, a Totality Concept redoubt abandoned two centuries ago.''

''Yes,'' Sam drawled patronizingly. ''Abandoned by none other than your most trusted adviser, Mohandas Lakesh Singh.''

''I know that,'' Cobalt said impatiently. ''He listed it as completely inoperable, gutted and cleaned out long ago. Not worth salvaging. A year or so ago I lost a Magistrate Division squad I had dispatched to search the place. I believe old Lakesh was right.''

''Actually,'' interposed Sam smoothly, ''he was only half-right. Old Lakesh did indeed abandon the place, right before the nukecaust. But he reactivated it some thirty years ago, refurbished and restocked it. He also reinhabited it with himself and his friends.''

Cobalt scowled. ''Friends?''

''You may be acquainted with a few of them, Lord Baron. Kane, Grant and Brigid Baptiste, to name but three.''

Baron Cobalt stared at him in silent, stunned disbelief, his mouth dropping open. His face sagged in an expression of astonishment that was almost comical.

"Oh, yes," Sam said in a conspiratorial whisper. "I do indeed know whereof I speak. I've even visited the place."

Cobalt snarled, his upper lip curling back over his teeth. He hugged himself, his small body quaking. Then he flung back his head and howled, a shriek of rage, betrayal and humiliation torn from the roots of his soul.

Sam nodded solemnly. "Yes, that was about the kind of reaction I expected."

Chapter 16

The long dugout rounded the river bend in the steaming jungle dusk. The Brahmaputra River, wide and swift as it rushed over half-submerged rocks, foamed brown and white, splashing over the canoe's prow. Brightly plumaged birds, disturbed in their perches among the great fronded trees overhanging the river, squawked angrily. A flock of them went flapping through the jungle toward the flaming orange shimmer of sunset in the west.

The paddles slashed in and out of the river's surface in a frantic, fast rhythm. The urgency of it matched the tense postures of the two people who paddled the canoe with a single-minded concentration, as though their lives depended on it—and they did.

A young woman and man gasped and strained over the long wooden paddle handles. Madi sat in the bow of the canoe, her sari soaked through with sweat. She had deep brown eyes and jet-black hair, which was caught into a bun at the back of her head by an ivory clip. The light color of her sari contrasted dramatically with her dark amber skin.

Ramja wore only a ragged loincloth. His scarred face was contorted in exertion and pain. A puckered weal bisected the right cheek and lifted his lip, revealing several missing teeth. He was a head taller than Madi, but his hair was just as black, his eyes as dark and his bare arms and legs just as brown. He was also as thin as she was, his skin drawn tight over the bones. Both people looked to be on the verge of starvation, and both of them wore leather collars around their necks.

The shrill, angry yells floating down the river behind them reminded Madi that her life and that of her companion rested on the fast-waning strength in her arms and shoulders. She continued to work her paddle, sucking in great lungfuls of air as she and Ramja slid the flat wooden blades into the water, pulled and then mechanically repeated the motion. They had been repeating it for nearly an hour on the roiling brown river that slashed through the forested vastness like a great knife wound.

Earlier, Ramja had estimated they had a half-hour lead on the soldiers of the Scorpia Prime, but evidently their absence had been discovered from the slave quarters sooner than expected. Fortunately, the river's many twists and turns hid them from their pursuers, but the shouts and yells had drawn steadily louder over the past few minutes.

Their canoe entered a broad, straight span, and Madi cast a glance over her shoulder. Outlined starkly against the reddening sky she saw the long wings of several vultures. The birds didn't flap their wings but simply soared over the treetops as they glided, tilted and banked. The hideous creatures seemed to sense an abundant feast in the offing.

Madi repressed a shudder, then around the last

bend came three canoes, each one of them bearing four soldiers. She didn't need to get a close look to know they were brandishing streamlined and skeletal firearms, or that their faces under black turbans were painted red on the left side and dead white on the other. On the right cheek of each soldier, starkly imprinted in black, was the stylized silhouette of a scorpion.

Ramja's brow ran with sweat and he blinked it back. Hoarsely, he said, "Watch where we're going!"

Madi turned and saw they were approaching another bend. A crocodile slid lazily out from the muddy bank. It started to swim toward them, snapped its jaws once and submerged, out of sight.

"Guess he wasn't as hungry as he thought," Ramja managed to husk out.

Madi had no breath or inclination to respond. She lifted her gaze away from the dark surface of the river and glanced at the broken line of mountains. They formed a great hairpin obstacle at the mouth of the valley, many miles to the north. She could barely make out the rocky peaks of the Naga Hills, dwarfed by the snow-clad, titanic bulk of the Himalayas. According to legend, the mountains were the home of ancient gods and the guardians of India's northern wall. At the moment, Madi wished she and Ramja were on the uppermost peak of the Himalayas. At least they would be closer to Shiva, despite the freezing temperatures.

The paddling had become so automatic Madi was hardly conscious of the motions of her arms and shoulders anymore. But her muscles ached with a fiery fury that got worse with every passing second. The pain crept down her arms and settled into her wrists and fingers.

She knew they couldn't maintain the pace for much longer. She was astonished that Shiva had granted them the strength to go as far as they had, since they were both half-starved.

Madi thought again of the shrine to Shiva she and Ramja had arbitrarily made their objective. Supplicants often left offerings of food there, but now she despaired of ever reaching it. Already a humid evening mist was settling in, more oppressive than the noon heat of the jungle and it would hide the landmarks.

Ramja suddenly blurted, "We've got to get there soon, Madi!"

"It's very close," she replied between soft grunts of exertion, even though she had no facts to back up her assertion.

Ramja managed a short, breathless chuckle. "I'm glad you're so certain. I might have given up hope by now." His words were punctuated by gasps of effort and the steady splashing of his paddle.

Madi didn't respond. She wondered if her memory had failed her or if she'd simply miscalculated the distance of the shrine from the Scorpia Prime's temple. The river took another bend, and a slightly fresher breeze cooled her sweat-filmed cheeks. She could see nothing ahead but more river and more jungle, with steaming fog beginning to collect between the trunks of sal trees.

Their canoe rounded a small overgrown promontory, startling a deer that had come to the river's edge to drink. It leaped through the brush, and Madi's eyes followed its panic-stricken flight automatically. Then she saw the small stack of water-smoothed stones between the high grasses.

Ramja saw the makeshift marker at the same time Madi did and he whooped in delight, or tried to. It sounded more like the croak of a half-dead crow. They frantically drove the wooden dugout to the bank. Before the hull had fully grounded against the hard-packed mud, the two people leaped overboard into the shallows and waded ashore.

Madi staggered as a brief spasm of vertigo assailed her, but she kept her footing. Then she and Ramja ran, not thinking about where they were going, only that they had to put as much distance between themselves and the river as soon as possible. They slapped aside thickly fronded plants, ducked beneath dangling, flowering lianas and crashed through thickets, heedless of the thorns.

They ran stumbling through a bog, the ground little more than a soupy marsh, and at every step their bare feet sank ankle deep into the muck. They waded through stagnant pools and climbed over rotten logs. Twice they circled broad puddles from which bubbles of sulfurous swamp gas rose and burst, releasing a nauseating stench.

After a few minutes of running, they heard a distant, ululating cry from their pursuers. Apparently, their dugout had been discovered. The human cry was answered almost immediately by a nonhuman one, the harsh coughing growl of a great tiger. Madi and Ramja knew tigers didn't roar, and the beast's terrifying snarl sounded angry.

Madi and Ramja continued to sprint through the moist, heat-sodden forest. When the terrain became less swampy, they stumbled to a halt and rested in the low fork of a tree. Gulping the damp air, Ramja asked, "How far?"

Madi looked around the darkening jungle and felt the fingers of despair clutch at her heart. She saw nothing familiar, and the triumphant cries of the Scorpia Prime's soldiers when they found their trail nearly made her burst into tears.

She had convinced Ramja to join her in the escape attempt by telling him the Shiva shrine would be a storage vessel for food that they could take with them in their journey to escape Assam. If she couldn't find the shrine, then Ramja, the boy she had grown up with, the boy who had professed his love for her, would die—and she would be responsible.

Of course, according to the Nirodha philosophy that had lately taken root in her country, since life was ultimately meaningless, death was equally insignificant. But she did not—she could not—subscribe to those beliefs, nor to the assertion that the Scorpia Prime was an Apsara, one of the alluring wives of Vishnu.

Madi knew the ancient legends about Apsaras winging down to Earth and taking mortal men as consorts. But goddesses didn't need men with guns to round up followers or slaves. The Scorpia Prime had drawn the majority of her soldiers from the Naga tribespeople of northeastern Assam.

They were serpent worshipers and though they enthusiastically participated in the Tantric sex rites, she knew they didn't necessarily believe in the Nirodha. But with an age-old tradition of head-hunting to draw upon, the Nagas made excellent warriors and trackers.

"Are we lost, Madi?"

She turned toward him, blinking back tears of shame. "I'm sorry," she murmured. "I know how hungry you are."

Ramja grinned. "It's just as well. You wouldn't want me getting fat and lazy."

From behind Ramja came a stealthy rustle of foliage, as of someone trying to move silently through the jungle and almost succeeding. Madi stiffened and when Ramja saw her fearful reaction, he swallowed hard and slowly turned.

The brush rustled again, and then out marched a huge yellow-and-black Bengal tiger. The huge cat was a male, the most enormous tiger either one of them had ever seen. It was massively muscled, measuring nearly fifteen feet from its bewhiskered snout to the tip of its striped tail. It looked as if it weighed in the vicinity of five hundred pounds.

The tiger made no move toward them, but regarded them both inscrutably with tawny, yellow-green eyes. Its gaze was piercing, almost hypnotic. A deep rumble rose from its throat.

"Don't move," Madi breathed.

"Don't worry," Ramja whispered in response.

The tiger opened its huge, wet red maw. Its long

yellow fangs glistened as it uttered a frightening combination of growl and protracted cough. It dug the great, curving claws of its forepaws into the ground, inscribing deep, parallel channels in the soil.

The cries of the Scorpia Prime's soldiers suddenly cut through the deepening dusk. They sounded very close. The tiger swung its head toward the sounds with a snorting growl. It gazed at Madi and Ramja steadily for a few seconds, then slowly, majestically turned its blunt-eared head in the direction it had come. The movement seemed very significant.

Then, muscles rippling, the tiger gathered itself and bounded forward, leaping over them and disappearing into the vegetation. Ramja's forehead ran with rivulets of sweat and plastered his hair tight to his scalp. Between quivering lips he muttered, "He meant us no harm."

Relief swept over Madi, leaving her momentarily weak. "No," she replied in an excited whisper. "He was sent to help us, a servant of Shiva to show us the way to his shrine."

Ramja looked at her doubtfully, and she said urgently, "It's true. Tigers are not mindless killers, but human in their own way, without the lust and greed of man."

Madi paused for breath. Before she could say anything, a prolonged scream knifed through the forested silence. The terrible masculine scream seemed to go on for an unbearably long time, and then it was joined by others. Interwoven with the shrieks was a grisly crunching and then they heard the triple-jackhammer stutter of automatic weapons. A deep-throated cough overlaid the cacophony of shots and screams. The tiger's hoarse bellow was filled with rage, triumph and the promise of a painful death.

The shots and the screams seemed to stop simultaneously, and silence pressed down over the jungle again, an oppressive quiet as if a giant bell jar had been placed over it. Ramja and Madi exchanged swift, fear-filled glances, then they began running again.

This time their flight wasn't as wild. They carefully looked for the path made by the tiger and followed it, an almost invisible trail that zigged in one direction then zagged in another. Within a few minutes, full night settled over the jungle, but it brought almost no relief from the humidity.

Madi and Ramja reached a break in the foliage and stood upon a slope that declined away to a small structure. Although the moon hadn't fully risen, the stars illuminated its flat stone roof and three walls. The shrine wasn't large, perhaps eight feet tall and made of flat slabs of stone. But it was draped with garlands of flowers, blossoms growing in white profusion. From within flickered a dim radiation, probably from an oil lamp lit by a supplicant.

By its glow Madi was able to make out the three-foot-tall statue of Shiva on the rear wall. The god resembled a potbellied man of middle age, with four arms and a stern but paternal face. A crescent-moon headpiece adorned his brow, right above his third eye. When Shiva was angry or offended, his third eye shot forth supernal flame that destroyed everything nearby.

All of the accumulated tension and fear of the past

two hours rushed out of Madi in a gasping sigh.
"There it is. Shiva showed us the way."

"Blessed be to Shiva," Ramja intoned.

They started down the slope toward the structure,
the warm caress of a breeze feeling like the touch of
a comforting hand. Ramja touched her shoulder and
whispered, "Thank you, Madi."

She turned toward him—just as he cried out in
shrill pain. His back arched as if he had received a
blow between the shoulder blades, and he reached up
with both hands, groping for the back of his neck.

Gaping at him in shock, Madi watched as Ramja
fell forward, first to his knees and then onto his face.
His cry became a gurgle. She saw, sprouting from the
base of his skull, a feathered shaft like a short arrow
or a long dart. She recognized the sticky sap with
which it was coated—Tamil root extract, a poison
used by the Nagas. A full dose brought instant death,
and apparently Ramja had received one.

She bent over him, trying to bite back a scream
when shadows shifted around her. Figures stole from
the crest of the slope, slender dark men with black
turbans and red-and-black painted faces. There were
only four of them, and two were splashed with a wet
crimson that was not paint. It was blood, either from
wounds inflicted by the tiger or that shed by their
fellow soldiers.

She saw that one of the Nagas carried a short
wooden bow, and he was nocking yet another poisoned shaft into the string. With a scream, more of
anger than fear, Madi ran across the face of the slope
and toward the shrine. Still, she was encouraged a

little. If the Nirodha soldiers were forced to use their bows, that meant they had either lost their firearms or emptied them.

Madi chanted a prayer to Shiva as she sprinted toward the shrine, her temples throbbing. From the men behind her she heard a twist of cruel laughter. The prayer changed to an invocation, a plea for him to interfere, even if it meant bringing about the dance of Tandava.

Her lungs labored and her chest seemed to close in on itself as she ran. Within a few yards, she was reeling on rubbery legs. She wondered bitterly why she was running at all. There seemed to be no point except to provide entertainment for the Scorpia Prime's soldiers. It was cold comfort and a small consolation, but she took a bit of satisfaction in the realization the tiger had forced them to pay dearly for their sport.

Her foot struck an irregularity in the ground and she fell heavily, almost within arm's reach of the shrine. Lifting her head dizzily, blinking back the amoeba-like floaters obscuring her vision, she saw the flicker of luminosity within the shrine seem to glow brighter, increasing in intensity. Even the interior was adorned with ferns and chains of flowers.

Then fear descended on Madi like a wave. Crooked fingers of energy suddenly stabbed through the narrow interior. She crouched motionless, watching with awe and dread as thousands of crackling threads of light coalesced in the center of Shiva's shrine. A faint, high-pitched whine like that of a distant mosquito flitted in and out on the edge of her hearing.

A tingling, prickling sensation covered her body,

and she felt the fine hairs on her arms and legs stir and bristle. The damp air pulsed like the beat of a gigantic heart. A heat-wave-like shimmer rose from the floor of the shrine, and the blossoms of the flowers vibrated, some of the petals coming loose and swirling about as if borne by a breeze.

They swirled about an object that appeared on the floor of the shrine, a shape resembling a pyramid made of smooth, gleaming metal. It exuded a wavering funnel of light that fanned out to completely fill the stone structure. Madi could only gape at it, her thought processes paralyzed as if by a dose of the Tamil root.

A yellow nova of brilliance erupted from the pyramid. Madi felt a concussion slap against her face. Her eyes stung, but she couldn't look away. Through the blurred afterimage of the flare, three shadowy shapes stepped out of the fan of light. The edges of the shimmery fan peeled back and disappeared into the pyramid. Three figures stood within the shrine, all of them identically dressed in black.

The man in the lead stepped forward and spoke to her in Hindi. On the far fringes of her awareness, Madi knew he had asked her name, but she didn't give it to him. Instead, she flung out her arms and screamed, "Lord Shiva! Shatterer of worlds! It is the time of the Tandava!"

Chapter 17

Baron Sharpe flung out his arms in a sweeping, expansive gesture as if to embrace all of creation. In a loud, stentorian voice he announced, "Someday, Crawler, my boy, this will be all yours."

"Thank you kindly," came the sarcastic response. "You can keep it. And don't call me 'my boy.' I'm at least twenty years older than you are."

Sharpe opened his mouth to retort, then sneezed violently, not even bothering to cover his nose. "Bless me," he snuffled.

"Like hell," Crawler snapped, wiping away the spattering of saliva and mucus from his shaved head. Then he sneezed himself, the violence of it puffing up the powdery dirt upon which he lay. He sneezed a second time.

Baron Sharpe tittered, but the acidic air that irritated his sinus membranes and triggered the sneeze reflex also stung his tongue. He stopped giggling long enough to spit. This time he considerately turned his head away from his chief councillor. He stepped away from the sheltering rock overhang and glanced into the sky. At the far edge of audibility he heard a faint, keening whine, but he saw nothing.

Despite his inborn sensitivity to high light levels, Baron Sharpe did not squint when he looked up.

Thick, fleecy stratums of clouds always overlay Washington Hole, casting it into a form of perpetual twilight. For a time, following the nukecaust of two centuries earlier, the entire Earth lay beneath a canopy of clouds.

Massive quantities of pulverized rubble had been propelled into the atmosphere, clogging the sky for a generation, blanketing all of Earth in a thick umbrella of radioactive dust, ash, debris, smoke and fallout.

The exchange of atomic missiles did more than slaughter most of Earth's inhabitants. It distorted those ecosystems that weren't completely obliterated and resculpted the face of the planet into a perverted parody of what it had been.

After eight generations, the lingering effects of the holocaust and the nuclear winter, skydark, were more subtle, an underlying texture to a world struggling to heal itself—except in Washington, D.C., where the injuries had never healed but had simply scabbed over.

Only a vast sea of fused black glass occupied the tract of land that once held the seat of American government. Seen from a distance, the crater lent the region the name by which it had been known for nearly two centuries. Washington Hole, the premier hellzone of the country, still jolted by ground tremors and soaked by the intermittent flooding of Potomac Lake. A volcano, barely an infant in geological terms, had burst up from the rad-blasted ground. The peak dribbled a constant stream of foul-smelling smoke, mixing with the chem-tainted rain clouds to form a layer of stinking sulfur and chlorine.

The smell was so cloying, so fetid that new arrivals found it necessary to wear respiration masks until they grew accustomed to it. Of course, there weren't many new arrivals. The shantytowns that once ringed the outskirts of Washington Hole had been razed long ago, during the first year of the Program of Unification. Most of their inhabitants had succumbed to rad sickness years before. The former District of Columbia fell under the jurisdiction of Sharpeville, although the barony itself was located many miles away, in the former state of Delaware.

Although the center of Washington and all of its inner suburbs had dissolved in the first three minutes of the nukecaust, the outer rim still contained a few crumbling ruins. Beyond the hollow shells of buildings lay an expanse of rolling tableland, broken by hill ranges. Thirty miles to the north of the crater's epicenter rose a rampart of tumbled stones. Sharpe and his high councillor stood upon the rampart, waiting for whatever would happen next.

Sharpe was the third man to hold the title of baron. His close-cropped blond hair topped a high, smooth cranium. He was small and slender, no more than five and a half feet tall and weighing around 130 pounds.

His eyes were a milky blue, the cold color of glacial meltwater. They were very large, shadowed by sweeping supraorbital ridges.

Sharpe also had inherited a few of his namesake's eccentricities, though he knew some few people referred to them as insanities. One of Sharpe's eccentricities was a fondness for picking through predark articles of clothing stored in the archives of the

Historical Division and wearing whatever struck his whim at the moment. Depending on his fancy, Baron Sharpe would outfit himself in white tie and tails, complete with a silk top hat and silver-knobbed walking stick. On another day, it might be a backless evening gown of gold lamé, with a teased-out bouffant wig as a shock-value fashion statement.

A few years before, while pawing through the archived clothing, he made a discovery that became his personal uniform and statement of belief. It was a violet jumpsuit, with huge belled legs, flame-colored satin facings and a bat-winged collar. Long fringe streamed from both sleeves. Worked in glittering rhinestones on the back were three letters: TCB.

At a sigh from Crawler, Sharpe flicked his gaze downward. His high councillor scrabbled forward on heavily muscled arms. Thick calluses covered his elbows. His pale legs trailed behind him, like a pair of boneless tentacles. He wore a leather harness and velvet loincloth. The harness displayed his exceptionally well-developed upper body. His torso looked to be all muscle from the neck down to his hips.

Whereas the harness showed off his bulging biceps and dinner-plate-sized pectorals, the loincloth did nothing to disguise his shriveled, atrophied legs. They stretched out behind him like flaccid, flesh-colored stockings half-filled with mud. Even in the overcast light Sharpe could make out the red scars bisecting the backs of his knees.

Lifting his head, Crawler gazed at Sharpe speculatively with his dark eyes. "You're upsetting Commander Grady."

Sharpe frowned. "Did he think something?"

Crawler sighed again. "He didn't have to."

Sharpe stepped back beneath the overhang formed by huge chunks of rock and concrete. The partially open vanadium sec door was sunk deep within a rock-ribbed hollow about halfway up the slope. Clumps of scraggly brush grew around it, masking the depression so effectively, it was only by chance he glimpsed the dull reflection of light against the smooth alloy.

"Commander Grady," Sharpe said loudly, autocratically.

A black figure stepped out from the recessed entrance. He resembled a statue sculpted from obsidian, somehow given life and movement. The weak sunshine struck dim highlights on the molded chest piece and shoulder pads of the polycarbonate body armor. His face was completely concealed by a black helmet, except for his mouth and chin. A red-tinted visor masked his eyes.

A small, disk-shaped badge of office in crimson was emblazoned on the arching left pectoral of the chest plate. The badge depicted a stylized, balanced scales of justice, superimposed over nine-spoked wheels, symbolizing the Magistrate's oath to keep the wheels of justice turning in the nine villes.

A holstered Sin Eater was strapped to his right forearm.

Grady ducked his head deferentially. "Yes, my lord baron?"

Sharpe gestured to Crawler. "My councillor advises me that you are upset."

The swift, instinctive glance Grady shot Crawler

was one of pure terror, despite his visored eyes. He knew the creature called Crawler was a doomie, a doomseer, a mutant gifted—or cursed—with the psychic ability to sniff out forthcoming death. He also knew Baron Sharpe had more than once killed staff members who had displeased him, including his predecessor, Ericson.

"I'm not upset, my lord," Grady stated quickly. "But only cautious. Redoubt Papa is not the safest place for you, as I'm sure you realize."

Sharpe grinned bleakly. "Fuckin' A."

He unzipped the front of his jumpsuit halfway to his belly. A white stellate scar surrounded a raised, puckered ring on his upper chest. "I'm the one who was shot the last time I was here."

Grady didn't mention that the baron wasn't the only victim of gunshot wounds during his last visit to the redoubt. Even though he had been moved up the ranks of the Magistrate Division after the death of Ericson, Grady had fervently hoped never to hear about Redoubt Papa again, much less actually set foot in it.

Upon his promotion to division commander, Grady had been briefed about the secret installations. A major component of the Program of Unification had been the seeking out and securing of all redoubts within the territories of the villes. When the program was being ratified nearly ninety years earlier, anyone who spoke of having knowledge of them, even based on hearsay, was ruthlessly hunted down and exterminated. Inside of a generation, tales of the redoubts were suppressed to such an extent that they became baseless legends, much as stories about Atlantis and Avalon had been dismissed in earlier centuries.

He had been told about the Totality Concept, the gateways and the goals of Project Cerberus. He never knew how much to believe, but regardless of the actual truth, a gateway unit had been installed in every Totality Concept redoubt, including the one near Washington Hole, code-named Redoubt Papa.

Grady accepted the story he had been told, knowing he would be better off if nothing pertaining to gateways and redoubts ever came his way. But the day before, a very troubled clerk in the division comm staff brought him a message. The message had arrived in Sharpeville over a radio frequency used exclusively for division administrators to communicate with hard-contact Mags out in the field.

The clerk had transcribed the voice message. It was addressed to Baron Sharpe and was very much to the point: "Grant and Baptiste need to meet with you on a matter of extreme importance. Future of your ville at stake. Washington Hole, Redoubt Papa, tomorrow, noon."

Although the frequency on which the voice message had come was not a secure channel, the clerk could offer no opinion how anyone could possibly patch into it—particularly since such technological items as tight-band wireless transmitters were restricted to the elite of the villes. Grady had no idea, either.

But since assuming Ericson's position, Grady had tried to keep close tabs on the activities, movements and sightings of Grant, Brigid Baptiste and Kane.

Like most of the other Magistrate Divisions in other baronies, Grady had been largely unsuccessful. He knew, however, that Baron Sharpe had gotten embroiled in their activities on at least two occasions.

The first time was nearly two years before, deep inside Redoubt Papa. Kane had shot and seriously wounded Sharpe, though astonishingly, he seemed to bear him no ill will.

The second time, a little over six months earlier, was when Baron Sharpe struck an alliance of convenience with Grant and Baptiste on the eve of the battle of Area 51. Since then, verifiable sightings of the three seditionists had been sporadic. Kane and Grant had last been reported in the Area 51 zone only a few weeks ago, but the entire story was hard to accept—eyewitness accounts had them piloting strange aircraft and destroying several Deathbirds and Sandcats. Grady found the tale almost impossible to believe. The identification of Grant and Kane as the culprits was hardly spot-on, either.

When Grady brought the message to Baron Sharpe, he had no idea what his reaction might be. Before his promotion, he had never dreamed he would stand in the presence of Baron Sharpe, since he understood that audiences with barons were exceedingly rare and conducted with great ceremony and secrecy.

He had heard stories of the barons of course. Anyone serving in any division in any ville had heard them. Part of his mind knew that maintaining a baron's mystique was contrived, an intimidation strategy, an old psychological gambit. But still, the baronial oligarchy ruling the nine villes was more than the governing body of postnukecaust America—they were god-kings, serving as a bridge between predark and postdark man, the avatars of a new order.

Sharpe, however, wasn't as preoccupied with ceremony as his brethren, but still Grady didn't think the baron would react as if he had just been invited to a social function by long-lost friends. He tried to point out to the baron how obvious a trap it was, but Sharpe dismissed his objections.

Grady realized it was futile and possibly fatal to oppose the baron's will. From what he had heard, when Ericson had attempted to do that very thing, Sharpe shot him in the face.

Although he couldn't dissuade the baron from attending the rendezvous, he at the very least managed to convince Sharpe to allow him to accompany the baron and Crawler to Redoubt Papa.

"With the utmost respect, Lord Baron," Grady ventured, "I am here to keep you from being shot a second time."

Sharpe smiled at him almost pityingly. "I thought you knew."

Grady cocked his head at him quizzically. "Knew, my lord?"

"I cannot die." Sharpe made the pronouncement very matter-of-factly. "Isn't that right, Crawler?"

The councillor gazed unblinkingly at Grady. "Oh, so very right."

Feeling the pressure of the doomie's gaze, Grady's flesh went clammy. Before meeting Crawler, Grady had assumed that doomies didn't exist anymore. Most of the mutie strains spawned after the nukecaust were extinct, either dying because of their twisted biologies, or hunted and exterminated during the early years of the unification program. Stickies, screamers, scabbies, swampies and almost every other breed exhibiting warped genetics had all but vanished. To find a doom-sniffer and then act subservient to him was almost more than he could bear.

"I see, Lord Baron." Grady backed toward the open sec door. "Then I will await your further orders here."

Crawler cast Sharpe a sly, knowing grin. The baron returned it and went back to the edge of the rockfall and scanned the skies beneath shading hands. In truth, Baron Sharpe wasn't worried about becoming a victim of Grant and Brigid, since he had already survived two face-to-face encounters with them and Kane. He was absolutely positive he couldn't die, because Crawler had told him so.

Part of Sharpe's legacy from his human greatgrandfather was a small private zoo of creatures that had once crept and slithered and scuttled over the Deathlands. The monsters had been fruitful and multiplied over the decades, and one of them was a doomie called Crawler.

It was more of a title than a name, bestowed upon him after his leg tendons had been severed. The psimutie had displayed a great cunning and propensity for escape from his compound, no doubt employing his mental talents to find the most opportune time and means to do so. After his leg tendons had been severed, his psi-powers availed him nothing, inasmuch as he was restricted to dragging himself around his cell by fingers and elbows.

After recovering from a near fatal illness, Baron Sharpe visited Crawler one sultry summer midnight. He gazed in revulsion at the human face staring back at him from a wild, matted tangle of gray beard and long, filthy hair. The baron had no idea of Crawler's age, but he understood that he was one of his ancestor's last acquisitions before his mysterious death some ninety-five years before. He knew the doomie was very old, but some muties possessed remarkable longevity.

"I have a question," Baron Sharpe announced, "about my death."

Wheezing whistles issued from Crawler's hair-rimmed lips. For a moment, the baron thought the mutie was undergoing an asthma attack and would expire, but then he recognized the sound as laughter.

In a high, whispery voice, Crawler said, "That question has no meaning, my lord baron. You have died and crossed back. You no longer need fear death, for it is behind you, not ahead of you."

Baron Sharpe was so delighted, he came close to bursting into tears of gratitude. His hopes had been realized; his fear of death proved groundless. That very night, he ordered the release of Crawler from his cage, saw that he was bathed, fed, shaved, cropped and pampered. He installed him as a high councillor, ignoring the outraged reactions of his personal staff.

And now Crawler was the only creature he trusted, even though the doomie had tried to orchestrate his murder at one point. After that, both of them realized they were linked in some fashion and knew that if one died, so would the other. The notion made no real sense and couldn't be tested without incurring lethal results, so they decided to trust each other implicitly from then on.

When Sharpe found the violet jumpsuit with the rhinestone-studded letters, he remembered Crawler's phrase about crossing back. He realized delightedly the letters meant To Cross Back, and thusly the baron decided that by wearing the outfit, he said to the world that he had died and crossed back to the land of the living.

He reflected on the irony that he had worn the jumpsuit the first time he met Kane, within Redoubt Papa, which made him the second baronial victim of the mad Magistrate. Baron Cobalt was the first victim, and it could all be traced back to the night Kane was inducted into the Cobaltville Trust.

As Sharpe understood it, Kane, whose father had been a member of the Trust, was recommended for recruitment by Salvo, his former Magistrate Division commander. Kane was informed that his father was a member of the Trust, and therefore he had to accept the honor offered to him. Like his father, he would belong to the elite that literally ruled society in secret. Henceforth, like his father, he would work for the evolution of humankind.

Kane accepted the offer—and after that, everything went to hell on a slide. Sharpe was never briefed on exactly what happened in the twenty-four hours following Kane's entrance into the Trust. He knew the Magistrate escaped Cobaltville with Brigid Baptiste, a seditionist awaiting execution, and his partner of many years, Grant. Salvo was badly injured trying to stop the escape, and a few Magistrates were killed.

Kane reappeared only a day later when Baron Cobalt arrived at the Dulce facility for his annual medical treatment. Kane had attacked and humiliated him and escaped after killing a number of hybrids.

But all of that was just prologue. Only a few months later, Kane and Grant led a raiding party into the very heart of the Admin Monolith where they not only killed a pair of the Baronial Guard, but they also abducted Lakesh and Salvo.

Sharpe never learned the entire story of the raid and the abductions. The version put forth by Baron Cobalt explained some of it, but by no means all of it. Upon examination, there seemed no reason for the kidnapping of his fellow members of the Trust. In the intervening months, no ransom demands had been made in exchange for their return. It was as if both Lakesh and Salvo had fallen off the face of the earth.

The high-pitched whine Baron Sharpe's inhumanly keen ears had detected earlier was now much louder. Tilting his head back, he glimpsed two dark specks streaking across the sky. Within a heartbeat and a half, the specks had grown in size and he was able to make out their configurations.

They were aircraft, that much was obvious, but they were of a type he had never seen, heard of, or even viewed pix of. Sheathed in bronze-hued metal, the ships held the general shape and outlines of sea-going manta rays, and as such they were little more than flattened wedges with wings.

Stepping closer to the edge of the rock tumble, Sharpe exclaimed, "What wonderful toys!"

Crawler squirmed closer, taking up a position near his knees. "I don't think they're toys. Not in the least. Remember the recent reports of the attack on Area 51. One of the staff there theorized the ships might be Transatmospheric Vehicles...TAVs."

Baron Sharpe nodded in comprehension. "Oh, yes. You're right, my boy. They would hardly be toys at all."

The wingspans of the two TAVs were roughly twenty yards, and the fuselage was probably fifteen feet long. A short tail assembly was tipped by an ace-of-spades-shaped rudder.

The pair of airships hovered above the rockfall for a long tick of time, the engines making a peculiar sound between a muted rumble and a steam-kettle whistle. Then both ships dropped straight down. Tripodal landing gear unfolded from the undercarriages, and the craft rested gracefully on them. Fine clouds of dust puffed up all around.

The composition of the hulls appeared at first glance to be made of a burnished bronze alloy, but Sharpe was sure that wasn't the substance at all. Intricate geometric designs covered almost the entire exterior surface. Deeply inscribed into the metal were interlocking swirling glyphs, cup-and-spiral symbols and even elaborate cuneiform markings.

Neither craft had any external apparatus at all, no ailerons, no fins and no airfoils. The cockpits were almost invisible, little more than elongated oval

humps in the exact center of the sleek topside fuse-
lages.

As Sharpe and Crawler watched in fascinated silence, the engine sounds faded away into inaudibility.
The cockpit canopies slid back and allowed two people to climb out of one ship—a huge man Sharpe
recognized instantly as the renegade Magistrate,
Grant, and an exceptionally small but very well pro-
portioned blond man. Both of them were attired from
throat to heel in black garments that fit them as tightly
as doeskin gloves.

From the second TAV emerged a woman with a
long mane of sunset-colored hair. Brigid Baptiste
wore an identical black uniform. Although Sharpe
kept a welcoming smile on his face, he could see
another figure in the cockpit of the craft Baptiste had
flown in. He said nothing until all three people had
clambered down from the TAVs and stood at the foot
of the pile of lichen-patched stone.

"Hello, all," he said loudly, waving to them.
"Nice to see all of you again, even if this is a trap."

Chapter 18

Gazing down at the babbling, terrified girl groveling on the grass at Lakesh's feet, Kane demanded, "What the hell is all that gibberish about?"

Lakesh speared him with a frosty glare. "I will thank you not to refer to my native language in such an ethnocentric fashion."

Lakesh, Domi and Kane stepped out of the narrow, rectangular structure, avoiding the skeins of energy that still crawled and sizzled over the gleaming alloy skin of the interphaser, despite the shadowsuits they all wore. Kane had christened the one-piece garments *shadowsuits,* and though they didn't appear as if they could offer protection from a mosquito bite, they were impervious to most wavelengths of radiation.

Lakesh leaned over the girl and spoke to her soothingly in the singsong language Kane had heard him employ on very rare occasions in the past. He started to kneel beside her when, in reaction to a torrent of words spilling from her lips, he straightened, eyes narrowing.

"What is it?" Domi demanded, guessing from his body language that something the Indian girl said had aroused Lakesh's fears.

In a tense, low voice, he answered, "The girl says

she's being chased by the Nirodha, warriors in service to the Scorpia Prime.''

''Chalk up another one for the future me,'' Kane muttered, moving farther away from the shrine. He automatically flexed the tendons of his right wrist, and his Sin Eater slid from the forearm holster and slapped solidly into his waiting hand. The sensitive actuator ignored all movements except the one that indicated the weapon should be drawn.

''She thinks they're still out there in the jungle,'' Lakesh continued quietly and swiftly. ''Watching and waiting.''

''I don't see anything,'' Domi said in a terse whisper, her crimson eyes scanning the moonlit vegetation at the top of the slope. Her hand rested on the butt of the Detonics Combat Master holstered at her right hip.

''Ask the girl if they're armed,'' Kane said to Lakesh. ''And if so, what with.''

Almost as soon as the request left his lips, he heard a faint thrumming. He caught only a glimpse of dark objects arcing through the sky. One of the wooden shafts flew short and buried itself in the ground between Kane's feet. The second struck him in the lower chest, directly below his left pectoral. Stinging pain flared through his torso.

Kane's reaction was immediate. His index finger depressed the Sin Eater's firing stud. Flame and thunder gouted from the barrel as he loosed a long, stuttering full-auto volley into the foliage. The 248-grain rounds slashed through shrubbery and crashed into tree trunks, shaving away bark and ripping loose branches.

Drawing her Combat Master and holding it in a two-fisted grip, Domi fired in the same direction as Kane, but a little to the left. The fusillade of gunfire whipped the foliage with the fury of a gale-force wind.

Before he emptied his clip, Kane relaxed the pressure on the trigger button. Domi stopped shooting when he did, but she had fired her .45-caliber pistol dry. Moving with expert ease, she toggled the empty magazine from the pistol's butt and slapped another one home in almost the same motion.

They waited for more projectiles to be hurled their way. Lakesh knelt by the girl, his arms around her. The palms of her hands were pressed together, her steepled fingers touched her forehead. She was murmuring rapidly through some sort of invocation.

"What's she saying?" Kane demanded.

"A prayer to Shiva."

"Tell her to knock it off," Kane snapped, still questing for a target. "She's distracting me."

Lakesh cast him a sour glance, but spoke briefly to the girl. Almost immediately she fell silent. Her dark eyes flashed as they flitted from Lakesh to Domi to Kane. She didn't appear to be frightened, but she was definitely wary. Apparently, she was beginning to realize that Lakesh was not Shiva, nor were his companions even lesser gods. Still, Kane wouldn't have blamed her for believing them to be demons.

The shadowsuits definitely lent them a sinister aspect, particularly Domi, with her red eyes and skin as pale as milk. However, they had become important items in their ordnance and arsenal over the past few months. Ever since they absconded with the suits from Redoubt Yankee on Thunder Isle, the garments had proved their worth and their superiority to the polycarbonate Mag armor if for nothing else than their internal subsystems.

The suits were climate controlled for environments up to highs of 150 degrees and as cold as minus ten degrees Fahrenheit. Microfilaments controlled the internal temperature.

Manufactured with a technique known in predark days as electrospin lacing, the electrically charged polymer particles formed a dense web of formfitting fibers. Composed of a compiled weave of spider silk, Monocrys and Spectra fabrics, the garments were essentially a single-crystal metallic microfiber with a very dense molecular structure.

The outer Monocrys sheathing went opaque when exposed to radiation, and the Kevlar and Spectra layers provided protection against blunt trauma. The spider silk allowed flexibility, but it traded protection from firearms for freedom of movement.

The inner layer was lined by carbon nanotubes only a nanometer wide, rolled-up sheets of graphite with a tensile strength greater than steel. The suits were almost impossible to tear, but a heavy-caliber bullet could penetrate them and, unlike the Mag exoskeletons, the suits wouldn't redistribute the kinetic shock. Still, the material was dense and elastic enough to deflect an arrow, but Kane knew he would have a hell of a bruise the next day.

Lakesh reached over and tweaked the short shaft from the ground, revolving it between gloved thumb and forefinger. The girl shook her head in furious negation and slapped it from his hand, speaking very brusquely.

"Now what?" Kane asked.

Squinting as he listened to her, Lakesh said, "She's speaking in a dialect that's a form of Hindi mixed in with some other local tongues, like Bengalese, but it sounds like some Dravidian in there, too. It's hard to gather more than half her meaning, but apparently the arrow is poison. She doesn't want us to touch it."

Madi uttered another stream of fluid vowels, which Lakesh laboriously interpreted. "I can't be sure, but I think she's claiming a friend of hers was killed by the poison arrows. His name was Ramja. He's up there on the hill. He helped her escape from the slave compound…wherever that might be."

Domi grunted softly in sympathy. "She's just a kid, maybe thirteen or fourteen years old."

Kane nodded toward the tree and foliage line at the crest of the hill. "I think we should check out the zone, make sure it's secure. We either ran off the Scorpia soldiers or killed them."

Domi's lips tightened. "Hope it's the second option."

Kane slid out of his backpack and dropped it near Lakesh. Domi carried a war bag containing three flash-bangs, two high-ex V60 minigrenades, four incends and two CS grens over her left shoulder. She dropped it carefully to the ground, but made no move to touch the knife with the nine-inch-long serrated blade sheathed to her right calf. A black knit balaclava was pulled down around her throat. She could tug it up to conceal her hair and most of her face within a couple of seconds.

Kane led the way up the face of the slope, walking heel-to-toe as he always did in a potential killzone. Domi walked behind him, pistol at the ready. The air was hot and steamy, and despite the environmental controls of his shadowsuit, sweat gathered at Kane's hairline.

Taking his night-vision glasses from a pouch attached to the small of his back by a Velcro strip, Kane slipped them on his face. The specially treated lenses allowed him to see clearly in deep shadow for approximately ten feet, as long as there was some kind of light source.

They encountered the corpse of a man with one of the short arrows piercing the back of his neck. Domi carefully worked the shaft free, not concerned about its toxicity because of the shadowsuit's gloves. She turned him over and saw a dark young man, his malnourished face locked in a death rictus.

The two of them went farther up the slope. When they reached the wall of shrubbery, Kane carefully eased himself through a ragged opening. His nostrils recoiled from the faint coppery tang of fresh blood and the whiff of a perforated bowel.

A pair of corpses floated in widening puddles of blood that continued to flow from torsos riddled with bullets. They were small men, with ropey muscles and spindly limbs. Both of them were attired identically in simple uniforms consisting of bright red sleeveless jerkins, shorts and black turbans. Small wooden bows lay near their lifeless hands.

"They're not going to be reporting back to anybody tonight," Domi observed sagely.

Going back to Ramja, Kane grasped the corpse by the wrists and dragged him a few yards away into a clump of shrubbery, so at the very least he would be out of the girl's field of vision. He briefly considered trying to dig a shallow grave, but he wasn't sure if burial was the custom of disposing of bodies in Assam.

Domi and Kane returned to Lakesh and the girl. "Did you ever get her name?" Kane inquired.

Lakesh nodded. "It's Madi."

"Ask Madi if it's safe enough to make camp here for the night."

Lakesh translated the question. Madi frowned in confusion and Lakesh repeated it, using a few different words. This time the girl nodded and replied. "She thinks so," Lakesh stated. "She says not even the Nagas are crazy enough to come downriver into the jungle after dark."

"Good," Domi said. "Let's get some food into her. She looks half-starved."

"She is," Lakesh confirmed. "One of the reasons she and her companion were coming to the shrine was in the hopes of finding food here."

Kane gestured toward the upright structure. "Lakesh, check over the interphaser and recalibrate it if necessary."

Lakesh's shoulders stiffened at Kane's peremptory tone, but he rose and walked over to the narrow building. The interphaser rested on the floor at the feet of the Shiva statue, and he couldn't help but wonder if its placement was significant.

Dropping to one knee beside the little metal pyramid, he pressed a seam on its smooth surface. A flat keypad popped out from its base. As he tapped in a numerical sequence, he announced, "Recalibration doesn't seem necessary. The Parallax Point program is still locked in with this particular vortex node."

Domi smiled wanly. "Whatever that means."

"It means," Kane interjected, "that we'll be able to phase out of here when we want." He paused and added, "Right?"

Lakesh chuckled. "Right, friend Kane."

The interphaser was more than a miniaturized version of a gateway unit, even though it employed much of the same hardware and operating principles. The mat-trans gateways functioned by tapping into the quantum stream, the invisible pathways that crisscrossed outside of perceived physical space and terminated in wormholes.

The interphaser interacted with the energy within a naturally occurring vortex and caused a temporary overlapping of two dimensions. The vortex then became an intersection point, a discontinuous quantum jump, beyond relativistic space-time.

According to Lakesh, evidence indicated there were many vortex nodes, centers of intense energy, located in the same proximity on each of the planets of the solar system, and those points correlated to vortex centers on Earth. The power points of the planet, places that naturally generated specific types of energy, possessed both positive and projective frequencies, and others were negative and receptive. He referred to the positive energy as *prana,* which was old Sanskrit term, meaning "the world soul."

Lakesh was sure some ancient peoples were aware of these symmetrical geo-energies and constructed monuments over the vortex points in order to manipulate them. He suspected the knowledge was suppressed over the centuries. Kane had no reason to doubt the suppression of such knowledge, even if he was skeptical of everything else.

Apparently, the knowledge had been rediscovered by the technicians laboring for Operation Chronos. A few months earlier, inside the Thunder Isle facility, they had discovered a special encoded program called Parallax Points. Brigid and Lakesh made several visits to the facility, salvaging what could be salvaged. Most of the machinery was damaged beyond any reasonable expectation of repair, but the data pertaining to the so-called Parallax Points was retrieved and put to use including the black, protective garments Kane had named shadowsuits.

After weeks of study, they learned that the Parallax Points program was actually a map, a geodetic index of all the naturally occurring vortex points on the planet. That discovery spurred Lakesh to build the second version of a device he referred to as an interphaser, or to be technically precise, a quantum interphase matter-transmission inducer.

Decrypting the Parallax Points program was laborious and time-consuming, and each newly discovered set of coordinates was fed into the interphaser's targeting computer.

Kane, Grant and Brigid had endured weeks of hard training in the use of the interphaser on short hops, selecting vortex points near the redoubt—or at least, near in the sense that if they couldn't make the return trip through a quantum channel they could conceivably walk back to the installation. So far, the interphaser hadn't materialized them either in a lake or an ocean or underground, a possibility that Kane privately feared. He knew an analog computer was built into the interphaser, which automatically selected a vortex point above solid ground.

Due to the wide usage of the interphaser, which wasn't bound by the limitations of the mat-trans units, the Cerberus redoubt reverted to its original purpose for the first time in two centuries—not a sanctuary for exiles or the headquarters of a resistance movement against the tyranny of the barons, but a facility dedicated to fathoming the eternal mysteries of space and time.

One of the vortex nodes downloaded from the Parallax Points program happened to be within the shrine to Shiva, in the Goalpara province of Assam. This in itself wasn't unusual, since many holy sites were constructed above naturally occurring vortices. Most temples and places of worship in the ancient world were built on intersection points of geomagnetic energy.

As Lakesh completed his check of the interphaser, Kane pawed through his backpack, examining the labels on the MREs. He found one marked Rice Pilaf and under Madi's mystified gaze, he opened it and mimed eating the contents. Then he handed it to her.

The girl sniffed it tentatively and after a moment's

hesitation, placed a delicate pinch of the food in her mouth, as if she were doing so only to be polite. She chewed slowly, her eyes narrowed with concentration. Then suddenly, her eyes widened and her face lit up in a wide smile. She began stuffing the food into her mouth with her fingers.

Domi laughed. "I think she likes it. I guess the kid ain't eaten since her last meal."

Kane grunted, eyeing the girl's stick-thin limbs and sunken, dark-ringed eyes, her belly swollen with malnutrition. "Which was a long damn time ago."

Lakesh sat down across from Madi, but said nothing. He felt a cold sickness surging in his belly. He remembered from his youth how the poverty-stricken in outlying areas of Kashmir treated females from poor families. He knew Madi would spend her young life in sexual servitude either among the stronger of her people, or for sale to anyone who could afford her. Once she was worn out or lost her appeal, she would be cast out to survive on her own or die.

As Madi blunted the sharpest edge of her hunger, Lakesh drew a story from her in start-and-stop spurts. It wasn't an inspiring tale, nor had he expected it to be.

Her people had lived in the Goalpara province near the banks of the Brahmaputra river region for many, many generations. Their settlement was located on high ground and they drew sustenance from groves of mango and plantain trees. They also grew rice and fished the river. It might not have been a rich life, but it wasn't as hard as it could have been.

Unfortunately, her people lived in a state of perpetual hostility with the Naga tribe, who dwelt primarily in the hills. Although the struggle for survival in the harsh realm was often desperate, the Nagas and her village observed semicivilized rules of warfare.

After Lakesh translated that bit of information, he added approvingly, ''The Nagas were very formidable warriors. They helped resist Japanese encroachment during the Second World War.''

As Madi continued, she described the situation between her village and the Nagas as essentially antagonistic, but during infrequent engagements, no massacres were conducted by either faction, nor were captives enslaved. Their chief, a man named Avanisa, who enjoyed a reputation of being tough but not a monster, was rumored to have embraced a philosophy known as the Nirodha. The general consensus was that Avanisa was so enthralled by the Nirodha movement that he no longer had any interest in earthly matters. Then the situation changed.

Almost within the time period of a single day and a night, a plague struck—not just Madi's village, but the surrounding region, as well. A devastating plant blight had consumed the area only a short time before, information the travelers from Cerberus had already deduced before embarking on their hyperdimensional journey. Satellite pictures showed miles-long bands of brown and dead vegetation.

The pattern of plant death was strangely geometric, the areas cut in cleanly, with sharply defined boundaries and parameters. The implications were disastrous. If Sam—or Thrush—could contaminate the soil and plants of the world whenever and wherever he wanted, he could conceivably starve humanity into submission, threatening to overwhelm entire countries with seas of plague. He would promise food or the antidote only if his demands were met.

And of course, Sam would keep an ace-on-the line to play—certain lands and even nations would continue to be productive and provide food for his followers—followers who swelled in ever growing numbers as their stomachs shrank. The imperator could simply bide his time until famine and riots held sway, slowly turning the knife in the bellies of the starving masses.

According to Madi, over the next few weeks signs of Naga activity all but disappeared, and her fellow villagers began to suspect they had perished or migrated. Then one dawn, the Nagas surrounded their settlement and they were armed not with bows and arrows, but with guns.

Chief Avanisa announced they were now subjects of the Scorpia Prime. The young men of the village would be indoctrinated into the way of the Nirodha, and the girls would eventually be initiated into the Shakti sisterhood.

Those too young, too old or too infirm were fitted for the slave collars. Those simply too uncooperative were killed on the spot—more than twenty of Madi's people were shot dead, including her mother, younger brother and two uncles.

The survivors were marched downriver to the ancient site of the Shakti temple, which had lain largely forgotten and overgrown by vines for many, many centuries. They were put to work rebuilding the temple and if the work was hard and unrelenting, they at least were given food—enough to keep them alive, at any rate.

Domi shook her head in disgust. "Same old story, no matter where we go. The strong enslaving the weak…and the weak enslaving the weaker."

Kane opened his mouth to speak, then a cold prickling crawled over his flesh. The jungle had fallen silent with a startling and ominous swiftness. There were no chirps of insects, no birdcalls, no rustle of foliage. Suddenly, there was no sound at all, as if the jungle itself held its breath and watched them with unseen eyes.

Domi, with her half-feral, wilderness-honed senses experienced the same shuddery sensation, and her hand tightened around the checkered walnut grip of her pistol.

With a swish of palm fronds and a crackle of shrubs, a king cobra slithered out of the shadows, long, powerful coils disappearing into the murk. In the panic-stricken half second Kane gaped at it, he realized he had no idea of the serpent's length—but the hood flaring on either side of its wedge-shaped head was over a foot across.

The forked tongue flicked out from its scale-coated snout, testing the air. The hue of the cobra's scales was splotchy, mostly dark greens with a dash of leaden gray thrown in. A thick blue circle collared its neck.

Madi stared and cried out happily, "Vasuki!"

Chapter 19

Grant surveyed the heap of stone rising before him. Evidently, the massive slabs and chunks of rock had once been the upper floors of a multilevel complex. Sheared-away reinforcing rods jutted out of the edges of some pieces like rusty, skeletal fingers. Two centuries of hell weather had scoured the rock mercilessly, rounding the jagged edges, smoothing the corners, filling in cracks with grit. Scraggly thorn brush hung by tenacious roots over the rockfall.

As Brigid and Sindri stepped up beside him, a burst of static filled his head, and then he heard Philboyd's voice echoing inside his ears.

"Testing," Philboyd intoned. "One-two-three. Testing."

"Got you," Grant said softly. "Calibrate the audio pickup for Brigid, too."

Brigid tapped her right ear. "My Commtact is calibrated. Reading you, Brewster."

The Commtacts fit tightly against the mastoid bones behind their right ears. Implanted steel pintels embedded in the bones slid through the flesh and into tiny input ports in the small curves of metal. The Commtacts had been found recently in Redoubt Yankee, and Philboyd had described them as state-of-the-art multiple-channel communication devices.

Their sensor circuitry incorporated an analog-to-digital voice encoder that was subcutaneously embedded in the mastoid bone. The pintels connected to input ports in the comms themselves. Once they made contact, transmissions were picked up by the auditory canals and the dermal sensors transmitted the electronic signals directly through the cranial casing. Even if someone went deaf, as long as they wore a Commtact, they would still have a form of hearing.

The Commtacts were still being field-tested, since in order to make them operational, surgery was required and few people wanted to make that sacrifice. But the surgery to implant the sensors was very minor, with only a small incision behind the ear to slide them under the skin.

The Commtact's five-mile range was superior to the handheld trans-comms. The range of the radiophones was generally limited to a mile, but in open country, in clear weather, contact could be established at two miles.

"I only see two people at the top of the heap," Philboyd said from the cockpit of the TAV he had piloted from the Bitterroot Range, with Brigid sitting on his lap.

"That's all we expected in the way of a welcoming committee," Grant replied.

"Yeah, but there's a door or something up there, too. It's half-open. Nice place for an ambush."

"That's why you're staying put," Brigid told him. "To cover us with the missiles."

"That sort of fits the definition of overkill, doesn't it?" Philboyd inquired uneasily.

"If a situation arises that forces you to launch the damn things," Grant retorted testily, "it won't be."

Sindri inhaled and the acrid air seared his throat. It took a great effort not to succumb to a coughing fit. When he recovered, he asked Grant very quietly, "You sure it's a good idea to go up there unarmed?"

Grant shook his head, "I don't know what's a good idea nowadays. But we won't get any cooperation from the fused-out little bastard at gunpoint."

He glanced back at the Manta ships, repressing the urge to touch his nose with his index finger and snap it away in the "one percent" salute. It was a private gesture he and Kane had developed during their Mag days and reserved for undertakings with a small ratio of success. But Brewster Philboyd, not Kane, sat in the cockpit of the TAV and covered him with its weapons.

Brewster Philboyd was an accomplished pilot of the transatmospheric craft found on the Manitius Base. Of Annunaki manufacture, they were in pristine condition, despite their great age. Powered by two different kinds of engines, a ramjet and solid-fuel pulse detonation air spikes, the Manta ships could fly in both a vacuum and in an atmosphere.

Looking down at the base of the slope, Grant gazed at a heap of slag, metal that had turned molten, then hardened again. It had no identifiable configurations, but he knew the slag had once been a Mag-issue Sandcat. Sooty steel fragments lay scattered around it. A looping crescent-shaped scorch mark had fused the ground to black glass, and it intersected with the heap of metal.

Spread out over the boulders at the foot of the slope, he saw a splattering of obsidian gel. By staring hard, he was just able to discern what might have been a forearm and hand, now glued to the bulwark of stone.

Grant glared down at Sindri. ''Do you get a thrill seeing your handiwork from the last time you were here?''

Sindri shrugged, but said nothing. He knew Grant was making a very unsubtle reference to the time, well over a year before, when he had briefly occupied Redoubt Papa and experimented with a molecular destabilizer brought down from the *Parallax Red* space station. The subjects of the experiment were Magistrates and a Sandcat dispatched from Sharpeville.

Grant began clambering up the face of the rockfall, Brigid and Sindri following closely behind. The climb wasn't particularly rugged because the heaps of fallen rock and concrete formed a crude stairway.

When he reached the top, he saw what Philboyd had described, a half-open sec door within the recessed double frame beneath a shelf of granite. He also saw the bizarre figures of Baron Sharpe and Crawler, both of them beaming at him as if he were a long-lost friend. Grant didn't need to see the blasterman to know he was there. Although he had never boasted of possessing a point man's sense like Kane, he knew a baron would never expose himself to the possibility of assassination or abduction without taking protective measures.

From his prior experience with Baron Sharpe and

his high councillor, Grant also knew the doomie was a far more reliable barometer of intentions than the characteristic baronial paranoia.

Sharpe's cold blue eyes flicked up and down Brigid's lissome form, the contours hugged tightly by the shadowsuit. "Fashionable outfit, Miss Baptiste."

"Thanks," she replied straight-faced. "Yours, too."

Sharpe looked levelly at Grant and gestured to the TAVs. "Where'd you get the flying toys?"

"Maybe I'll tell you later," Grant rumbled. "We'll see how this parley goes first."

Baron Sharpe focused his fatuously smiling attention on Sindri. "And who might you be, my dear little fellow?"

Sindri scowled first at Sharpe, then at Crawler and finally swung an angry gaze up to Brigid. "Is this affected punk for real?"

"As far as the baronial hierarchy is concerned," Brigid said, voice purring with barely repressed amusement, "he's fairly unique."

"'Unique' wouldn't be the word I'd choose," Sindri muttered peevishly. "But since you asked, Lord Baron, my name might be Sindri."

Sharpe laughed in genuine merriment. "Fabulous name. And you're as cute as a bug, too."

He reached out to tousle Sindri's hair, but the little man slapped his hand away. "Fuck off, freak."

"Look who's talking," Crawler sneered.

Sindri bared his teeth and tensed his body as if he intended to kick the doomie in the mouth. Grant stepped forward, announcing gruffly, "That's enough.'' He eyed the partially open sec door and the gloom beyond it. ''Sharpe, if you have some blaster-men in there, tell them to stand down. We're here to help you.''

Sharpe regarded Grant with an expression of in-genuous surprise. ''Help me? Correct me if I'm wrong, but the last time we saw each other, weren't you shooting at me?''

''Only because your Magistrates were shooting at us.'' Brigid's reply was calm and matter-of-fact, free of rancor or accusation.

The baron bowed his head graciously. ''That's very true. But you'll understand if I'm reluctant to make myself completely vulnerable to you, human nature being what it is.''

Grant nodded. ''Not to mention the tendency to-ward baronial treachery being what it is.''

''You know us so well.''

''Keep in mind,'' Brigid stated darkly, ''that we have a friend in one of our flying toys, and he has missiles aimed right at us.''

Sharpe squinted toward the grounded Mantas, then glanced down at Crawler. ''Give me a read.''

Crawler's eyes widened, his lips peeling back from discolored teeth. He shivered, moaned softly, clutched at his brow. Both Grant and Brigid had witnessed the mutie's performance before, as if invisible antennae sprouted from his psyche and quested for answers to the baron's question. At one time Grant would have thought it was a sham, but a very good piece of im-provised theater on the part of the doom-sniffer. But now, as before, he felt a wispy touch against the surface of his mind, like a gritty texture against a softer one.

Crawler focused his eyes next on Brigid. She stiffened, drawing in her breath sharply. Blinking his eyes rapidly, the doomseer stared around as if he expected to see some place other than the exterior of Redoubt Papa. Sindri shuddered and sidled away from Crawler, taking up position beside Brigid. In a flat, uninflected voice, he declared, "They speak the truth. One wrong move on our part and boom—that's us all over."

"One bona fide established," Sharpe said with a rueful smile. "On to the others. Why are we here, why does this moment exist? What do you have to tell me of such extreme importance that you risk your lives to do so?"

Pulling in a deep breath and then pushing out slowly, Brigid stated, "You might find it rather unbelievable, but Crawler can attest to our veracity. Baron Cobalt is not dead. Right at this moment, he's off somewhere building an army so he can wage war against the imperator and his allies. He intends to reclaim Area 51."

Baron Sharpe's high, smooth forehead acquired a horizontal line of consternation. "I was never convinced that brother Cobalt had perished during the siege of his ville. Since the most important thing in his life was his life, he would safeguard it above any and all considerations. Nor do I find it particularly improbable that he's attempting to regain his territories.

"However, no baron is willing to oppose the imperator. I've heard rumors that several have actually made plans to do so, but to date, no single one wants to step up and be the first to defy him...and therefore be held responsible for starting a civil war and breaking the new unity.''

Neither Grant nor Brigid was surprised to hear about the barons' growing discontent with their roles as Sam's viceroys, mere plenipotentiaries in their own territories. Quavell had essentially confirmed Sharpe's opinion.

''There's a difference now,'' Grant said grimly. ''Sam is the one who wants the civil war. He intends to finance it with Cobalt acting as his puppet general, his manufactured threat to unity. Sam will give Cobalt everything he needs to stage a war. Most likely he'll get the matériel from the Anthill.''

For the first time, Sharpe appeared shaken. The Anthill was built in the late twentieth century as the most ambitious of the Continuity of Government installations. COG was viewed as the ultimate insurance policy against an atomic attack and to this end, many subterranean command posts were constructed all over the country.

The Anthill was by far the most extensive, built inside of Mount Rushmore, using advanced digging and tunneling machines. By the time the machines had done their work, the layout of the complex resembled a vast ant colony. All of Mount Rushmore was honeycombed with interconnected levels, passageways, stores, theaters and even a small sports arena.

After the nukecaust and the Program of Unification,

the Anthill became not so much a forgotten installation but a feared installation. Many of the barons viewed it as both a threat and an untapped treasure trove. But inasmuch as all the villes were standardized, equally matched in terms of technology and firepower to maintain a perfect balance of power, none of the barons dared mention what unclaimed wonders lay within Mount Rushmore.

Even a word of wonder about it might be construed as evidence of ambition, a prelude to a territorial war. Inasmuch as such ambitions were strictly forbidden by the tenets of the Archon Directorate, the Anthill became a taboo subject, a no-baron's-land.

"After a few years," Grant continued, "the war will end. By then almost all of the baronial territories will have been destroyed. Then Cobalt will turn on the barons who supported him and join with the imperial forces. After that, Sam will easily win the war and execute all surviving barons."

A faint smile touched his lips beneath his mustache as he added, "Including you, I presume."

Sharpe was so stunned, he could only gape up at Grant for a long moment. Then his mouth twisted in a grimace. "How do you know this? How *could* you know this? As far as I know, none of you have precognitive powers."

Sindri stepped forward. "I told them all about it. Less than seventy-two hours ago, I came from the future whence all of this had come to pass. I've been to your future, Lord Baron. And it ain't pretty."

Nostrils flaring, Sharpe snorted rudely. "And how did you pull off that miracle, Pee-wee?"

Sindri bit off a profane comeback, casting his eyes toward Brigid. "Shall I tell him?"

"I think you should," she answered calmly.

Staring boldly into Baron Sharpe's face and with a challenging, insolent smile on his lips, he began to talk. He spoke for less than five minutes, and long before he was done, the baron's high-planed face had gone as stiff as if it were molded from enamel. By degrees, his eyes narrowed to slits.

When Sindri finished his tale, his mobile mouth still creased in a mocking smile, Baron Sharpe whirled on Crawler. His "Give me a read!" was a shrill plea of desperation. Crawler peered penetratingly at Sindri, who pretended not to notice.

After a few seconds, the crippled doomie sighed in frustration. "All I can tell you is that *he* believes what he's just told you."

"But what did you see?" the baron cried.

Crawler's voice lowered as he spoke hesitantly. "I saw flashes of red...of purple. I saw war...I saw horror...cities burning...monstrous, slouchy things I can't understand."

The doomseer squeezed his eyes shut, wincing as if in pain. "I can't tell you the difference between his perceptions and objective truth. However, I can suggest no reasonable alternative other than he did indeed speak the truth about his visit to the future, his exposure to the imperator's Great Plan and how he came to be here."

Sharpe chewed his lower lip, brow tightening in a deep frown. He examined Sindri closely. He didn't speak, and Brigid realized he was processing all that he had heard, extrapolating and weighing all of the implications. He opened his mouth and closed it. Then he exploded incredulously, ''The Great Plan?''

His eyes searched Grant's and Brigid's faces, almost as if he were seeking a clue that they were only seconds away from bursting out laughing, congratulating themselves on the elaborate practical joke they'd successfully pulled off.

Grant crossed his arms over his thick chest. ''That's apparently what Sam calls it. The plan to eventually control all of humanity. Both new and old human are in the same boat—marked to be ruled or destroyed.''

Baron Sharpe's eyes clouded over with the intensity of his emotion. In a distracted half whisper, he said, ''Academically, I can see a certain logic to it. If the control mechanisms are installed at key points throughout history, then the nukecaust will not be necessary.''

Quietly, Brigid said, ''I know we've dropped a lot on you. Some of our claims are very wild and impossible to prove. The final decision as to whether we're right or wrong is up to you.''

Baron Sharpe blinked, then his eyes frosted hard. ''What do you expect me to do?''

''Spread the word to all of the other barons,'' Brigid answered. ''Maybe the fact that you now know Sam's ultimate objective might be sufficient to alter the timeline. Form a consortium of barons and pool your resources to occupy Area 51. Do whatever you have to do to fight the future, to keep the imperator's adaptive Earth from coming to pass.''

Sharpe cocked his head, regarding all three people intently. "And what of you?"

"We have our own fronts to fight on," Grant responded brusquely.

"I see." The baron fell silent, pondering, lips pursed thoughtfully. A titter broke his silence. "I'll say one thing...you apelings never fail to surprise me."

He drew a deep breath. "My world is on the brink of ending, yet we, the Homo superior, must rely yet again on the ape-kin to maintain it."

Impatiently, Grant snapped, "It's ever been thus, hasn't it? Have you heard enough, Sharpe?"

The baron glanced down at Crawler. "Have we?"

The doomie smiled wryly. "To a point we have. However, we might be able to hear even more. The mind of that one—" he nodded toward Sindri "—is very remarkable. It contains visions of the kind I have never before encountered. I think it would be a shame if we were not able to tap into them."

Sindri's spine stiffened. "What do you mean by that?"

"He means," Sharpe answered smoothly, "that in order to show your good faith, you should have no objection to coming with us and accepting the hospitality of my barony."

Crawler bobbed his head enthusiastically. "Capital idea."

Grant knotted his hands into fists. His jaw muscles bunched. "I don't think much of it."

Baron Sharpe angled a haughty brow arch at him.

"And I don't think your opinion means much at all. *Grady!*"

Before the echoes of the cry had even begun to fade, a man armored in Magistrate black swiftly stepped out from underneath the sec door. He trained his Sin Eater on Grant.

"See?" Sharpe inquired mildly.

"We see," replied Brigid. "But do you see the aircraft out there with its missile pods aimed directly at us?"

Philboyd's voice echoed within her head. "I don't think he'll buy your bluff."

Sharpe shrugged dismissively. "Of course I do, Miss Baptiste. But as you should recall, I don't fear death. I can't die, as your friend Mr. Kane learned."

"If he had meant to kill you," Grant growled, "he would have."

Baron Sharpe chuckled derisively. "I have no intention of wasting any more of my time arguing with you, Mr. Grant. This Sindri fellow will accompany me, Crawler and Commander Grady back through the mat-trans unit to my ville. He will be of enormous help to me in drafting a great plan of my own."

Grant gazed blandly at Sindri, then lunged for him. With almost supernatural speed, Sindri sidestepped, ducking under Grant's arm and taking up a position behind Grady. Staring at him in astonishment, Grant snarled, "You *want* to go with him?"

Peering around the Mag's polycarbonate-encased hip, Sindri retorted, "Frankly, I think it's a capital idea myself."

Sharpe raised his hands palms outward. "There you are."

Angrily, Brigid spit, "Sindri only wants to go so he can use you, Baron!"

"By a pleasant coincidence, that's pretty much why I want him to go with me." Sharpe favored Sindri with a speculative stare. "A mutually beneficial situation, wouldn't you agree?"

"I would," Sindri replied smugly.

"You can't trust him, Sindri," Grant gritted through clenched teeth.

Sindri laughed loudly, contemptuously. "But I can trust you? What did you intend to do with me after this crisis passed? Let me go on my way?" He shook his head in disgust. "Please."

"We wouldn't have harmed you," Brigid countered hotly.

"Perhaps not," retorted Sindri. "More than likely you would have kept me as a permanent prisoner. At best you would've tried to return me to Mars, but in such a manner so I could never return to Earth."

Sharpe shot him a startled glance. "Mars?" he repeated skeptically.

No one responded to Sharpe's inquiry. "At least you'd be alive," Grant argued. "With the baron here, you'll never know where you stand. He could tire of you tomorrow and have you sent to Area 51 so your liver could be pureed and added to a chem bath."

"At least we're the devils you know," interjected Brigid.

Sindri shrugged. "'He casteth out devils through the prince of the devils.'"

Sharpe frowned at Sindri. "I don't quite know what you meant by that, but I have the distinct impression I've been insulted. Still, on that note—"

Baron Sharpe swung his right arm out from the shoulder in a fringe-whirling circle, then stabbed a finger directly at the redoubt's entrance. "Let's take care of business."

Sharpe, Sindri and Crawler stepped toward the opening. Grady maintained a steady aim on Grant, the bore of his pistol trained directly at the center of his chest. Before they walked underneath the sec door, Baron Sharpe paused long enough to say, "Regardless of how this meeting turned out, I thank you for the warning about the imperator's plot. I promise to do what I can to insure it never comes to pass."

Sindri put in cheerfully, "And that's what this whole long, strange trip has been about, right?"

Grady followed them into the dark maw of the redoubt and within seconds the heavy vanadium-alloy portal descended, sealing the installation with a thud and a crunch of gravel.

Philboyd's voice floated into his ears. "If you want, we can try to blast the thing open with the Manta's rockets."

Grant didn't react to the suggestion. He closed his eyes the way a man in pain did. Lines deepened around his eyes and mouth and his jaw muscles worked. He gusted out, "*Zurui chibi*...sneaky dwarf. I should've taken that literally."

Opening his eyes and turning to face the TAVs, Grant said, "Never mind, Brewster. Prep your ship for takeoff."

Brigid forced a resigned smile to her lips. "Sindri was right about one thing, you know. We hadn't discussed what to do with him. You know Kane wouldn't have agreed to simply setting him free."

Grant nodded absently. "I suppose so. We've done all we can do here. Let's go."

Climbing down the tumbles of rock was no more strenuous than climbing up them. As they strode toward the Mantas, Brigid asked, "So it's a straight shot now to Assam?"

"For me it is, yeah. You're going back to Cerberus with Brewster. Monitor the ELINT signals that come in from the villes, so you can get an idea of Baron Cobalt's movements—if there are any."

Brigid was too shocked to say or do anything except to continue walking beside him. Her thought processes seemed numb. Finally, almost too stunned to formulate words, she forced herself to husk out, "I'm not going with you?"

"No, you're not." Grant's tone brooked no debate as he continued walking.

Brigid grabbed him by the arm and pulled him to a halt. "Why?"

With an expression as impassive as if it were carved from teak, Grant turned to face her. "The same reason Shizuka isn't going."

Brigid blinked at him incredulously. Her senses stumbled. "I don't understand."

Flatly, in a voice that was edged with fear, Grant declared, "Kane and I discussed this before we left. We're doing it this way to further knock the timeline out of true, to put more obstacles in the way of Sam's Great Plan.''

"What's that got to do with sidelining Shizuka and me?'' Brigid demanded.

Grant gestured with both hands. "It's got everything to do with it. We have to change things in the here and now, and that means we shouldn't undertake actions that mirror those in the future.''

With sudden clarity, Brigid exclaimed, "Four plus years from now, both Shizuka and myself are killed in Assam. So you and Kane figure if we don't go near the place, you'll doubly insure that aspect of the future never happens. You're trying to create a probability wave dysfunction.''

Grant shook his head gloomily. "To be honest, we don't really know what the hell to think or what to do. We're just guessing. But we know it makes sense to minimize the risk to you and Shizuka as much as possible.''

Brigid regained some of her composure although her mind still raced. She realized Kane was driven to protect her through any means possible, and her initial reaction was anger and resentment.

"I see,'' she whispered as she felt the familiar ache fill her whenever she thought of Kane. Questions always surrounded their relationship, and knowing they were to be married a few years in the future did little to reveal much to her.

Yet, if the shared memory they'd experienced during a bad mat-trans jump to Russia was correct, they had been together before. A sick knot twisted through Brigid's stomach. The memory hadn't had a good ending, and there'd been no guarantee how together they'd been. Even Morrigan had told them they'd been together and separated a number of times in past lives.

Grant levered his body atop his Manta's wing. "I hope you won't argue with me about this, Brigid—or do something like fly back to Cerberus to pick up Shizuka and then meet us in Assam."

"No." Brigid's tone was studiedly casual. "This is an unprecedented set of circumstances, dealing as we are with temporal fault and fracture lines. We might be able to repair one breach, but then another crack could open up—and it might be the one that swallows me, Shizuka and everyone else."

Grant dropped into the cockpit and strapped himself into the pilot's seat. "Try to explain it that way to Shizuka, will you?" He grinned sheepishly. "I'm afraid she thinks I'm coming back for her."

Brigid nodded. "I understand. I'll do what I can so she will, too."

Philboyd pushed himself up from the cockpit of the second TAV and called, "I know you've got the GPS correlated with the Parallax Point so your navigational computer will home in on Assam—but you could probably use more help over there."

Grant's teeth flashed in a broader grin. "Thanks, Brewster...but I won't know until I get there and by then it might be too late to holler help."

Looking down at Brigid, Grant said, almost gratefully, "Thanks for understanding. Kane didn't think you would."

Brigid smiled lopsidedly. "Kane is the predictable one, not me."

In actuality, neither person was predictable. Both Kane and Brigid had their individual gifts. Most of what was important to people in the postnuke world came easily to Kane—survival skills, prevailing in the face of adversity and cunning against enemies. But he could also be reckless, high-strung to the point of instability and given to fits of rage.

Brigid, on the other hand, was structured and ordered, with a brilliant analytical mind. However, her clinical nature, the cool scientific detachment upon which she prided herself, sometimes blocked an understanding of the obvious human factor in any given situation.

Regardless of their contrasting personalities, Kane and Brigid worked very well as a team, playing on each other's strengths rather than contributing to their individual weaknesses. It had taken her several months to grudgingly admit she learned a great deal from Kane, from her association with Grant and Domi.

She had learned to accept risk as a part of her way of life, taking chances so that others might find the ground beneath their feet a little more secure. She didn't consider her attitude idealism but simple pragmatism. If she had learned anything from her friends, it was to regard death as a part of the challenge of existence, a fact that every man and woman had to face eventually.

But the questions surrounding her and Kane's relationship still remained mysteries. It was possible they already knew the answers and feared to face them, not wanting to draw any closer than they already were in order to fulfill whatever grand scheme they were supposed to fulfill.

All the supposing made Brigid's head hurt. It was also possible that she and Kane just found each other to be too much of a pain in the ass. That put a damper on love and sex, whichever it was they felt for each other.

Grant pulled a bronze-colored helmet down over his head and slid shut the cockpit canopy. It sealed almost instantly with a faint pop, indicating the interior was now airtight.

Brigid backed away as, with a droning whine, the Manta slowly rose, a small and brief blizzard of dust swirling beneath it. The landing gear retracted automatically into the TAV's underbelly.

The ship's ascent halted at one hundred feet and Grant waggled its wings in a farewell. Then the pulse detonation wave engines engaged and the Manta hurtled across the sky like an arrow flying from a bow. The sonic boom sounded like a thunderclap over Washington Hole.

Brigid watched until Grant's TAV was a barely discernible speck in the sky. Then she turned toward her own Manta, telling herself repeatedly that the cold, leaden weight settling in the pit of her stomach was only due to tension, not a prescient warning of death.

Chapter 20

The cobra rose from the jungle floor in a beautifully graceful vertical glide. The forked tongue darted from its mouth as it rose at least four feet from the ground. Assuming a posture like an L, the serpent swayed slightly, its eyes gleaming like gemstones.

Kane took a hasty aim with his pistol, aware that Domi had leveled her own semiautomatic. Madi suddenly swatted out with both arms, slapping at their weapons. She yammered in a shrill, rapid-fire rhythm, her tone urgent, almost outraged.

Domi and Kane held their fire but very reluctantly. "What's she saying?" Kane asked, his voice pitched low to disguise the tremor of fear in it.

Lakesh pursed his lips in concentration. "I'm trying to figure it out, but it's evident she doesn't want you to shoot the snake."

Kane kept his eyes on the cobra's hypnotically swaying head, feeling his nape hairs tingle. His loathing of serpents wasn't pathological or due to any kind of inborn phobia, but drawn from a recent series of unpleasant experiences.

First there had been his encounter with Lord Strongbow and his mutagenically altered Imperial Dragoons, with their scale-ringed, snakish eyes and reptilian odor. Then there was his terrifying battle with a gigantic constrictor atop a ziggurat in South America, one the natives had decked out in a feathered headdress and christened Kukulkan, in homage to the ancient Mayan god. That incident was followed only a short time later by walking a gauntlet of diamondbacks in California. His fear of things reptilian was reinforced a few months before during his nightmarish bareback ride on a tyrannosaur he had christened Monstrodamus through the jungle of Thunder Isle.

Of course Domi had been present during almost all of those incidents, as well, but she didn't seem particularly upset by the appearance of the cobra, despite its huge size. She was revolted more by bugs than by reptiles.

In a voice tinged with frustration, Lakesh said, "Madi is chattering something about the cobra being a friend, sent by Shiva—"

He broke off, forehead creasing thoughtfully. "I think I understand now."

"Well, let us in on it," Kane bit out, the cobra's bobbing head still framed within his Sin Eater's sights.

"Mythology," Lakesh stated flatly. "During the time of creation, some minor deities used the giant cobra Vasuki as a rope to churn milk. Torrents of venom flowed from the fangs of the suffering snake. The poison grew into a river and threatened to destroy all creation. Shiva came along, freed Vasuki and drank up the poison. It burned his throat and made it permanently blue."

He nodded toward the serpent, saying, "As you can

see, the scales on the creature's throat are blue. Apparently, Madi thinks that has marked it as a special cobra, a servant of Shiva.''

Domi smiled wryly. "And what does she think old Blue Neck doing here? Checking up on us?''

Lakesh put the question to Madi, who responded with a relieved laugh. "Yes,'' Lakesh translated. "That's exactly what the cobra is doing. After all, we're at a shrine of Shiva, and it served as a doorway for his warriors to step through and end the tyranny of the Scorpia Prime.''

"Warriors?'' Domi repeated dubiously. "What warriors—oh, she means us, right?''

Lakesh nodded. "Right.''

Madi spoke again, this time directing her comments to the cobra. Her voice was soft, reverential and she steepled her fingers, touching the tips to her forehead. The serpent stopped swaying and gazed directly at the girl. Despite knowing that snakes lacked conventional organs of hearing, Kane was almost positive the cobra listened to her. He discarded the notion as ridiculous, then reconsidered when the huge cobra majestically turned on its sinuous coils and disappeared into the undergrowth.

"Apparently, the snake believes Madi that we're friends,'' Lakesh announced.

Kane exhaled his pent-up breath in a profanity-seasoned sigh and lowered his pistol. "Friend or not, I can't say I'm sorry to see the damn thing go.''

"According to legend,'' Lakesh said conversationally, "many animals are associated with Shiva. He is generally represented as wearing no clothes, except a tiger skin wrapped around his waist and hips, and snakes coiled around his arms and neck. These animals act as his eyes and ears, and they make sure no sacrilege is committed against his temples or shrines.''

''Will Shiva send animals to help us?'' Domi couched the question to sound almost playful, but Kane detected the sincere note underscoring her words. Raised in the Outlands, Domi was steeped in superstitions and folklore, and sensitive to omens.

When Lakesh interpreted Domi's question, Madi shook her head gravely and responded very quietly. ''She's afraid not,'' Lakesh said. ''But Shiva will not hinder us, either, since the Scorpia Prime is defiling the name of the great Mother Goddess, Shakti.''

''With the Tantric sex rites performed at the temple?'' Kane inquired.

''Actually,'' Lakesh said, ''not in themselves. Madi knows about sex, since she's close to conception age. And Shiva is the god of regenerative functions and of sexual powers, after all. No, what she finds objectionable on the part of both Shiva and Shakti, is that the mystery and ceremony surrounding the Tantric practices at the temple are being used to lure people to do evil. A reverence to the eternal principle of female sexuality, an aspect of the Mother Goddess Devi, the wife of Shiva, is an accepted part of her culture, and the Nirodha are distorting it.''

Kane shrugged. ''Frankly, I don't find the Shakti cult any worse than some religions Grant and I ran across in the Outlands when we were Mags.''

Lakesh nodded in silent agreement, realizing to

what he was referring. Following skydark, a few old, ugly Judeo-Christian and fundamentalist Islamic cults were revived. Their tenets were that women were little more than cattle, created solely for man's benefit and they were inherently wicked creatures whose sensual natures had to be subjugated and suppressed, even if that meant murdering them.

"At any rate," Lakesh went on, "the Nirodha, the followers of the Scorpia Prime, have a false god—or goddess in this instance. They have no courage and no honor. Or so Madi claims."

"Madi has made a lot of claims so far," Kane remarked dourly. "I don't know how many of them are reliable, though."

Domi threw him a slit-eyed stare. "What reason would she have to lie to us?"

Kane shook his head, deciding not to make further comments about the girl and her beliefs. Madi was their only source of intel, and they couldn't afford to alienate her.

"Will she guide us to the temple of Shakti?" Domi asked.

Lakesh put the question to her, but the girl only mumbled and seemed reluctant to commit.

"She's afraid of being enslaved again." Lakesh tapped his neck and pointed to the leather collar around her neck. "And I can't say I blame her."

Domi hissed in anger between her teeth and drew the knife sheathed at her leg. She knee-walked over to Madi, reaching out for her. Whimpering in sudden fear, the girl cringed from her touch and the knife, but subsided after Lakesh spoke a few words to her.

The razored point of the knife easily sliced through the leather binding Madi's neck without touching the skin beneath. Domi hadn't been so careful when she used the knife to cut Guana Teague's throat. The former Pit boss of Cobaltville, Teague had found Domi in the Outlands and smuggled her into the Pits with a forged ID chip.

In exchange, she gave him six months of sexual service. When seven months passed without his releasing her from their agreement, she terminated the contract by cutting his throat—and saved Grant's life in the process.

Domi spit on the collar and flung it contemptuously away into the shadows, a melodramatic gesture not lost on Madi. Rubbing her neck, the girl smiled gratefully at Domi. The albino smiled back, saying, "Tell her if she leads us to the temple of Shakti, we'll do the same with all collars around the necks of all her people."

Lakesh chuckled fondly. "I think she's made that connection, darlingest one."

Domi giggled and fell into Lakesh's arms. They embraced and kissed passionately, and Kane stopped short of sighing in exasperation.

Being privy to the relationship between Domi and Lakesh caused Kane a bit of discomfort. He felt a quiver of embarrassment mixed in with a little guilt. A few months ago during a mission to Utah, when he and Domi had shared a room, she made it clear she wouldn't be averse to sharing more than that with him. He had dashed cold water on her amorous advance by reminding her of her devotion to Grant. That had been the end of it and he'd never mentioned the incident to anyone, not to Brigid and certainly not to Grant.

Now he wondered if he should have. He remembered Domi's wild behavior when she believed Grant had rejected her love in favor of Shizuka. Without Grant as the mitigating influence, the authority figure, what little self-restraint the girl ever practiced was completely discarded. All her bottled-up passions were unleashed, but turned from love to violence. Her shame, her mad desire for vicarious revenge against Grant, had been released during the mission to Area 51 and set in motion a dramatic sequence of events, the fallout of which Cerberus was still dealing with.

Shaking his head to drive away the memories, Kane peeled back a Velcro-lined strap on his wrist and consulted his wrist chron. "If everything went according to plan in Washington Hole, Grant should be here no later than daybreak."

Lakesh gazed at him speculatively over the top of Domi's white-haired head. "Assuming Baron Sharpe attended the rendezvous at all. I still maintain he was a poor choice on which to hang the hopes of an imperator-free future."

"Other than Cobalt," Kane argued, "he's the only other baron any of us have met face-to-face. He may be fused-out, but he can still be counted on to react like a baron when his own best interests are threatened."

"Perhaps," Lakesh agreed dourly. "But we don't know the extent of Sam's influence over him."

"Funny," Kane said with icy sarcasm, "pretty much the same thing could be said about you."

Lakesh glared at him, his blue eyes suddenly glittering with anger. Kane met the glare with one of his own. He still hadn't grown accustomed to dealing with a robust—relatively speaking—Lakesh whose eyes weren't covered by thick lenses, whose voice no longer sounded like a reedy rasp and who didn't look like a hunched-over, spindly old man who appeared to have one foot in the grave.

Domi pushed herself away from Lakesh and snapped at Kane, "That's enough."

With her back to Lakesh, only Kane could see the meaningful lifting of her eyebrows, a silent plea for him to drop the topic. Kane nodded and Domi resheathed her knife with a flourish.

"You're quite right," Lakesh said. "We still have Madi to impress, her confidence to gain."

During the exchange between Lakesh and Kane, the girl's dark eyes had flicked nervously from one to the other. Kane forced a friendly, nonthreatening smile to his lips. "It's all right," he said, even though he knew she couldn't understand him. "Lakesh and I often interact like this."

"Yes, indeed," Lakesh drawled sardonically. "And more's the pity."

Kane couldn't help but agree that it was a pity, particularly when he remembered all the bitter disagreements he and the man had over tactics. In the past, most of the missions Lakesh concocted never dealt with head-on confrontations with the barons. Always they involved finding some way to strike cov-

ertly at the Archon Directorate, not at their plenipotentiaries who actually held the reins of power.

After Balam's revelation that the Directorate was
but a diversionary smoke screen created two centuries
earlier by corrupt government officials and military
men to mask their own ruthless ambitions, an entirely
new set of strategies had to be drafted.

The earlier tactics had been hampered by their own
belief they contended with a vast, omnipotent opponent, and by Kane's way of thinking they wasted a
lot of time and energy searching for ways to fight an
enemy that didn't exist.

But in retrospect he couldn't really blame Lakesh,
particularly in lieu of the fact he was the man who
came to the pivotal conclusion that the Directorate
was but a cunningly crafted illusion. Even so, he
seemed reluctant to accept the findings of his own
detective work, despite Balam's essentially confirming his suspicions. But little of it really mattered at
this point. Lakesh's self-assumed position as the final
authority in the redoubt was no longer absolute.

A smile tugged at the corners of Kane's mouth. It
wasn't as if he, Grant and Brigid had ever obeyed
him unquestioningly in the first place, but now any
proposals for action had to be agreed upon by a majority vote.

Kane knew the man bitterly resented this change in
procedure, but his plans had nearly gotten them all
killed—worse than killed—on a number of occasions,
often due to Lakesh's giving them just enough information to plunge them into serious trouble. He wondered if his sudden—and uncharacteristic—willing-

ness to take an active hand in this op stemmed from guilt over all those previous missions that had gone awry.

The decision of who would comprise the jump team to Assam hadn't been an easy one to reach. To Kane's surprise, there had been a number of volunteers among the Moon base refugees. He was further gratified that, when faced with the possibility of an assault on Cerberus, not a single one of them opted to cut and run. Of course the only familiar place to where they could have cut and run was the Manitius colony, but Kane was still impressed by the fortitude they displayed.

Lakesh, because of his facility with the linguistic groups of the Indian subcontinent, was a natural part of the team, despite his fear that Sam might interfere with the hyperdimensional channel opened by the interphaser.

He had done so only a short time before when he abducted Quavell, rerouting the gateway unit's matter stream to Australia. According to Lakesh, Sam practiced a form of energy manipulation and interaction once known as geomancy, the art of using the mind to tune in to the energy matrix of the planet. Sam had a natural ability to manipulate the global energy grid. The Cerberus mat-trans network Lakesh had so assiduously constructed over a period of many years was only a synthetic, technological imitation of Sam's geomantic powers.

When planning for the Assam mission, both Grant and Kane were adamant that neither Shizuka nor Brigid be a part of it. They weren't surprised by Lakesh's agreement to participate in a deception to keep the women out of harm's way.

"Anyhow," Domi announced, breaking Kane's reverie, "we've got a long time till daybreak, and there may be two- and four-legged animals there who aren't working for Shiva."

Kane nodded. "You're absolutely right. And since you're so absolutely right, you can take first watch."

"Had that in mind all along."

Domi rose to her feet, chambering a round into her Combat Master with a blood-chilling clicking and clacking of metal.

Kane watched the girl march toward the perimeter and wondered just what she had in mind. Skulking around in the jungle dark didn't sound like a pleasant way to spend the evening. But Domi was often motivated by little more than impulses, whims of the moment.

Kane lay back on the soft grass, apprehensive, keyed-up and tired all at the same time. He closed his eyes and after a time, slept.

Almost immediately it seemed he was awakened by a crash of static in his head, followed by Grant's voice demanding, "Vimana One to Ground Force. Anybody reading me?"

Chapter 21

Grant dropped the Manta's altitude to a thousand feet and cruised over a panorama of forested hills and wooded valleys. Colored by moonshine and starlight, the Goalpara jungle looked peaceful, almost bucolic. But he also saw huge strips of land where the jungle simply stopped, foliage and trees turned to acres upon acres of brown desolation. It looked as if a sea of plague had washed over the forests, the farms, the paddies.

Lifting his gaze, Grant looked out beyond the prow of the Manta at the snow-draped peaks and foothills of the mountains forming the spine of the Himalayas. They rushed up very fast, filling the inner curve of his helmet's visor, and he cut back on the Manta's airspeed, reducing it to under one thousand knots. The maximum atmospheric cruising speed for the little transatmospheric vehicle was Mach 25, but he hadn't seen the necessity to boom through the sky from Washington Hole to India at such an air-scorching velocity.

Grant's bronze-colored helmet was attached to the headrest of the pilot's chair. A pair of tubes stretched from the rear to an oxygen tank at the back of the seat. The helmet and chair were of one piece, a self-contained unit.

The instrument panel was almost shocking in its simplicity. The controls consisted primarily of a joystick, altimeter and fuel gauges. All the labeling was in English. But the interior curve of the helmet's visor swarmed with CGI icons of sensor scopes, range finders and various indicators.

The Manta transatmospheric plane was not an experimental craft, but an example of a technology that was mastered by a race when humanity still cowered in the trees from saber-toothed tigers. The ships were of Annunaki manufacture and design and had been found on the moon beneath the shattered remains of an incredibly ancient city, once protected by massive geodesic domes.

The Mantas handled superficially like the Deathbird choppers Grant and Kane had flown when they were Cobaltville Magistrates. But when he and Kane brought two of the TAVs down from the Moon, they reached the unsettling realization that the ships couldn't be piloted like winged aircraft within an atmosphere.

A pilot could select velocity, angle, altitude and other complex factors dictated by standard avionics, but space flight relied on a completely different set of principles. It called for the maximum manipulation of gravity, trajectory, relative velocities and plain old luck. Despite all the computer-calculated course programming, Grant learned quickly that successfully piloting the TAV through space was more by God than by grace. Skill had almost nothing to do with it.

Consulting the HUD grid-map icon, he saw he was within a five-mile radius of the Parallax Point coordinates fed into the computer before embarking from Cerberus. Activating the comm system, he hailed Kane at the other end of the Commtact line: "Vimana One to Ground Force. Anybody reading me?"

He wasn't sure about the meaning of his particular call designation except Lakesh had suggested it. Lakesh had made a brief reference to the Vimanas as ancient flying machines from Hindu mythology. Nor was he sure about joining Domi on an op.

The half-feral Outland girl had proved herself to be a tough and resourceful, if not altogether stable, partner on various missions together. At one point she had saved his, Brigid's and Kane's lives when the Cerberus mat-trans unit was sabotaged.

Grant had deliberately maintained a distance between himself and Domi, so if either she or he died— or simply went away—the vacuum wouldn't be so difficult to endure. He recalled with crystal clarity what she had said to him over six months ago, when she confronted him about his reluctance to bed her: "If you can't do it, if you're impotent, then let me know right now so I can make plans."

When he angrily denied a physical disability was the reason, she snarled, "Then it is me, you lying sack of shit." With contempt dripping from every syllable, she said, "Big man, big chest, big shoulders, legs like trees. Guess they don't tell the story, huh?"

That was pretty much the last private conversation they ever had. Her angry outburst cut him like the knife she turned on Guana Teague. When he remembered the recrimination in her voice, he knew he couldn't make up for anything he had done to hurt her. He knew he had hurt the girl dreadfully when she learned about him and Shizuka, but he was sure Domi knew his decision to relocate to New Edo wasn't based on pettiness.

Grant half expected to receive no response from the hail and so he was slightly startled when Kane's voice, which sounded exceptionally startled, responded promptly. "Where the hell are you?"

"Coming in low over Assam," he replied. "If I had my running lights on, you ought to be able to spot me."

"You're a couple of hours ahead of schedule," Kane replied. "Did you have any problems with convincing Brigid and Shizuka to stand down?"

Grant smiled within his helmet. "None to speak of. Brigid understood where we were coming from."

The Commtact accurately conveyed the relief in Kane's reply. "Good. I hope Shizuka is as understanding."

Grant's smile vanished. "Guess I won't know that until we get back." He purposefully didn't say "if."

"How'd it go with Sharpe? You make any progress?"

"Well..."

"Well what?" Kane demanded irritably. "Did you meet with the crazy bastard or not?"

"We met with him." Tersely, Grant told him all that had transpired. Kane's reaction to hearing about Sindri's decision was close to what Grant had expected.

After half a minute or so of venting expletives, Kane finally paused to catch his breath and Grant interjected, "If you're thinking that Sindri and Sharpe will team up, I doubt that will happen. They're too much alike temperamentally. They will most likely try to kill each other. Or one or the other will have to make a break for it to keep from being killed."

"Yeah, you're probably right," Kane agreed gloomily. "I guess they deserve each other."

Grant glanced down past his starboard wing. Through the helmet's infrared scanner, he saw the jungle blotched by patches of shimmering white. "Stand by, Ground Force."

Grant cut back on the Manta's speed and altitude, sending it in a wide spiral downward, soundless but for the hum of the low-power gravity modifier field. He searched the darkness below and saw a massed glow. He corrected the Manta's navigation, swinging wide so as to approach from the northeast. The light was dim, the glow among the trees a shimmering, pearly sheen.

Seeming to float in the air between his eyes and the visor, a column of numbers appeared, glowing red against the pale bronze. When he focused on a distant object, the visor magnified it and provided a readout as to distance and dimension. Now he focused on the structure rising from the lush tangle of foliage far below.

A minaret thrust up from the center of a huge stone mass. Lakesh had described the ancient walled temple as being made of blocks of red sandstone, constructed to serve as a palace during the days of the Mogul Empire. Under the blended light of the Moon and the stars, the walls held a rusty hue like old bloodstains.

"What's going on?" Kane's voice demanded. "Where are you now?"

"I'm about fifteen hundred feet above a pile of rocks in the middle of the jungle." Grant's tone was smooth and unconcerned. "My powers of deduction tell me that since it's the only pile of stones I've seen so far in the middle of the jungle, it must be our hit site."

"Brilliant conclusion," came Kane's dry response. "We met a kid who apparently was enslaved to rebuild the place. She'll guide us there at dawn, I hope."

"My scanners are picking up heat signatures," Grant said. "I'm going to make another pass, see what kind of sensor readings I get and try for a head count. Keep your comm frequency open and I'll trace it to you. Can I make a vertical landing there?"

"Yeah." Kane sounded uncertain, uneasy. "I don't know if it's such a good idea to buzz around the temple and advertise we're here."

"It's also not such a good idea to charge into dark territory without having an idea of the opposition waiting for us." Grant's reply sounded a little too sharply impatient, even in his own ears, so he mitigated it by saying, "I'll hook in the low-observability camouflage screen and glide in on the gravity modifiers. Unless somebody down there is expecting a spy from the sky, I won't be spotted. Besides, I thought we're dealing mainly with locals, strictly knives and arrows."

"Madi says the Nirodha soldiers have guns."

"I won't give them a target to shoot at."

"All right." Kane still didn't sound convinced. "But don't take too long. We've got some plans to make."

"I thought," Grant intoned flatly, "the plan was to blow the fucking place off the ass of Assam."

"We don't know the number of noncombatants. Any ass bombing will have to wait until after a hands-on recce."

Grant opened his mouth to voice an objection, then realized there was no point in trying to argue with Kane over the topic of acceptable losses among innocents. "Understood. I'll make a couple of LOC passes, then meet you at the camp."

He touched a switch on the control console, and electrical impulses fed through circuitry all over the hull of the Manta. Dark, ambient waves shifted over the bronze exterior, coating it as if by a film of India ink. Within seconds, the TAV was the hue of the night.

Grant dropped the craft like a stone for two hundred feet, then checked its descent. The wedge-shaped craft, now little more than a black blur against a deeper black, hovered almost directly above the temple.

Firelight stained the darkness within the perimeter of a half-tumbledown wall, glowing between the columns of the palace, with a flickering, lurid radiance intercut with black, sliding shadows. He couldn't discern any details.

Grant then slid the TAV forward and swept his gaze over the temple's architecture, noting the arches, the stairs winding up around a minaret. He saw a pattern of fluted columns, topped by snarling beast faces, the gaping mouths ugly with fangs.

The combination of starlight and moonshine altered perspective and muted all the colors. Even so, he saw how the pillars were luridly carved to represent every conceivable sexual joining of male and female, male and male, female and female. It was a monument to eternal lust.

A path stretched from the rear of the temple, down to a bend in the wide stretch of the great Brahmaputra River. Assembled there on the bank, he saw a small collection of buildings made of rough wood and roofed by jungle plants. They looked like barracks or storehouses. There were open sheds for cooking, and behind them were pens for the stabling of livestock.

When Grant's ears suddenly started buzzing, he jumped in his seat and swore. He was overwhelmed by astonishment when he recognized the sound as the radar-lock-on warning, piped from the forward sensor array into his helmet. Glancing out of the starboard side, Grant glimpsed a brief flash of flame in the jungle darkness.

For a half second he was too stunned to react, his eyes registering the missile lancing up from the forest, propelled by a wavering tail of fire, but his mind couldn't comprehend that the Nirodha had access to both radar and SAM emplacements.

Grant's hand closed around the joystick control and jerked back on it—then the night outside the Manta's canopy blazed with a sheet of flame. The TAV shuddered brutally under the jarring concussion of the surface-to-air missile's explosive impact.

The confines of Grant's helmet echoed with an electronic cacophony of alarms as the pile-driving thunder of the warhead's detonation against the Manta's undercarriage flipped the craft over on its port side. The sky and jungle reeled over, the horizon tipping up and then down, spinning in a mad kaleidoscopic tumble.

The TAV plummeted like a rock tossed down a well. He struggled with the stick, trying to bring up the nose, but the tree line swelled in the canopy. There was nothing left to do but pray.

Grant managed to bellow, "I'm hit! Going down!" before the blackness rushed in and engulfed him.

Chapter 22

Kane leaped to his feet as Grant's roar of "I'm hit! Going down!" seemed to lift off the top of his skull.

Cold terror tightening like a fist in his midsection, he watched the green jungle hills to the north, in the general direction Madi had indicated the temple of Shakti lay. His eyes searched and scanned and finally caught a brief, almost subliminal glimpse of a firefly flicker of flame. It fluttered to earth, shedding a stream of sparks.

Then it was gone, swallowed up by the night, as if it were nothing more than the final, dying arc of a shooting star halfway around the world.

Kane's heart beat fast within his chest as he called Grant's name three times without a response. Neither Lakesh nor Domi was outfitted with the Commtacts, so they regarded Kane's sudden agitation and skyward stare with expressions of questioning surprise.

"Grant just said he was hit, that he was shot down," he told them grimly.

Incredulity shone in Lakesh's eyes as he rose to his feet. "Shot down by what?"

"He didn't have time to make a positive ID," Kane replied coldly, "but it doesn't take a lot of imagination to guess it was a surface-to-air missile."

He gestured in the direction of the pyrotechnic display in the sky. "Something sure as hell went down in flames."

Domi followed his hand wave, eyes wide. "They have missiles in that temple?"

"Worse," Kane grated. "They have a means of detecting stealth technology so they can use their missiles."

Addressing Lakesh angrily, he demanded, "Fetish-worshiping natives don't usually have such things in their juju huts, do they?"

"No, they don't," Lakesh countered. "Therefore, we must assume Sam has advanced further in building the Nirodha movement than your future self knew."

Kane swung away from him, staring down at a sleepy-eyed Madi. "Will you guide us to the river right now?"

The girl only stared at him, confused and frightened by his aggressive tone and stance. "She doesn't understand you," Lakesh said acidly.

"Then ask her yourself, goddammit!"

Although he glared at Kane, Lakesh knew better than to chide him about his manner. He did as the man ordered, putting questions to Madi. The girl reluctantly nodded, replying in her own tongue.

"She'll do it," confirmed Lakesh, "but doesn't think much of the idea. It'll be far safer to wait until dawn."

"Safer for us," Domi stated curtly. "Not for Grant."

Kane picked up his pack and slipped into the straps. "Get all our gear together and let's get it done."

Within a few seconds, they were plunging through

the damp, humid jungle. Domi's Nighthawk microlight emitted a 5,000 minicandlepower beam, and it illuminated their path. They passed bloody, disemboweled remains, already crawling with ants. Madi identified the corpses as the Scorpia Prime's soldiers, dispatched by Shiva's tiger.

They saw no sign of the great cat and Kane was just as glad, servant of the god or not. Two of the corpses were completely ripped in two, huge sections of their spines missing, intestines looped across the jungle floor. The Nirodha had not died easily.

As they slogged across a stretch of marshy ground, they heard a liquidy growl from a copse of purple-leafed brush ahead of them. The four people came to a halt, and the Nighthawk's amber beam touched a pair of round, tawny eyes that shone like two yellow-green moons.

Kane automatically tensed his wrist, and his Sin Eater popped into his hand. A huge tiger limped slowly out of the bush. His black-and-gold striped coat glistened dully with a mixture of water, mud and blood. Madi spoke in a voice choked with grief and made a motion as if to render the enormous cat aid. Domi drew her back by an arm and lined up the bore of her Combat Master with the tiger's broad head.

"This is the beast who saved her and her companion from the Scorpia Prime's soldiers," Lakesh translated. "Who showed her the way to the Shiva shrine. It was obviously wounded by gunshots."

"Mortally wounded, I'd say," Kane murmured, feeling a surge of pity for the great animal.

The tiger lowered its head, and its immense jaws

hung open as it panted. The long fangs gleamed with slaver and blood. Madi said something sorrowful, eyes brimming with tears.

"She wants us to put the poor creature out of its misery," Lakesh interpreted.

Kane waited for Domi to volunteer, but she did not. Instead, she glanced at him expectantly over her shoulder. He shook his head, frowning. "It's not my place."

"Then whose place is it?" she asked waspishly. "Tiger is suffering."

Kane lowered his pistol. "I don't feel I should—"

The rest of Kane's objection was drowned out by a hoarse, snarling cough as the tiger leaped, muscles rippling under its scarlet-streaked hide. The cat bounded straight at him, a blur of black, gold and red. Domi cried out in fear.

Automatically, Kane jerked up his gun hand and fired the Sin Eater. Even as he did so, he felt bitterly sorry. The full-auto fusillade drove the tiger back, breaking the momentum of its charge. Jaws foaming with crimson, the cat staggered, regained something of its balance and began another lunge.

Hand trembling a little, Kane aimed carefully and squeezed off a single shot, putting a round into the tiger's head. Voicing a gasping growl, the beast slammed down heavily on the ground, its long tail lashing the air for a moment. Then the tiger expired, dying very quietly for such a fierce animal. Kane turned away, swallowing hard, shaking his head.

Madi stepped forward and knelt beside the tiger,

gently stroking its massive head as if it were a sleeping housecat. She whispered tenderly to it.

Lakesh said quietly, "She thanks him and wishes him well on his journey to his next life. She says they will meet again."

In a very unsteady voice, Domi declared, "We got no time for this."

Lakesh urged the mourning, weeping girl to her feet. She regarded Kane with eyes like wet black diamonds and after saying a few words she turned away, back toward the trail.

"She thanked you, friend Kane," Lakesh told him softly. "The tiger made the decision for you. In you, he recognized a kindred spirit, a warrior's heart who understood his own. So don't blame yourself."

Kane didn't reply, but only started walking again. Within twenty minutes of struggling through ferns, fronds and vines, they glimpsed the Brahmaputra River, a wide, glistening ribbon. Under the combined radiance of the moon and the stars, it had become a running sea of silver, rolling between jungled banks.

In a hushed tone, Lakesh said, "From mystery above it flows, to mystery below."

Kane didn't ask him what he meant. After a couple of minutes of searching, he found the dugouts. The four people piled into the longest. Domi pushed the craft out into the current of the river with a long steering oar.

All four of them paddled. Although the current wasn't exceptionally powerful, to make any progress at all required all of them working in tandem, pulling and straining at the oars. Once they were past a small section of rapids, the course became easier.

The dugout wasn't a clumsy craft, despite its crude appearance, but even paddling against a sluggish current, the canoe moved slowly through the shrouds of mist. Even at the halfway point between midnight and daybreak, the heat and humidity were oppressive. The air was heavy with moisture, tainted with the muddy, tropical fecundity of the jungle that brooded on either side of the river. Sweat gathered on Kane's face despite the temperature controls of his shadowsuit.

He strained to hear any sound in the night that didn't belong there, like human voices or mechanical noise, but all he heard was a chorus of frogs and insects. Despite his long training in staying focused on gaining an objective, Kane found his thoughts wandering to Brigid. He thought he had made his peace, as much as he was able, with whatever demon haunted their relationship, but knowing they were to be man and wife in the future—*a* future, he mentally corrected himself, not *the* future—affected him deeply. And it was a future he was now working to keep from coming into existence.

He swallowed a sigh, wishing that he and Brigid could define once and for all the bond between them, but he doubted it could ever be done. The possibility of marrying threw any conjectures he might make even further into a bottomless pit of unfulfilled what-ifs.

Lakesh suddenly uttered a groan and withdrew his paddle from the river. When Kane glanced at him, the man gave him a sickly, shamed grin and panted heavily. Unaccustomed to long periods of physical exertion, he tired quickly. Breathlessly he said, "Almost completely around the world in a second with the interphaser and now maybe five miles per hour in a boat."

Wincing, he worked his shoulders back and forth. "I feel like a stove-up Hiawatha."

"Who's that?" asked Kane, still paddling without breaking rhythm.

Lakesh snorted. "Sometimes I feel very sorry for you, friend Kane. You've no frame of reference for much of anything. You don't know the myths, the legends, the folklore of your own culture."

Kane cast him a searching over-the-shoulder glance. "We're making new legends for a new culture, Lakesh. All of us."

Lakesh pondered that for a thoughtful moment, then slid his paddle into the water. "I suppose we are," he admitted.

The river narrowed, the strength of the current slackening somewhat. The prow of the canoe continued to slide forward, propelled by the steady paddling. Insects whirled in such abundant clouds, Kane knew that if he, Domi and Lakesh hadn't been wearing the shadowsuits, not an inch of their bodies would've remained unbitten. He felt sorry for Madi, who endured the discomfort with silent stoicism.

Domi suddenly stiffened, straightening and staring intently ahead. The moonlit river swept around a curve, and a mile ahead of them, just visible above the treetops, loomed a dark tower, black against the star-speckled sky.

Madi muttered something, and it didn't sound encouraging.

"That," Lakesh said confidently, "would be the temple of Shakti."

Domi nodded. "And get a look at what's waiting for us there."

Chapter 23

Grant awoke to a nostril-clogging stench, to heat, to a murmur of voices. He blinked in the dim light and saw a place where sewage and garbage were dumped. All around were stinking pools of slime. He was naked and chained to a wall.

His head ached abominably and thirst burned his mouth and throat. His belly quivered with nausea. The fact the stink in the room caused his stomach to slip sideways told him just how virulently repulsive the odors were. His nose had been broken three times in the past, and always poorly reset.

Unless an odor was extraordinarily pleasant or astonishingly repulsive, he was incapable of detecting subtle smells unless they were right under his nostrils. A running joke during his Mag days had been that he could eat a hearty dinner with a dead skunk lying on the table next to his plate.

He heard the muted, distant babble of many voices, but he couldn't pick out any single word. Whatever language the voices spoke in, it sounded like gibberish to his ears. Slowly, he surveyed his surroundings. In the gloom, things looked blurred, out of focus on the edges. Grant wondered briefly if he had suffered serious damage to his skull. A naked lightbulb on the ceiling offered feeble illumination.

He closed his eyes, palming them, felt the tug of the manacles and heard the clink of chains. Shackles encircled both wrists, and the chains from them looped through eyelets on the metal belt locked around his waist. A chain at the rear of the belt was bolted to a bracket on the damp stone wall behind him.

Experimentally, he opened and closed both eyes one after the other and realized the vision in his left one was impaired, as if covered by a translucent film. The flesh around it was swollen, very sore and tender to the touch. Grinding his teeth, he tried to stand.

Cramping needles of agony shot up through his shoulders and arms. Nausea became a clawed animal trying to tear its way out of his stomach. It was all he could do to swallow the column of burning bile working its way up his throat—not that vomit would do much to spoil the ambiance of his surroundings. He stayed where he was for a long moment, breathing deeply. He was helpless, half-blind and sick.

When he felt better, using the chain welded to the belt as support, Grant pulled himself into a standing position, staggered on unsteady legs and fell against the wall. He remained where he was, breathing hard. After a minute he began checking himself expertly for broken bones and more severe injuries. He touched a lump at the back of his head, and his fingers came away damp and red. His head throbbed, in cadence with his pulse. He figured he was suffering from a concussion.

His right rib cage burned as if a hot, saw-bladed knife had been inserted there. He wasn't sure if he was suffering from broken or cracked ribs, but either way, his torso felt as if it had been substituted for an anvil. The swelling on the back of his head was more worrisome. Reba would probably diagnose it as a closed-skull injury, and he knew from his years as a Magistrate that head traumas were always tricky. He could have sustained a skull fracture and be suffering from a subdural seepage of blood, for all he knew.

Mentally, he played back the glimpse of the missile flaming up from the dark jungle. He remembered the explosion and the dizzying spin into oblivion, but his recollections were hazy. His shadowsuit would have cushioned the impact of the crash, even protected him from burns. That he survived the crash was not open to conjecture since he hurt so much, but he had no idea of who had retrieved him and chained him naked to a wall. More importantly, he had no idea why.

Feeling a stinging sensation on the inside of his left elbow, he saw a tiny crusted-over pinprick. Despite the cloying heat, he shivered. Not only had he been pulled from the wreckage of the Manta, but also he had been drugged, no doubt to keep him tractable while he was searched and stripped.

Grim determination steeled his mind. Despite the blurred vision in his left eye, he examined the chains. The links were thick, too strong to break, made of high-grade steel. The bracket in the wall looked deeply sunk into the stone, but he pulled anyway. It did not stir, nor had he really expected it to.

A multilegged insect scuttled over his foot and crawled toward a noxious puddle on the floor, startling him so much he couldn't stop himself from blurting out an obscenity.

"That will do you no good, you know."

Grant whirled, releasing the chain. A young man stood framed in the open doorway. Almost emaciated in appearance, he wore a white linen suit and matching shoes that showed not a trace of mud. He apparently had not ventured into the cell before now. His face, despite its look of genteel starvation, was still a boy's face, pale, angular and even rather cherubic, despite the dark glasses masking his eyes.

His silvery hair swept across his high forehead. His appearance struck a faint chord of recognition, but Grant couldn't immediately place him. Still, he exuded a force, a broodingly powerful aura, that Grant could sense and his nerves throbbed in reaction to it.

"Who are you?" demanded Grant, making no attempt to cover up his nakedness.

"You don't remember me, Mr. Grant?" The man's voice was a beautiful, musical contralto.

Grant was in no mood to play guessing games, but he forced himself to mutter, "I'm not sure."

"Take a guess." The young man reached up and removed his sunglasses, revealing a pair of haughty golden eyes that shone like polished ingots. His mouth curved in a vague smile, but it didn't affect his eyes. They were old, old with an age beyond human understanding. They were eyes that had seen birth and life and death in an endless stream, eyes that preferred death. Grant had seen those eyes before, even though the color wasn't the same.

"Colonel Thrush," Grant said quietly.

The young man's slender body stiffened. His lips moved, twisted almost as if in agony. His upper body leaned forward with a desperate hunger and he demanded, "Do you know who I really am? Tell me!"

"Don't you know?" Grant asked with a forced calm.

"I'm told my name is Sam." He spoke in a distracted, almost dreamy whisper. "That my title is imperator. But sometimes I don't think that is right. It's almost as if part of me, the true part, is sleeping—"

He broke off, clearing his throat, as if catching himself before he broke a confidence. He folded the earpieces of his sunglasses and tucked them into a breast pocket of his blazer.

Knotting his big fists, Grant inquired quietly, "Why don't you come closer, Sam? I'll put *all* of your parts to sleep."

Surprised, Sam snapped his head toward him and rubbed his hands together in agitation, making a dry, papery rustle as of scales sliding across leather. He glared at Grant in sudden rage. The sheer homicidal fury in his eyes and face rocked Grant back like the blow of a fist.

"Don't dare wake all of me!" he shouted. "Not until I have built the world I want, rebuilt this one to suit me so it will truly be a part of me. It will be the world of my dreams—even the people in it!"

"What makes you think you can build anything?" Grant asked, voice heavy with undisguised contempt. "Much less a world?"

The question didn't upset Sam. His expression became vague and preoccupied. "I am not too young to be a god, am I?"

"You're just a boy."

Sam nodded in grudging agreement. "A boy who doesn't age, but who evolves, who possesses all the wisdom from the beginning of time. But no one has ever been as alone as I. So I must build my own world, where I will never be alone again."

"And how," Grant asked, "will you do that?"

"By making everyone who ever lived, who ever will live, a part of me. And me a part of them."

Grant stood frozen, inwardly shrinking from the quiet self-confidence in the young man's tone and bearing.

Sam put his hands in the pockets of his blazer and looked down at the toes of his spotless white shoes. Musingly, as if he were talking to himself, he said, "I know what happened to the cities in the Black Gobi, to Kharo-Khoto, to Sumer…to the civilization of Angkor…to the temples of the Maya and the Aztec. Somehow I know. And because I do know, that isolates me. I was born alone. No one in history has ever been as alone as I."

The young man laughed, a low, bitter sound. He glanced up, staring intently at Grant as if seeing him for the first time. "How did you find out about this place, Mr. Grant? Do you know what I'm doing here?"

Grant's reply was toneless. "What makes you think I know anything about anything?"

Sam's mouth twisted in a moue of mockery. "Oh, yes, naturally, you know nothing!" His tone was brittle with sarcasm. ''Naturally, you must deny knowing anything about anything—about the perfectly unique aircraft you were flying, about the hows and whys of you just happening to be flying it over this province in Assam, about whether I can expect your friends, Mr. Kane or Miss Baptiste or even Mohandas Lakesh Singh, to drop in at any moment.''

''Judging by your missile and radar emplacements,'' Grant retorted, ''it wasn't like you never foresaw something like that happening.''

Sam's response was sullen. ''I believe in being prepared to deal with all contingencies.''

''I've heard that about you.''

Sam stepped farther into the room. ''Really? What else have you heard?''

Grant refused to reply; he only shook his head.

''The fact you have *not* asked me any questions tells me you know quite a bit about my affairs. Far, far more than you should, by any laws of logic. You know where you are, don't you?''

Grant didn't move or speak. His face remained impassive.

''I suppose I could tell you a few things,'' the imperator continued blithely. ''For example, before another month is out, almost all of Assam will be under my control. Before another month and a half passes, that quaint little mountaintop retreat of yours will be destroyed.''

Grant let out a long breath. ''All right, Sam. I do know a few things, some of which you don't know, but really want to know. But I'll expect to receive some information from you, too. For example, what's so special about Assam?"

Sam's golden eyes glinted with sudden humor. "Very little, actually, except for its long historical association with a variety of Tantric sex cults. At this point it's a culture dish, in more ways than one."

Grant shook his head. "I don't get you."

Patronizingly, Sam stated, "Perhaps it would be more accurate to refer to Assam as my laboratory, wherein I gather empirical data about the human race's primary motivators. For example, humanity functions by responding to the overwhelming commands of its visceral needs and its survival.

"Humankind's single most overriding need is to eat, so at the head of my data list is to induce hunger. It's simple, isn't it? Eat or die."

Grant nodded, wishing the young man would come close enough so he could launch a kick. "Yes, that's simple enough."

"Then when a belly is full," the imperator continued, "sex assumes the dominant position of visceral demands. As far as your kind is concerned, sex transcends simple procreative needs. You find it satisfying, intoxicating. Every human society throughout your sordid history has followed this basic pattern. I meet these two basic drives with the Nirodha movement. This country, this province, is only a pilot experiment. I'll be exporting it abroad soon enough."

Grant nodded casually. "I figured as much. You need to test the audience before you fully draft your so-called Great Plan."

Sam's lean body suddenly seemed to freeze. His

expression did not alter, his eyes did not blink, his hands did not move. He did not appear to breathe. When he finally spoke, his voice was barely above a whisper.

"Now that *is* interesting, Mr. Grant. How could you possibly have heard those two words in connection to me?" His eyes shone brightly, hot aureate pools of suspicion and anger.

Grant tried to shrug, even though the motion pained him. "I have my connections, Sammy."

"What are they? What brought you here?" Sam's tone had lost all pretense of amiability. "Have I been betrayed? Did my mother—?" He bit off the rest of his question, as if he could not bring himself to utter it.

Grant brayed a short, scornful laugh. "Who the hell would betray you? Nobody gives enough of a shit about you."

In a voice pitched so low it was almost a sibilant hiss, Sam intoned, "You are so very, very wrong about that, Mr. Grant." He turned his head and called, "You may come in now. I'm afraid I'll need you after all."

Instantly, a woman stepped into the room, moving with a lithe, danceresque grace. Grant had expected to see Erica van Sloan, but he didn't recognize the dark-haired woman who responded to Sam's summons—however, he recognized her as a type. She was a hybrid, and a stirringly beautiful one, too.

Grant noticed immediately that she was nearly a half head taller than most hybrids he had seen. The long sleek hair that framed her high-planed face and her dark, back-slanted eyes gave her an exotic, almost barbaric flair. She wore the black imperial uniform, the satin tunic stretched taut across her small breasts and cinched tight at her narrow waist. She carried a slender silver wand, which tapered down to a very narrow tip. Grant's belly turned cold when he recognized it as an infrasound wand.

"This is Baron Beausoleil," Sam announced. "Also known as Scorpia Prime."

By great effort, Grant managed to keep the astonishment he felt from registering on his face. He knew Domi had encountered the female baron at Ayers Rock during the mission to rescue Quavell, but he hadn't expected to ever see her face-to-face. Just the concept of a female baron was surprising enough, so actually seeing her in the flesh was almost shocking.

"The baron enjoys wringing answers from mysteries," Sam went on. "She has been a great comfort and help to me in my various endeavors."

As Sam spoke, Beausoleil absently swished the rod back and forth. Grant was assailed by an instant of irrational dread. He knew the infrasound batons converted electrical current to sound waves by a maser and were very deadly weapons. He had been on the receiving end of their kinetic punch once before, and it had taken him days to recover.

"Mr. Grant, I want you to tell me how you came to be here." Sam spoke very authoritatively. "After all, you owe me a little consideration. I could have left you to die in your aircraft."

"You wouldn't believe me if I told you," replied Grant.

"Try us," Beausoleil suggested icily.

"We received a message from the future," Grant said earnestly. "It laid out your entire Great Plan, how you intend to starve the world with a plague, then set up the Nirodha movement and stage a devastating war. By the time you're all done with it, you'll have built the world you talked about. You'll never be alone again, because you'll be linked with every human brain alive on the planet."

"Ah." Sam nodded as if he had expected the answer. He nodded to Beausoleil and then to Grant. "If you would be so kind?"

The woman danced forward and slashed Grant viciously across the left cheek with the point of the infrasound wand. Fortunately, it wasn't powered up. If it had been, most of his facial bones would have been fractured. As it was, the unexpected force of the blow staggered him. If not for the chain at his waist, he would have fallen.

"The imperator put some simple questions to you, Mr. Grant." She spoke very crisply, very matter-of-factly. "He expects you to answer them, and if you do not, he expects me to compel you to do so."

"He's liable to be very disappointed," Grant grunted.

Sam turned toward the door and said genially, "I'll leave you two alone. I've the sunrise ceremony to arrange."

"Hey, Sammy," Grant called out.

The young man paused, turning his head to look at him. Grant dug the toes of his right foot into a puddle of fetid muck and kicked a slurry of slime in his direction. Sam didn't get all of it, but his spotless white coat was spattered with dark brown-green splotches. Recoiling, he shrieked in disgust and anger.

Grant kicked then at Beausoleil, who danced back out of the way of his big muddy foot with a mincing step that was surprisingly swift. In the same motion, she thumbed on the power switch of the wand. The humming, shivering tip of the wand inscribed a short arc and swiped him across the ankle. Crying out, Grant reeled backward, a numbing pain running up and down his leg.

"That wasn't even notched to half power," the baron stated, a dangerous edge to her voice.

"Get answers out of that son of a bitch!" Sam's maddened voice shook with wild rage. "Do whatever you have to do!"

He whirled through the door and was gone. Baron Beausoleil flashed Grant a very smug, very self-satisfied smile. He tried to straighten, favoring his right foot. He didn't think the ankle bone was broken, but the nerves in it felt as if they had been dipped in acid.

Beausoleil slowly ran her gaze up and down his body, eyeing him speculatively. "You are a superb physical specimen," she almost crooned, "for an apeling."

She extended the vibrating tip of the infrasound wand toward his genitals, continuing to smile at him. He resisted the urge to cup his hands over his groin. Even if the length of the chains encumbering his wrists allowed it, he knew it would do little good. Having been on the receiving end of the ultrasonic kicks delivered by the wands, he knew how quickly they could disable. He recalled how the focused energy had once liquefied a hybrid's brain. The notion of what it could do to his testicles caused cold sweat to break out all over his body.

"You have a true man's physique," Beausoleil said in a feral purr. "Strong, powerful, virile. It's a pity sex holds no appeal for me." She paused, her smile broadening as she added, "A pity for you."

Grant did his best not to let the fear filling him show on his face. If Domi was tempestuous in her passions and Shizuka a fierce warrior-queen, then Beausoleil was a terrifying symbol of female power. She was more predator than woman, driven by a lust that could only be satiated by pain and blood. She did not just want it; she demanded it.

The point of the baron's little wet red tongue popped out and touched her lips as she stepped closer, the tip of the baton humming like a swarm of insects. Beads of sweat ran down his backbone.

"There's no point to this," he rasped. "There's nothing I can tell you."

"On your knees." She snapped out the words in a haughty, imperious voice. "On your knees before your baron."

The fear in Grant didn't exactly ebb, but it was replaced by a stronger, hotter emotion. He felt his face locking into a mask of angry resolve. "No."

The tip of the rod stabbed forward, touching his left shoulder. Grant jerked at the sting of it against bruised flesh. "Hurts just a little, doesn't it?"

Then she began flailing at him with the wand, using

it with skill and speed and sadistic expertise. A series of nerve-shredding shocks tore at his body. Through a red mist of agony, Grant twisted, fought the restraint of his bonds. He didn't try to snatch at the wand. Not until the vicious bitch was within his reach did he dare act.

"Why did you come here?" The point of the wand struck before Grant could answer, stroking his knee, his stomach, his chest. "Answer me, you ape-kin scum! Answer!"

Despite the agony consuming him, Grant understood the interrogation technique. Baron Beausoleil had probably picked it up from her ville's Magistrate Division—questions followed by the application of pain, then more questions with no opportunity for answers. It was a standard Mag practice, meant to break the spirit and encourage unthinking responses.

Grant refused to answer or to be broken, even though the wand seared his nerves, bruised his flesh and muscle and ruptured capillaries all over his body. "Told you already," he gasped out.

"Do you expect me to believe that idiocy about a message from the future?" Beausoleil's voice was a screech of fury—or excitement. Her eyes blazed with a wild light and perspiration slicked her face. "Do you take me for a fool?"

"No," Grant spit. "A diseased little slut."

The baron tensed with rage, her face taut as she raised the infrasound wand, holding it like a rapier, the humming tip circling inches from Grant's eyes. She hissed, "Do you think you can be as uncooperative without the use of your eyes? Don't you know how easy it would be? Pop-pop and you're blind for life.''

Beausoleil had worked herself up to a mad fury, converting it to pleasure, taking almost orgasmic enjoyment in the pain, the fear she caused. "Do you know where you are?" she demanded breathlessly. "Where the cultists put their garbage, their offal! Because that's all you really are, your entire species, only secretions and excrement!''

"And what does that make you?" he asked hoarsely, his eyes blurred by pain. "Since you're spending so much time with me, that makes you a sanitation expert, doesn't it? A sewer worker?"

Baron Beausoleil's cold marble face didn't alter. She extended the shivering tip of the wand until it touched his forehead. Like a bolt of lightning, pain ripped through Grant's nervous system. His brain seemed to catch fire, electric with agony. He writhed and convulsed and cursed, the links of the chains clinking and rattling.

He was only dimly aware of sagging in his chains, the manacles cutting cruelly into his wrists. His head hung loosely. All he could see was the damp ground and the toes of Beausoleil's polished boots.

In a tone heavy with mock sympathy, she asked, "How much longer will you allow this to go on— until you're blind, crippled, impotent?"

Grant had no breath or inclination to answer. He could barely move. Even blinking brought pain, and respiration was an exercise in agony.

"As you wish," the baron murmured almost sadly. "As you wish."

The wand's bee-swarm hum grew louder, filling his ears. Then the room seemed to move as if a giant boot had given the foundation a ferocious kick. Grant heard objects falling over, and the ceiling cracked, showering the room with dust and grit. The lightbulb exploded with a crackle and a spray of sparks.

Then Grant dared to act.

Chapter 24

Avanisa didn't like guns, particularly not the spindly machine guns called SIG-AMTs that had been doled out by the Scorpia Prime's foreign minions. He much preferred his own rawhide twelve-plaited whip as a symbol and tool of discipline and violence. He took a secret pride in the knowledge that the whip itself marked him as an overseer, not the colored uniform or the face-paint with the scorpion insignia.

Unlike most of the Naga people, Avanisa was a gnarled, knot-muscled little man, stringy and lean, like a half-starved cat. A shag of iron-gray beard clothed his lower face. His hair was just as gray, but at least the red-and-black turban covered that. His skin was as dark and tough as cured leather, and his obsidian eyes glinted from nests of wrinkles. As much as he prided himself on the whip, he took a great deal of satisfaction in believing his eyes saw everything.

In the hour preceding dawn, Avanisa roused the slaves from their barracks, ordering them down to the riverbank to bathe and make themselves presentable for the weekly benediction performed by the high priestess of Shakti.

The blessing bestowed by the servant of the Scorpia Prime was meant to inspire the workers to labor with more dedication in the restoration of the temple.

As far as Avanisa was concerned, more food and fewer hours toiling in the brutal heat would accomplish that, with no man-hours wasted on pseudoreligious ceremonies. A bit of consideration given to the limitations of human endurance would greatly improve morale.

At the moment, morale was in a precarious balance. Two of the young slaves had escaped from the barracks the evening before, stealing a canoe and taking it down the Brahmaputra. He had dispatched a retrieval party, but they had yet to return.

Although he didn't find their absence particularly significant, since he knew they wouldn't try to come back upriver at night, he knew the other slaves were anxiously waiting to learn if the escapees would be returned after daybreak. If they were not, then Avanisa feared the pair of young people would become heroes, sources of inspiration. As it was, he had already heard murmurs among the laborers that Shiva was greatly displeased by the defilement of the temple of Shakti and would soon intervene. Those murmurs had become pronounced after the strange events of only a few hours before, when the spear of the Scorpia Prime pierced a flying machine, like Shiva's Vimana mentioned in the *Ramayana*, and brought it to earth.

Avanisa wasn't a superstitious or religious man. He didn't necessarily disbelieve in the gods or the old ways, but by the same token he had a great appreciation for reality. And at this point, the simple reality was that the Scorpia Prime held the reins of power in Goalpara. She saw to the feeding and clothing of the people and their entertainment. Whether she was really an incarnation of Shakti or not, all Avanisa cared about was whether he ate and was laid on a regular schedule. So far, the Scorpia Prime hadn't let him down.

Avanisa and three of his fellow Nagas watched as the people clustered at the water at the riverbank, washing and grooming themselves so their stench wouldn't be an affront to the Scorpia Prime's high priestess, a tall foreign bitch who behaved as if everything in Assam was an affront to her.

So he waited in the predark murk for the twenty-eight people to complete their ablutions. When it seemed they were taking an inordinately long time, he barked a command and cracked his whip in the air to catch their attention.

Slowly but obediently, the slaves began trudging up the slight incline, the women drawing closed their saris and the hoods of their robes. In a tight mass, they marched toward the temple. Avanisa led them past the irrigation ditches and the worktables.

The eastern horizon glowed with red-gold bands when they entered the temple through a courtyard full of shadows and overgrown shrubbery. Cracked pillars thrust up their pinnacles into the sky, some of them topped by eroded, horrific faces of demons and *rakshahas*.

The entrance foyer was partly fallen in, but the portico, upheld by four marble columns, was still intact. Along the edge of the roof a row of horn-headed stone gargoyles leered down—statues of monsters of bygone epochs, half human and half beast.

Inside the temple, Avanisa followed the distant
thumping of drums and the people followed him.
From a wide corridor, they walked into the vast central hall serving as the temple of Shakti. The area was
illuminated by flaming braziers and lanterns that
threw a shimmering veil of color over the walls,
which depicted passion-twisted figures locked in a
wide variety of sexual positions.

The high priestess stood upon the round altar stone,
slowly beating a drum with the heel of one hand. Her
features were painted in red-and-black designs, her
long black hair tossed over a shoulder in a thick braid,
intertwined with garlands of flowers. Her graceful,
swanlike neck led to a voluptuous body draped in a
thin, gauzy silk that only blurred, not obscured her
long legs and firm, round breasts. Taut nipples
pressed against the thin fabric as if she were in a high
state of sexual arousal.

Avanisa stood aside as the slaves filed into the
chamber. He wasn't particularly anxious to attend the
benediction, since the ceremony would end only with
the distribution of bowls of rice, not with an orgy.
The Scorpia Prime herself was not present, and therefore such activity would not be proper.

As one of the female slaves strode by him, body
wrapped in a sari from head to ankle, Avanisa noted
absently that she didn't shuffle. He also caught a brief
flash of white from beneath the linen hood. It required
a moment for the anomalies to register fully, and by
then most of the laborers had crowded into the temple.

Suspicions flaring, Avanisa shouted an order and

all the people lurched to a halt. The overseer ignored
the glare of disapproval from the high priestess, as his
eyes swept over the bowed, linen-covered heads. He
pulled a laborer from the line, more or less at random
and yanked the hood back, revealing the frightened,
seamed face of a middle-aged woman.

Avanisa pushed the woman aside and stepped to
the next person in line, a small figure he guessed was
a teenager. He pulled her hood back roughly—and
gaped at the white-skinned, white-haired, red-eyed
devil who smiled sweetly up at him. He started to
bellow an alarm, then Domi shot him, right through
her sari.

THE REPORT of the Combat Master boomed and echoed in the vaulted chamber. It sent out a wave of
eardrum-compressing sound. The .45-caliber round
caught the bearded man Madi had identified as Avanisa dead center, crushing his clavicle and ripping both
of his lungs apart.

The overseer didn't cry out, but just left his feet,
catapulting backward into one of the free-standing
braziers. It toppled over amid a storm of sparks,
clanging loudly against the stone floor.

The slaves, many of them clapping hands over their
ears, fell into a mindless panic, despite being told earlier by Madi what the three outlanders had in mind.
The laborers had been overjoyed to see them in the
girl's company when they floated to the riverbank.
They were ecstatic when Madi explained they intended to free them from servitude and were more
than eager to help smuggle them into the temple.

Now, with the death of their cruel overseer, they screamed and ran in all directions at once. The few who didn't milled around aimlessly, confused as to the correct reaction.

Kane knew the sound of the gunshot would draw other Scorpia Prime soldiers into the temple and he shouted to Lakesh, "Grab Erica!"

The high priestess, standing frozen by shock on the altar stone, dropped the drum. Lakesh saw the light of recognition dawn in her overly made-up eyes as he fought his way through the terrified workers toward her.

His feet tangled in the hem of the robe hanging from his shoulders, and he stumbled, falling to the floor. He managed to catch himself with both hands, but before he could lever himself upright again a frantic slave stepped on him, using his back as a springboard and slamming him face first to the floor.

Cursing, Lakesh got to his feet in a lunging rush, elbowing two people aside. He ripped off his robe as he did so, catching only the briefest of glimpses of Erica van Sloan racing toward a narrow doorway at the rear of the chamber.

He glanced over his shoulder and saw Domi and Kane struggling out of their robes. At the same time, a group of turbaned, face-painted men pounded into the temple, the barrels of the subguns in their hands spitting flame and thunder. Three of the workers screamed and fell, clutching at themselves.

Kane caught Lakesh's eye. *"Go!"* he roared.

AS THE LAST OF THE SLAVES ran screaming from the temple, Domi and Kane reacted instantaneously, simultaneously, reflexively. They depressed the triggers, and their handguns roared.

A turbaned soldier's cry of warning ended in a gargled grunt as the 9 mm blockbusters from Kane's Sin Eater tore blood-bursting gouges in his throat and knocked him backward. Miniature volcanoes erupted crimson geysers all over his torso.

The six warriors rushing into the temple uttered wild, undulating screams, shouldering their SIG-AMTs. The Nagas, savages though they might be, had an instinctive grasp of tactics. They spread out across the area, some trying to cut their quarry off from a retreat.

Shots cracked and boomed. A bullet hissed past Kane's ear and another tugged at the collar of his shadowsuit. He dived behind a carved pillar that displayed a relief image of a ménage à trois among a man, a woman and a cobra, his finger depressing the trigger of his Sin Eater.

Three bullets took the right ear off the head of a Scorpia Prime soldier, bit deeply into his neck and hammered him between the eyes, blowing out the back of his turban in a gout of blood, bone chips and brain matter.

Domi went to her knees behind the altar stone and her semiautomatic pistol thundered as she chose her targets carefully. A pair of .45-caliber slugs hit a man bearing a long, wavy-bladed dagger with a hollow-point one-two punch, knocking him backward.

A barrage of bullets spewed from two subguns thudding into the stone, chopping out fragments but not penetrating it. Domi kept her head down and continued working the trigger of her pistol. The thunder of the gunfire was deafening. The walls of the huge chamber beat it back and magnified it.

A keening Naga raced directly for Kane's position, swinging a curved sword over his head and working the trigger of a SIG-AMT. Kane shifted the barrel of his Sin Eater and let loose a triburst. The warrior doubled over, bleeding from three wounds in his belly. He fell facedown at the base of the column, right beneath the stone representation of a male sexual organ.

A lucky bullet knocked a dust-spurting gouge in the altar stone, sweeping Domi's face with stinging rock particles and drawing blood. Shrieking a profanity, she fired the Combat Master in return. Two rounds pounded the man who had scored the lucky shot off his feet, his limbs twisting and convulsing.

She knew she needed to reload, then she saw Kane, still laying down a left-to-right pattern of fire, pitch a metal ball with his left hand. For Domi's benefit, he shouted, "Gren!" before ducking behind the pillar and burying his face in his arms. Domi dropped flat, arms over her head, bracing herself for the explosion.

One of the turbaned soldiers saw the object bouncing across the ground, and he opened his mouth to scream a warning. A thunderclap blast slammed his words back into his throat.

For a microsecond, the temple was haloed in a red flash. Then flying tongues of flame billowed outward. The detonation of the incendiary grenade hurled fire-wreathed bodies into the air, the concussion shattering bones and rupturing internal organs.

A fine rain of dirt, pulverized pebbles and droplets of blood drizzled down. Domi and Kane looked up and saw a warrior thrashing around in blind agony, screaming as he tried to beat out the phosphorus flames on his clothes and hair.

Kane shot him quickly, one merciful bullet to the head. He and Domi climbed to their feet, surveying the killzone with swift, appraising stares. The unit of Scorpia Prime's soldiers was thoroughly neutralized, their bodies scattered like broken, bloody dolls. The air held a throat-closing reek of smoke and cordite. The sweetish odor of seared human flesh made both people want to hold their noses.

Looking behind them worriedly, Domi said, ''There may be lot more soldiers in this place and Lakesh is unarmed. We need to—''

There was no time to complete her thought. A wedge of Scorpia Prime warriors, at least half a dozen, drove into the temple from the opposite end of the wall in a milling rush. Their subguns were out, and when they caught sight of the outlanders, they shouted commands. The warriors behind them began to fan out warily but swiftly.

Domi and Kane sprinted swiftly through the doorway that Lakesh had run through. Domi plucked a gren from her war bag, slipped the spoon and lobbed it around the curve in the wall. Eyes wide and fearful, the Naga soldiers dug in their heels and tried to stop, but the men behind them continued to push them onward.

The high-ex compounds detonated in a tremendous cracking blast, a blinding burst of dust and sand erupting from the floor. The sound of the explosion instantly bled into a grinding rumble of a stony mass shifting. The groaning grate overlapped the ringing echoes of the detonation, then overwhelmed it.

The grinding noise expanded into a rumbling roar. As Kane and Domi watched, a long section of the high ceiling was riven through with ugly black fissures, spreading out in a spiderweb pattern. It seemed to crack open like overripe fruit. Then the ceiling split in the middle and folded downward like a double lid.

It fell into the temple in a crushing torrent of bouncing blocks and spurting dust. All the Scorpia Prime's soldiers were engulfed by the tons of collapsing basalt and sandstone. The round altar was shattered and half-buried.

Kane and Domi stepped quickly away from the doorway, shielding their faces from ricocheting chunks of stone. After the rolling echo of the crash faded, there came a stunned silence, stitched through with a clicking of pebbles and faint moans. Grit-laden dust hung in the air like a blanket over the fallen mass of rock.

Tongue filmed with dust, Kane spit and said, "So much for the restoration."

Domi's eyes glinted ruby bright, ruby hard. "We haven't done enough yet. Find Lakesh, find what happened to Grant. Then we do more."

Kane nodded. "Let's start on that right now."

As THE EXPLOSION ROCKED the foundations of the fortress, causing little showers of dust to sift down from above, Baron Beausoleil gaped up at the ceiling, eyes wide with astonishment.

Grant lunged forward, using his massive legs as springs. The slack of the chain on his waist snapped out taut and straight as the crown of his head caught the woman in the midsection. The impact was not as full-on as he had hoped, but still Beausoleil careened backward, her arms windmilling. All the air left her lungs in an agonized grunt.

The silver baton flew from her fingers and landed with a splash in a puddle of sludge. The vibrations sent slime splashing in all directions. Teeth set on a groan of pain, Grant leaned forward as far as he could, balanced on his toes. With tendon-straining effort, he extended his right hand and managed to pull the infrasound wand from the semifluid pool of muck.

As he did so, he saw Baron Beausoleil push herself to her feet, her lips writhing over her small perfect teeth as she tried to pull in oxygen. She clutched at her belly as she staggered erect.

Grant thumbed the wand's power switch to full output. The humming drone became a high-pitched buzz. He touched the vibration-blurred tip to the chains hooked to his manacles. The links split and fell with chiming sounds like the ringing of distant bells.

He twisted around to break the chain connected to the metal belt at his waist and free himself from the wall. Just as the links snapped apart, sickening pain burst up through his testicles like an explosion. He dropped the infrasound wand and clutched at his crotch, folding in the direction of the white-hot agony.

Through pain-fogged eyes, he saw Baron Beausoleil snatch at the wand on the ground, and he swatted at her, trying to drive her back. Beausoleil's right leg came up in a lethal kick. The toe of her boot caught Grant under the chin with surprising force.

He fell over backward and fought the urge to huddle up into a ball. Moving on sheer hatred and desperation, he rolled away, knowing as he did so she had retrieved the infrasound wand. Through the blood thundering in his ears, he heard her voice hiss, "Long ago, long before you were born, I learned all of your kind's weak and vulnerable points...and how to not just mete out pain, but to tolerate it."

With the wall at his back, Grant pushed himself to his feet, breathing deeply between clenched teeth. With a cold, mocking smile on her face, Baron Beausoleil feinted with the wand, but Grant didn't rise to the bait.

He slid to the left, his back pressed against the rough stone of the wall. The baron advanced slowly, thrusting with the baton toward Grant's face. Instead of recoiling, Grant took a swift sidestep, back toward the right. The motion disconcerted Beausoleil, who didn't have the time to get her weapon back in line for another straight-on attack, and she struck out in a poorly aimed backhand.

Leaning away from the clumsy blow, Grant's right hand shot out and closed around the woman's slender wrist. He pivoted at the same time on the ball of his right foot.

He pulled Baron Beausoleil forward, hooking his left arm over the woman's shoulder. Keeping his weight on the pivot foot, he extended his left leg between the baron's feet. With an outraged screech, she fell heavily to the muddy floor, but she maintained her grip on the wand, and Grant maintained a viselike grip on the woman's wrist, grinding the bone.

Staring into her eyes, Grant whispered almost lovingly, ''Tolerate this.'' He brought the baron's elbow across his knee with such force that the joint snapped with a sound like a stick of green wood breaking. She screamed with agony, and her fingers opened around the handle of the baton. It rolled across the floor, but Grant made no move to pick it up. Instead, he fitted his hand around the slender column of the woman's throat and began to squeeze.

Chapter 25

Lakesh sprinted flat-out down the corridor, Erica van Sloan's pale figure little more than a wispy wraith in the shadowed dimness. The passageway was very plain, with no carvings, no statuary, no frescoes anywhere in sight. He wondered absently if the Mogul builders had felt the temple itself was sufficiently ornate for anyone's tastes.

Lungs straining, Lakesh called out, "Oh, come on, Erica—this is ridiculous! I won't hurt you! I'm not armed."

Erica van Sloan ran for a few paces, then slowed and leaned against the wall, drinking in air. She stared at Lakesh with suspicious eyes as he stumbled to a halt near her. The gown she wore draped her figure in such a way that the fabric stretched tight over the mounds of her breasts, the swell of her hips and thighs. It was a garment designed to enhance femininity, but there was nothing soft about the expression on her face or in her eyes.

"What the fuck are you doing here, Singh?" she husked out.

Lakesh smiled condescendingly. "A little more formal now than the last time we saw each other."

Fear and fury warred for dominance in Erica's voice and bearing. "How did you get here?"

He shrugged, approaching her. She sidled away from him, lips compressed. "You think you can stop Sam?" she demanded, as if she found the concept itself too scandalous to be put into words.

Lakesh's smiled broadened. "By my calculations, he's already been stopped. The timeline has been altered just enough so his dreams of an adaptive Earth can never be realized…at least not by the method of staging a war and creating a phony religion."

Erica's overly made-up eyes widened in surprise, but she tried to laugh scornfully. "This? It's only a small loss. Sam can deal with it and go on to the next phase. He's free of all the poisons that degrade the rest of us. He has all the tools he needs to reshape the world."

"Tools like you?" Lakesh asked softly. "That's all you are to him, you know. Once you're worn out, you'll be discarded."

"So self-righteous."

Lakesh whirled at the sound of Sam's voice, heart suddenly pounding within his chest. The young man in white bared his teeth in either a grin or a grimace. "You're my tool, too. I thought you understood that, Mohandas."

"I understand about the nanites that you used to make me fairly youthful again." Lakesh saw the cold, sneering mask of Erica van Sloan's face change a little.

Lakesh said to Sam, "You didn't tell her, did you? That your fountain-of-youth miracle had nothing to do with energy, but was due to the introduction of molecular machines into her body?"

Sam half turned toward Erica. "Does it matter how it was done, Mother? You're young, beautiful and vital again, commanding far more power and influence than you ever did in your former life."

"Tell her the rest, Sam," Lakesh suggested, a taunting smile stretching his lips.

"The rest?" Erica repeated numbly.

"Not only is he not human, but he's a mass murderer, a destroyer of souls. He's the latest incarnation of a conniving monster that has walked Earth for aeons."

Lakesh cocked his head at Sam. "Tell me, Imperator—what will happen to you if you do manage to build your adaptive Earth and everyone on it dies? Will you go on living, trapped forever in an immortal body, your program running on automatic?"

Sam's eyes were veiled and remote. "You misjudge me. I want only the opportunity to open minds...to seek affinity between them...thought to thought, dream to dream."

Lakesh shook his head in disgust. "No, you want to open minds so you can empty them and put your own thoughts and dreams in there."

"Would that be so horrible? Think of the wonders the human race will accomplish, free of all their visceral emotions."

"I think of all the horrors they will commit, with their minds as merciless and as cold as yours."

"It's not like that at all," Sam blurted.

"Then tell me."

Sam opened his mouth, closed it and smiled again. "It's my game, Mohandas. If you're not going to join my team, then you have to figure it out for yourself. And while you're at it, you can figure out how much longer you have to live.''

Agony washed over Lakesh in a wave, deep, boring pains in his chest, in his legs, and then a fire burning behind his eyes. He was only dimly aware of crying and falling to the floor. He felt similar pain in the same areas of his body as before—where he had undergone surgeries to replace knee joints with polyethylene, a lung and heart transplant and where his glaucoma-afflicted brown eyes were changed out for bright new blue ones.

The nanites were attacking the weakest parts of his body on a molecular level, sending him writhing across the corridor floor in pain. Through the squall of pain roaring within the walls of his skull, he heard Sam's voice say faintly, ''I will concede my defeat on this occasion, Mohandas, but it's only a small move in a far larger game. But I'm the game master, and it's up to me whether I'll keep you alive to contend against me another day or kill you at a whim. I have plenty of time to make up my mind.''

Lakesh groaned, not with pain but with utter fear. He blinked to clear his vision, then felt small, soft hands touching his face and heard gentle words, soothing and tender.

Vision slowly clearing, he saw he lay on his back, his head cradled in Domi's lap. The fear he felt before was nothing to the terror that consumed him at the sight of her. He groped for her hand, knowing at any second he could age fifty years and never know her touch again.

Domi understood his sudden fear and she smiled down on him. "It's all right, Lakesh. We'll always have plenty of time."

RED-AND-BLACK MADNESS overwhelmed Grant's thoughts. He could think of nothing else but killing the monster who had tried to humiliate and kill him. Very dimly, on the edges of his awareness, he thought he heard Kane shouting his name.

Then he realized Kane was hammering at his wrists and forearms, trying to prize his fingers from Baron Beausoleil's neck. The pain of his blows was drowned in his hatred, which in turn became pain.

"Stop it!" Kane bellowed into Grant's ear. "Let her go! We can use her! Do you understand? *We can use her!*"

Finally, Grant allowed himself to be borne backward by Kane. Baron Beausoleil lay on the floor, twitching fitfully, breathing in little gasps, barely conscious. He sagged within the arms of his friend, totally exhausted, so worn out by pain and fatigue, all he could do was stare at the baron's body.

"Can you walk?" Kane asked him.

Grant nodded. "Think so."

Kane steadied him, released him, then knelt beside the baron, swiftly examining her. He had guessed who she was based on Domi's description. "The temple is on fire and will probably be falling apart in a few minutes. Domi went after Lakesh. Whether she finds him or not, we've got to get out of here—fast."

Grant nodded numbly. Kane heaved Baron Beausoleil's body over a shoulder and strode out of the cell. He pointed out Grant's shadowsuit lying just outside the door, wadded up on the floor. He waited impatiently while Grant drew it on.

By the time they were halfway down the passageway, Grant's step was more sure and firm, even though he limped. By the time they found the way out, the palace was in flames. Apparently, the incendiary grenade had ignited various flammables and the fire had quickly spread. Smoke lay in heavy sheets and boiled out of windows. Flames licked from every opening.

Lakesh and Domi were waiting for them in the courtyard. Kane cut off their questions, particularly those about the hybrid female slung over his shoulder. He hustled them outside the walls, where most of the former slaves were assembled, Madi among them.

The sun was only a hand's span above the horizon, the sky ablaze with brilliant molten colors only slightly less muted than those of the flame sheets spurting from the temple of Shakti.

Kane dropped Baron Beausoleil unceremoniously on the ground where she lay unconscious, the marks of Grant's fingers discoloring her throat. Turning to Grant, he asked, "What did that bitch do to you to make you try to strangle her?"

Grant didn't answer for such a long time Kane almost repeated the question. Then, at length, he said in a flat, bleak voice, "She showed me I can't retire…that I can't build a new life with Shizuka, until I've laid to rest all the demons that plague the old one."

Kane arched an eyebrow. ''And that's why you tried to kill her with your bare hands?''

Grant gave him a level stare. ''Wouldn't you?''

A thundering column of flame suddenly mushroomed from the temple. Rolling balls of orange-red fire billowed up into the blue sky, and burning debris was hurled in all directions. The former slaves cried out and retreated, backing away toward the jungle.

Domi looked at the monstrous, crackling pyre roaring into the dawn sky and whistled appreciatively. ''Looks like this mission wasn't a waste of time after all.''

Kane squinted away from the roaring flames and glanced down. Baron Beausoleil was gone. He stared unblinkingly at the ground, then covered his eyes with one hand.

''I'm not so sure,'' he said darkly.

Stony Man is deployed against an armed
invasion on American soil...

ECHOES OF WAR

Facing an unholy alliance of Mideast terrorists conspiring
with America's most dangerous enemies to unleash the
ultimate—and perhaps unstoppable—bioengineered
weapon of horror, Stony deploys righteous fury against
this rolling juggernaut, standing firm on the front lines
of what may be their last good fight.

STONY MAN®

*Available in
October 2003
at your favorite
retail outlet.*

DEATH LANDS®

Devil Riders

*Available in September 2003
at your favorite retail outlet.*

Stranded in the salty desert wastes of West Texas, hopes for a hot meal and clean bed in an isolated ville die fast when Ryan and his companions run into a despotic baron manipulating the lifeblood of the desert: water. But it's his fortress stockpiled with enough armaments to wage war in the dunes that interests Ryan, especially when he learns the enemy may be none other than the greatest—and long dead—Deathlands legend: the Trader.

GDL63